To the Dolls
Deirdre, Olivia, Liz and Siobhán

The Estate

Liza Costello

HACHETTE
BOOKS
IRELAND

First published in Ireland in 2021 by
HACHETTE BOOKS IRELAND

1

Cataloguing in Publication Data is available from the British Library

Trade paperback ISBN 978 1 52935 011 1
Ebook ISBN 978 1 52935 012 8

Typeset in Garamond by redrattledesign.com

Excerpt from 'Ghost House' by Robert Frost from COLLECTED POEMS
OF ROBERT FROST edited by Edward Connery Lathem. Copyright © 1962
by Robert Frost. Reprinted by permission of Penguin Random House.
All Rights Reserved.

Printed and bound in Great Britain by
Clays Ltd, Elcograf, S.p.A.

Hachette Books Ireland policy is to use papers that are natural, renewable and
recyclable products and made from wood grown in sustainable forests. The logging
and manufacturing processes are expected to conform to the environmental
regulations of the country of origin.

Hachette Books Ireland
8 Castlecourt Centre
Castleknock
Dublin 15, Ireland

A division of Hachette UK Ltd
Carmelite House, 50 Victoria Embankment, EC4Y 0DZ

www.hachettebooksireland.ie

'I know not who these mute folk are
who share the unlit space with me.'

– Robert Frost, 'Ghost House'

PROLOGUE

I had the dream again last night. As usual when it woke me, before my alarm went off, I was drenched in sweat and breathing as though I'd been running. Which I had, in the dream. Or, at least, I'd been trying to run, towards the entrance of the estate. It's always dark in that dream. Rain slapping the ground around me, mud sucking my sandals, like the night I ran across to Michael's house. The entrance always the same distance away, the houses enormous, all looking down at me. Looming.

No people. Just me and the houses and the mud and the rain.

I cried out when I woke. And afterwards I lay there in the dark, half wondering if my mother might knock on my door to check if I was okay. The delusion still there. What is it they say about habits of the mind? That it's easier to prevent than break them? Something like that.

No knock came, of course. The only sound was my rapid breathing, blood rushing in my ears, the sheet whispering against my skin.

Mother. I looked up the word in the dictionary earlier and almost laughed at the simplicity of the definition: 'a woman in relation to her child'.

How long have I been writing here? Two months? Three? Every day, sitting on this bed, opening my laptop, typing away, just like I am now. Trying to get it all down. Always with only that same wretched view for company – the low laurel that separates the garden from the road beyond, the horse chestnut, which is still leafless. The whole time I've been doing this, not a trace of new green has pushed through anywhere on those grey limbs. All you can see are sticky-seeming shiny things protruding from the branches. The more I look, the more of them I see. They're everywhere. Hard and poisonous-looking.

· And here are the fruits of my labour. I have achieved what I set out to do. Every moment of what happened is down here in black and white, in sentences I can read back to myself. So I can finally see, once and for all, that that nice female guard was right when she said I had nothing to feel guilty about. That, if anything, I was a victim. Really, I should be celebrating. Maybe I am, in a way. Haven't I just opened this last bottle of wine? Haven't I finally allowed myself to take this little jar from the chest of drawers? Cool and smooth to the touch. The glass shining darkly. The delicate sound when I shake it is almost pretty.

The hardest part was deciding when to begin. When does anything really begin? That was not so straightforward. But once I realised it had all begun with Jason – that last night out with the girls – nothing could have stopped me. There had been no need, after all, to worry I wouldn't be able to finish it. Of all the hurdles I'd feared – Mum trying to have me admitted somewhere, Helen coming home early, the guards calling me in for more questioning, or an inquest being held after all, at which they conclude that I may somehow have been complicit – not one materialised.

Though the last was unlikely. That's what they call being paranoid. It is only me, after all, who suspects me of murder.

1

What I liked about Jason the first time I saw him, there on the street outside the nightclub at two in the morning, was the way he was smiling right at me. Not Sarah, or any of the others, but me. Even as he sauntered over to me, the girls and I all watching, not once did he break that gaze to take in any of them. They might have disappeared in a cloud of smoke and I don't think he would have noticed. It was like I was the only person in the world. Or, at least, the only one who mattered.

He was very handsome too, of course, in a tall, broad-shouldered way. Despite all that gel in his hair and the way his stiffly ironed shirt was tucked into his jeans – not my usual type – you couldn't fail to register how good-looking he was.

I suppose that didn't hurt. That, and the fact that I'd just had a huge falling-out with all four of the girls. But I don't think I'm misremembering when I say, in that moment, I sensed something fateful about our first encounter, as random as it seemed to be on the surface. There was something so purposeful about him. So focused. Even as he was smiling at me. Even as we began to talk.

That was only last summer. This time last year, I didn't even know him.

That night, the girls and I were having a farewell party of sorts. We had been living together since college, but now Sarah and Alice were about to emigrate to Australia, Emily was starting a new job in Galway and Jane was moving in with her boyfriend. Which meant that I would be the last of us living in our house in Dublin, which we had shared for all those years. Four other people were due to move in the following week. People I had never met.

The five of us used to do everything together. Eat, go shopping and, of course, party. Thursday night was Takeaway Thursday, or Tinnie Thursday, as Alice used to call it, on account of all the cans of beer consumed. Friday and Saturday nights, we almost always ended up in a nightclub, sometimes continuing to party at home or at someone else's house. Sunday was Brunch Sunday, never complete without at least one round of Bloody Marys.

At first, I blamed the recession for ruining everything. After all, it was because of it that Sarah, Alice and Jane all lost their teaching work and Emily was let go from a marketing company. And it was because of that that they were all suddenly broke and in bad form, and we had to stop going out so much. That I'd got off relatively lightly – the information company I worked for as a junior technical writer making me freelance instead of an employee – didn't seem to help things. If anything, it made them worse. There I was, working from home, in front of them, while they scanned the internet for anything that would pay. I was busy a lot of the time, and would often have a drink once I'd signed off for the day. Nothing major – a gin and tonic maybe, or a glass of white wine. Just to unwind. Maybe that bothered them, though I always offered them one. In fact, I was always trying to make things a bit easier for them. For instance, they couldn't afford to go out for brunch any more so I made it at home, a couple of Sundays. Along with a very big jug of Bloody Mary. But they didn't even have one drink. They just ate the food as though they had to, then made their excuses and left pretty much straight away. One Thursday I got takeaways and a few cans, but no one seemed grateful. I even caught Emily giving Jane this look, as if to say, God, here we go again. Whenever I asked if anyone wanted a post-work drink with me, they'd always say no. And whenever I tried to get someone – anyone – to go out with me on a Friday night, they were always too tired or too broke or too something.

'We're not students any more,' Alice snapped at me once.

After that, I stopped trying to do anything nice. I even took to having my takeaway in my bedroom. Occasionally I went out alone, to a bar we used to go to. I had to get out of the house after working there all day. I needed a change of scenery.

There might have been a couple of occasions when, in retrospect, I hadn't behaved brilliantly. But nothing major. The kind of stuff that used to happen all the time before, that no one would even notice, or if they did they'd laugh it off. Like, on Emily's birthday, she had booked a table at this bar she liked, but by the time we got there, the doorman wouldn't let us in. He said I was too drunk. I must have apologised a million times, even though I don't think I'd drunk much more than anyone else. Another time, they'd all been out with their families. Father's Day, I think it was. And when they got home, they found me pretty drunk. I'd been on my own all day, and had just been so bored. Work was busy so I'd decided to chill out with some wine, watching old movies. But there was some kind of row when they came home, and the next day, Emily would barely look at me. I couldn't even remember what I'd said to her. Again, it wasn't as though I didn't apologise.

So, when Sarah and Alice announced that they were moving to Australia, I was not that surprised. The most hurtful part was sensing that Jane and Emily already knew. That this whole 'announcement' was just being staged for my benefit.

'You two decided against it,' I said, looking at Jane and Emily, to show them I knew. They were flustered. I'd been right.

'Actually, I'll still be moving out,' said Emily. She spoke in a really low voice and she was staring straight ahead instead of at me.

'You never said anything,' I said.

'I got a new job. Starts next month. In Galway.'

'Congratulations.'

'I'll be leaving too,' said Jane, hastily. 'Moving in with Rob.' Her boyfriend.

'Great,' I said. 'Good for you.'

'Do you think you'll stay on here?' said Sarah.

'Well, why would *I* move out?'

'No reason. Just, I suppose there'll be people taking over our rooms. We were wondering if you might prefer to move in with Helen maybe.'

Helen is my sister, but she's a lot older than me. We hardly ever see each other.

'Helen?' I said. I shook my head. 'Anyway, she's in London, these days.'

'You never mentioned that.'

I shrugged. 'Some new play over there.'

I wasn't sure why they thought I *would* have mentioned it. Let alone why they seemed to have decided among themselves that I might move in with her. But that was the problem with the girls. For some reason, they never seemed able to accept that my family is – how can I put it? – less emotionally demanding than their own families. Whenever I insisted that I was happy with my family life, or lack of it, I suppose, they just never seemed to believe me. Sometimes I'd even occasionally invent family stuff for their sake, like a meal out for my birthday, or my mother and I going to one of Helen's plays. Just to reassure them and to stop them getting concerned and wanting to talk about it. I even pretended that my mother had invited me along when she did her annual house swap in Spain at Christmas. Just to avoid their outrage on my behalf, even though to me it was no big deal that my family doesn't do stuff like Christmas.

'Or even your mother?' said Sarah.

'Move in with my mother?' I said. 'Why would I want to do that?'

'Well, I don't know. Just for a while. I mean, you get on with *her*, don't you?'

'Of course. We get on fine. You know that.' They were all gazing blankly at me. 'We're grown-ups now, girls, or did you all miss that? Mum does her own thing.' I shook my head at the absurdity of it. 'Just because I'm not on the phone to her every night.'

'Okay,' said Sarah.

'Where would I even sleep? Her spare room is full of all her stuff.'

'Okay, okay, no worries. You're probably right.'

I wanted to ask Sarah why, if she was so worried about me, she hadn't invited me along to Australia. Sarah and I had been friends before any of the others. There was a time when we'd talked about everything, and always to each other first.

'Of course I'm right,' I said. 'Not everyone goes home to Mummy whenever something goes wrong.' This was a dig at Emily, who had once moved home for a month after her boyfriend broke up with her. But if she got it, she didn't say anything.

'Well, we know who we want in charge of the going-away night,' said Sarah. I almost expected her to pat me on the head when she said that.

'No problem,' I said. 'It'll be my pleasure.'

*

We started in the Westbury Hotel for cocktails, then went on to the Bank, where I'd arranged for platters of bar food – cocktail sausages, samosas, chicken wings – that kind of thing. That way, the party wouldn't be interrupted by a sit-down three-course meal somewhere, over which everyone half sobers up and gets sleepy. Everyone else agreed that was the best plan, or at least they didn't say anything against it, except Emily. She stuck a cocktail stick into a sausage and peered at it, like she didn't know exactly what to do with it. She looked at me.

'I thought we were going for an actual meal?'

'This is an actual meal, Emily,' I said. And I took her sausage and stuffed it into my mouth. 'See?'

'Just eat,' said Sarah. 'The samosas are all right.'

After we had cleared the trays of food and got in a couple of rounds, we went to another bar, and then on to Rí-Rás, a nightclub we always used to go to in college. By then, everyone was pretty drunk. We danced for ages. For a while, it felt like nothing had changed.

When the music stopped being good, I went to the bar to get in another round of sambucas. By the time I got back to the girls, Jane was gone.

'She has stuff on in the morning,' Sarah shouted in my ear.

'Stuff?'

'Family stuff.'

'Some friend she is,' I said. And I think that was when I started to get upset. There was a look, you see, between Sarah and the others when I said that. Just a quick flash. I pretended not to notice. I downed my shot and then I downed a second. Seeing as Jane wasn't there any more. 'Come on,' I said, 'drink up.' And I headed back to the dance-floor. When no one came with me, I danced with some strangers instead.

It was late when we walked out into the warm June night. Even though all the streetlamps were still on, there was that feeling of dawn having begun somewhere.

'Where next?' I said, once we were all on the path.

'It's two in the morning,' said Sarah. 'Our flight is, like, eleven hours away.'

'But you've packed, haven't you?' I said. 'We should keep drinking at home, and then go to an early house. You should go straight from the early house to the airport. That would be hilarious.'

'No, it wouldn't,' said Alice. 'We need to grab a taxi,' she added, to Sarah.

'C'mon, Beth,' said Sarah, linking arms with me. 'Let's call it a night.'

I stamped my feet in a mock tantrum. 'We cannot go home yet,' I said.

Emily and Alice exchanged glances. Again.

'I saw that,' I said. 'What's your problem anyway?' I was looking at Emily.

'I don't have a problem,' she said. 'I'm moving out, remember?'

'What's that supposed to mean?'

'It means what it means.'

'Fuck you, Emily.' I didn't shout it or anything, but it was definitely loud enough for her to hear.

'Oh, that's nice.'

'What have you suddenly got against me? It's not my

fault you had to get yet another job, on the other side of the country. How long do you think this one will last?'

The way she looked at me then, I thought for a moment she was going to strike me. I smiled at her.

'Why do you always have to do this?' she said. 'Why do you always have to ruin everything?'

People had started watching.

'Oh, Christ,' said Sarah.

'At least Emily's being honest,' I said. 'You may as well admit it. You all hate me now. Just because I managed to hold on to an income.'

'You need a cup of tea and your bed,' said Sarah. But she didn't say it in her usual voice. She sounded fed up.

'I don't want a cup of fucking tea,' I said. 'I want to stay out.'

'Jesus, hold her back!'

We all looked at the three men walking past us. One of them was smiling at me – that was how I knew who'd said it. It was Jason. Already smiling at me in that way.

I knew I had to do or say something quickly, or he would be gone.

'You get it,' I said, smiling back at him. I'm pretty sure Emily rolled her eyes. But I ignored her. Because it had worked. The three guys had stopped walking.

'Why don't you come with me?' I said to him.

His two friends laughed.

'I didn't invite you,' I said. That made them laugh more.

'Eh. Catch ye up, lads,' he said. Hands in his pockets, he made his way over to me, still smiling, in that who-have-we-got-here-then kind of way. His friends stood there for a bit, but soon they drifted off.

He really was very good-looking. Like someone out of an advert.

'So?' he said, when he was standing beside me. 'Come with you where, exactly?'

'Well, we can't go back to mine. They won't like it.'

'Will they not?' He looked quizzically at me when I said that. Only then did he smile at the girls.

'No. It's past their bedtime. Do you have any drink in your place?'

'Jesus. You don't waste time, do you?' He smiled at the girls again.

'Well, so long,' I said to them.

'What? You're taking off – with this guy?' said Sarah.

'I am.' I linked arms with him. The man whose name I still didn't know. 'Come on,' I said to him. I saluted the girls. 'Nice knowing you,' I said. 'Keep in touch.'

Emily looked away.

'Beth!' Sarah ran after me, pulled at my arm until I turned to face her. 'Beth,' she said again.

'What?'

You could see she wanted to say something important, but it was as though she couldn't figure out exactly what it was. She looked almost angry with me.

'I'm worried about you,' she said finally.

'What is there to worry about?' I said.

She turned to the man beside me. 'What's your name, anyway?' she said to him.

'Jason.'

'Jason. What's your surname?'

'Jason Maher. Don't worry, I'm not going to kidnap her or anything.' He was still smiling, like he was bemused by the situation he'd suddenly found himself in. Like he was trying to show he was just going along with it. That there was no reason to be concerned about *him*. But she didn't smile back. She just gazed at him, with her worried expression, and then she turned back at me.

'Are you sure you don't want to move in with your mother? Even just for a while?'

'Oh, for God's sake,' I said. 'I'm not even going to answer that.'

'You know there's nothing wrong with not being okay now and again? You don't have to pretend you're always fine.'

I didn't know what she was getting at. 'That's great,' I said.

'You're drinking too much, Beth,' she said then. 'You know that, don't you?'

'Oh, for God's sake.'

'You have a problem.'

'That makes zero sense.' I turned to the man beside me. To Jason. 'Where do you live?' I said.

'Beth, this is it,' said Sarah.

'Tragic, isn't it? Enjoy Australia.'

She gave me that worried look again. Then she pulled me to her, hugged me. 'You can talk to me anytime,' she said.

'Ha.' I smiled at Jason. 'She's going to the other side of the world in the morning. Did I tell you that?'

'Bye, then,' she called after us, as we walked away.

'Where do you think I'll be in the morning?' I asked him.

'I couldn't possibly say,' he said.

*

I woke in a small, dark bedroom in a strange bed. Beside me lay Jason, his face all relaxed and puffed out with sleep. He was snoring, very lightly. Every time he took a breath, there would be a tiny pause, as if that was his last. And then he would exhale.

2

I have this daydream. It's that Friday evening at the end of September when Jason and I go to dinner, after his meeting in Dunlone, and we form the Plan. In the daydream, I tell him I have to go to the bathroom. And I do go. But instead of making my way back to our table, I walk to the door, which was behind where he sat. I go outside and I call a taxi, which takes me straight to his place. There, I ask the driver to wait as I take all my things, or as many as I can manage. And then I go straight to my mother's house. She lets me in. She would have let me in, I think. The next day, I write Jason a letter, breaking up with him. And then I start figuring out how to leave Dublin.

I could have done all of that. It probably would have

worked. He hadn't met my mother and didn't know where she lived. If I ever saw him again, it would have been ages later, and by then it wouldn't have mattered. He would have got himself a new girlfriend and he would have forgotten all about me.

Of course, it never occurred to me to do any of that. Why would it? That summer, I had spent almost every single night in Jason's house, only ever returning to my own place to work or to collect something, maybe put a wash on. I barely met the people who had taken the girls' rooms. By the time I was sitting in that restaurant, waiting for him, most of my clothes had been squished into his wardrobe, alongside all his suits and shirts and jeans.

I'd got there early, so I'd found us a table by the window. It was a place we often went to – a big, high-ceilinged affair, which was almost always noisy and full, and did decent food and cheap carafes of wine. I ordered myself a glass, and passed the time watching people walking past outside. Already, the streetlamps had glimmered on, and the sky was that pale colour it goes just before it turns navy. The cars, too, had their headlights on and the bakery across the road glowed against the evening. The summer had already ended without me noticing.

It felt almost strange, being able to just sit there and think about whatever I wanted. Falling in love, I had realised by then, was overwhelming and exhausting. Very few days had passed that summer when we didn't see each other. When I wasn't working, I was usually either with him or on my way to him. Both of us were working a lot: I had picked up another couple of clients for freelance work and he was a project manager for a pharmaceutical company, in the middle of some big study. I never properly understood his job. Any time he talked about it, he would go into all sorts of complicated detail that I couldn't understand and I would find myself zoning out. Or it would seem to make sense when he was talking about it, but as soon as he stopped, I could never remember much of what he'd been saying. All I really knew was that he was responsible for getting a project finished on time, for everything to be done properly. That it was very stressful.

Once, I had asked him why he, like me, had few friends. I had made a joke of it, saying he was about as Billy No-mates as me. By then we'd been together about two months.

'Well, I do have friends,' he said. 'The lads at home. You'll meet them some time.'

He was a country boy, and had spoken before about his old school friends. But he had been home only once that summer for a weekend, and when he came back he was in an awful mood for days. I was going to ask him about that when he produced a photo of himself with a woman, slim and beautiful, his arm draping her neck, his hand hugging her shoulder. Both of them smiling. My ex-fiancée, he said. And he told me they had been going out together for three years. They'd looked at properties together, talked about having kids. They'd had the same big bunch of friends. And then one day he woke to find she had moved out, without telling him. And then he found out that all their friends had known before he did. That she had moved in with a couple they had once gone on holidays with. 'So they weren't really your friends at all,' I said, reminded of my own situation.

'Not exactly,' he said.

Then, he said, there was the time back in college when he'd been going out with someone else who, it turned out, had been seeing one of his so-called friends all along. 'Clearly I'm stupid,' he said. 'I'm the kind of person who falls hook, line and sinker for someone and gives them everything. I'm the idiot who keeps getting his heart broken.'

I put my arms around his neck and kissed him.

'What's your excuse?' he said then.

'What do you mean?' I said. He already knew about my falling-out with the girls.

'You don't have any other mates except those girls you were out with that night?' He sounded surprised.

'No. Not really.' I thought about it. 'I mean, I've had other friends but I suppose I lost touch with them over the years.'

He was looking at me.

'What?' I said. 'Is that awful?'

'No, no. Don't feel bad about it. Just a bit unusual, I suppose.'

'I didn't feel like I needed anyone else these past few years. The girls felt like a family.'

'Some family they turned out to be. What about your real family?' He was still looking at me keenly. I had already told him about Mum and Helen and he seemed not to have seen anything unusual in my relationships with them. He hadn't even seemed surprised when I told him I didn't know who my father was.

'Well, you know,' I said. 'Mum and Helen are busy. They've their own lives. It's all good.'

But he was still staring at me. I didn't know what to say. I started pulling little balls of lint off my cardigan.

'Poor little lost girl,' he said finally.

'Ha.'

He put an arm around me. 'Well, I still love you,' he said. 'Even if no one else does.'

'Are you sure?'

'Sure I'm sure. It's kind of romantic in a way,' he said.

'How so?'

'Just you and me. A pair of mavericks. Us against the world. We don't need anyone else.'

'I suppose not.'

'I mean, say you hadn't met me that night. What would you even be doing with yourself now? Who would you be hanging out with?'

I shook my head.

'Go on. Think about it. Who?'

'No one, I guess.'

'No one. That's terrible.'

'I suppose it is,' I said weakly.

'What a loser.' He elbowed me, to show he was joking. 'I've landed myself a friendless loser.'

'All right.'

'Ah, I'm only joking. Seriously, Beth. Look at me.'

It was difficult to return his gaze. I suppose I felt embarrassed. Ashamed, even.

'I see the good in you. Even if no one else does. Okay?'

'Okay.'

'You don't need anyone else. You have me. Fuck everyone else. Say it.'

'Fuck everyone else.'

'All right.'

'I love you,' I said, my eyes stinging, my voice wobbly.

'I love you too, loser.'

'Very funny.'

Occasionally that summer I saw flashes of the low moods that could descend on him. There was one weekend where he had to work because of some deadline, and we had arranged to meet in a pub on the Sunday evening. Every attempt I made at conversation fell flat. He just would not speak. All I could get out of him was the odd sullen nod. A group of people were sitting near us, and after a few minutes of this, I ended up in a conversation with one of them – a woman, about my own age. She had put her coat over my bag by mistake, that was what had us talking at all, and then we just chatted briefly about how packed the pub had become.

She said something about how she couldn't hear half of what was being said among her group, and I said something along the lines of 'I don't have that problem. This fella's playing the strong silent type this evening for some reason.' I looked in Jason's direction and she followed my gaze. She made some jokey remark about men being like children. He smiled when she said it. He even said something self-deprecating. I can't remember what it was, but I remember thinking, Oh, great, he's snapped out of it. He even started chatting to her, and while the three of us talked, he put his arm around my shoulders.

Soon afterwards he suggested we head home. I was a little surprised, but assumed he was tired. It was only when we were back out on the street that I realised he was upset. Once we'd gone down a side road towards our house, he stopped walking and turned to face me. He was holding my wrist and I remember his fingers dug in painfully but that he was too upset to notice.

'How could you insult me like that?' he said.

'What do you mean?'

'Don't pretend you don't know what I mean, Beth. Don't add insult to fucking injury, okay?'

I had never seen him like that.

'Do you mean when I was talking to that woman? It was just a joke. I'm sorry, okay? I didn't mean to insult you.'

We walked home in an awful silence. It was a couple of days before he spoke to me again. On the Tuesday, I curled up beside him on the sofa, bottle of wine in hand. In a quiet voice, I told him he could trust me. That I would never do anything to hurt him. That I could never leave him, not in a million years. I told him I loved him, even though we had only been seeing each other a couple of months. It doesn't matter that we have different taste in music, books and films, or that we don't have any of the same interests, I told him, because we have each other in common. We would be different, I told him, because we are a team. Isn't that what he had said? Us against the world? We wouldn't let each other down. We couldn't.

He stared at me long and seriously when I said that.

'What would you do,' he said, 'without me?'

'No,' I said. I shook my head. 'That can't happen.'

I meant it. The idea of being without him made me feel blind panic. I just couldn't see myself anywhere without him.

'You don't make sense on your own, do you?'

'No,' I said. 'I don't.'

Almost imperceptibly, he nodded. 'Come here,' he said, stretching out his arm. I scooched up beside him. Only then did I know I'd got it right.

After that, it felt as though we had made some kind of pact – that we were in this for the long haul. And if the silences and sudden flashes of anger seemed to happen more and more frequently, it was as though that pact had somehow created space for them. We were a team now. That was the main thing.

'You look comfortable,' he said.

It was Jason. I didn't know how long he had been standing by the table like that, watching me staring out the window, my almost empty glass. He was still in the suit he had worn to his meeting. His forehead was shiny with sweat. I remember that so vividly, and how his short hair shone too, from the gel he had applied that morning.

'Hey,' I said. 'You scared me. God, you must be tired. Did you drive straight back? How long did it take?'

He sat down.

'I got here early,' I said. 'I wanted us to get a good seat.'

He signalled to a waiter. He smiled at him. 'I'll have the burger,' he said.

The waiter looked at me.

'Me too,' I said. 'The burger. And can we get a carafe of the house red? And some of those olives and nibbly bits. So,' I said to Jason, 'how did your mysterious meeting in Dunlone go?'

'Fine. It went fine.'

'What does fine mean?'

'They've offered me a job,' he said.

'A job. Down there?'

'It's a massive pharmaceutical company. It's their biggest site in Europe.'

'Wow.'

'Yes. Wow. It would be a huge career leap.'

'When does it start?'

He looked at me, like he was trying to read something in my face. 'Not until January.'

'Right.'

'They want me now obviously, but there's no way I'm letting those morons get the credit for the past two years.'

'No, of course not.'

The waiter arrived with our drinks and the olives. I waited until he had gone. Then I filled our glasses.

'So. Are you going to take it?' I said. I tried to say it neutrally. Then I tried to seem distracted by some wine I'd spilled. The truth was, I didn't know what this meant for us. Neither did I know how he wanted me to respond. I didn't want that thing to happen, where I said the wrong thing.

'Maybe,' he said. 'I suppose it depends.' He was staring at me in a careful sort of way.

I tried smiling coyly. 'Would you commute? From here?' I said. 'It's too far, isn't it?'

'Yes, Beth. It's too far.'

I looked back out the window. Across the road, two young

women were coming out of an off-licence, all high boots and make-up. They were laughing.

'So,' he said, 'are you coming with me?'

At first, I didn't answer.

He looked down at his plate.

'Oh, my God,' I said. 'Jason! Are you serious?'

'Forget it.'

'No. Wait. I thought you were messing.'

He kept his gaze on the traffic.

'Jason. I've been half expecting you to break up with me!'

'Expecting or hoping?' He looked down at the olives. 'Jason makes a fool of himself again. I must be setting a record here.'

'What the hell are you on about? I would love to go with you.'

'Don't say things you don't mean.'

'No, seriously.' I put my hand on his, squeezed it until he looked back at me. 'I can't imagine being without you any more. What have I got in Dublin anyway? And I can work anywhere, can't I? Jason, it's perfect.'

'You're not bullshitting me?'

'I swear to God I am not bullshitting you,' I said. I took a drink of my wine.

'Because I've been thinking about it,' he said. 'I haven't explained everything. If we made some pretty big decisions around now, it could be life-changing. I'm not exaggerating.'

'Okay. Well, I'm definitely intrigued.' I gulped my wine again, refilled our glasses.

'You sure?'

'Eh – yes?'

He regarded me warily, his eyes all big and childlike. I squeezed his hand again and smiled.

He took a deep breath. 'Something – interesting happened.'

'I'm all ears.'

He frowned. 'Nothing actually happened. It's just – something got me thinking.'

I nodded at him. I beamed.

'After this meeting, I went for lunch with them. Someone asked if I'd sorted accommodation yet. I said I hadn't. Then this other guy mentions his brother-in-law has a small housing development in a village a couple of miles outside Dunlone.'

'He owns it?'

'He owns it. He's a developer. You know?'

'Right.'

'A nice village,' he said. 'With a golf course.'

'A golf course.'

'It's a really small estate. Like seven houses. High end, bespoke kind of thing. A ten-minute drive from work. So this developer wants to rent out one of the houses on it. Except this is the catch – there is no rent.'

'No rent. I don't get it.'

He smiled tightly, glanced out the window.

'Sorry,' I said.

'It's complicated. You might find it complicated. Stay with me, okay? Seven houses. Three finished. The rest in various stages of completion.'

'Right.'

'Like I said, a high-end, luxury-type estate. Two of the

finished ones have been bought. People living in them and everything. Now the developer, this guy Paul, has run out of cash. You might have noticed there's a recession going on.'

'Recession. Yes.'

'He's not in any crazy debt or anything. Treading water. He's pretty sure he can manage. All he needs to do is keep his head down until the economy picks up again and prices return to normal. Then he'll finish the last couple of houses, and sell the lot.'

'When will that happen?'

'A few years, I don't know. The point is, it looks better if there's someone living in the last finished house. And it keeps it from getting damp, run down, all that.'

'So, he wants someone to house-sit it.'

'Exactly. House-sit.'

'So. Whoever will move in won't pay anything?'

'They might cover the insurance. That'd be it.'

'But why doesn't he just charge rent? Sorry. I'm being slow.'

He sighed. 'The location. A village outside town, remember? Doesn't have much of a rental market. And, anyway, I think he's more interested in the calibre of tenants than the rent he might make from it.'

'Is it a ghost estate?' I said. 'I was reading about those.'

'What? No. It's not a ghost estate.'

'There's one outside Galway, with two families living in it and eighty empty houses. People come and break in at night. To the empty houses.'

'Is there?' He tapped the table top with his fingers.

'I was only saying.'

'Forget it. How was your day?' He glanced at me, then threw his gaze around the room.

'Sorry,' I said. 'Jason, I'm sorry. I wasn't listening properly.'

'Well, don't say it like that. You make me sound like a psycho. You can listen any way you like.'

'What was this guy saying anyway, about the estate?'

'It doesn't matter. It was just another way of trying to get me to start working there now. He wants someone to move in straight away.'

'Oh. And you can't do that, can you? You need to stay on in your job to get the full credit.'

'And obviously that house will be snapped up by someone in the meantime. I mean, a rent-free luxury house.'

'Sure,' I said.

'It could be ours if we moved in now, but . . .' He sat back. 'That's not going to happen.'

'No.'

He was looking at me as though expecting me to say something.

'What a pity,' I said.

'Yes, Beth. What a pity.'

'Imagine what we could save,' I tried.

'Imagine.' He pushed away his plate. He stared out the window.

'Hey,' I said. 'What if I moved down now?'

He turned back to me.

'Couldn't we do it that way?' I said. 'I mean, what's stopping us?'

'You want to move down now, to hold the place for us?'

'It's an idea.'

'What would your mother say?'

'My mother?'

He nodded, studying me carefully. 'And your sister.'

I was thrown by the question. 'Why would they mind?' I said.

'I suppose there's no reason. You're an adult.'

'They wouldn't mind.'

'What about your friends?'

'Friends? What friends? You mean the ones who moved to Australia without inviting me along? Or the ones still around who haven't contacted me all summer?'

'They don't sound too much like friends, when you put it like that.'

'No,' I said. 'They don't, do they?' I picked up an olive, put it down again. 'Friends who have not contacted me once, all summer. Who barely bothered to tell me they were moving out.' The anger crept back, just enough. 'And you'd be down every weekend, wouldn't you? It's not like I'd be on my own all the time.'

'Of course. I'd be with you every single weekend.'

'And we wouldn't be talking long.'

'You'd be talking about ten weeks. Eleven max. Wait. Are you serious about this?'

'I think I am,' I said. 'Imagine how much we'd save,' I said again.

'Well, exactly,' he said. 'We could save thousands. In this market, it could make us.' He ran his hand through his hair and then he put it on mine. I remember it felt a bit greasy from the gel.

'Hang on a minute, okay?' he said.

He left the restaurant. I watched from my window, as he ran across the street, disappearing into a Spar, soon emerging with a foolscap pad and a pen.

We must have sat in there for hours that evening, him scribbling notes, totting up columns of figures. How much we might save, between his income and mine. If we lived on a tight budget, of course. It would have to be very tight. Then how much we'd need for a deposit, how much time we had before the market might be expected to pick up, how much we might hope to get a property for, as against how much it had cost just a few years ago. How much it might cost in the future. At first, I hadn't realised that that was the plan – to save for a deposit on a property. When I did understand, it seemed so obvious to him that that was what we had been talking about all along, I was too embarrassed to say anything. And then he started talking about the kind of place we could buy, once we'd moved back to Dublin. A red-brick Victorian, right in the area where we were sitting – one of the nicest parts of the city.

'Imagine living here,' he said. 'I mean, imagine owning a house here. Imagine having children here.'

'I never thought of – where.'

He looked at me. He placed the pen on the table. 'I've gone too far.'

'It does all seem very – big stuff.'

'Yeah. Big stuff.' He rubbed his face. He squinted out the

window. By then, it had grown dark. 'I always go too far,' he said, and he pressed the heels of his hands into his eyes. He looked exhausted.

'Why not, though?' I said. 'Why not big stuff? Seriously, I mean it. We're in our twenties. We're proper grown-ups now. What am I waiting for?' I took his hand, squeezed it. 'I love you, Jason,' I said. 'I want to do big stuff with you.' I kept hold of his hand until he said it back.

'Yeah. I love you too. I can trust you, can't I?'

'You know you can. You can always trust me.'

'Yeah,' he said. 'This is different.'

'We could spend Christmas in that estate,' I said. 'Our first Christmas together.'

He stared when I said that. 'Yes,' he said finally. 'Our first Christmas together. We could do that. Unless you have other plans? Like with your family?'

I hadn't thought about what I'd be doing that Christmas. Trying to pretend it wasn't Christmas, as usual. 'No plans,' I said.

'Are you sure?'

'It's like what you said before. We're a team. We're making a go of this.'

He was still staring at me intently. 'You and me. A pair of mavericks against the world. Isn't that it?'

'That's it.'

A waiter came over, told us they were closing. The restaurant, besides us and the staff, was empty.

I drained my glass. 'We're celebrating,' I said to the waiter.

'Great,' he said, and walked away.

'This is what we should do,' I said. 'It's like Fate. Isn't it amazing that we only met three months ago?'

He nodded.

'Just sometimes things click into place,' I said, 'and you have to go with them.'

'We're actually going to do this,' he said.

'To a new life,' I said, raising my empty glass and waiting then, until he raised his, and we clinked. 'Even if it is going to be in the bloody midlands.' I made a silly sad face, then smiled to make sure he knew I was joking.

'A new life,' he said.

'I can't believe it,' I said. 'I'm going to live in the midlands. With you. Well, not straight away with you. But soon with you.' I drummed on the table. 'God, I'm so excited. It just feels right.'

3

This morning my mother who, since she picked me up from the hospital, has done her impressive best in pretending I'm not actually here, came up to me in the kitchen when I was making coffee and handed me a document. Typed, about four pages, stapled together. On the front page, it read, 'Eileen Sheehan. Assignment 3: Memoir'.

'It's from that writing course I did last year. I thought it might interest you.' Her voice was all nervous and shrill. That's the way it sounds any time she talks to me these days. As though she's frightened of me.

Maybe she is frightened of me.

Anyway, there is, of course, nothing unusual about her doing that. Once I read that an octopus can survive out of water for just half an hour and I immediately thought of my mother. If you replace water with being the centre of attention. It is completely typical of her that, after all that's happened to me, the only time she tries to reach out it's to make everything about her again.

I've read it, of course. I thought I'd better, in case she asked me about it. I'm certainly not going to bring it up with her. Anyway, it's not as though there was much in it that I didn't already know. Maybe not in so much detail, but I knew the outline. I mean, of course it's awful what happened to her. Shocking, even. But it was such a long time ago. And things have been pretty good for her since then, as far as I understand it. It's pathetic, really. Like the time she, Helen and I went for dinner after going to see Helen in her first play – this was years ago. Instead of praising Helen, she started saying how hard it was for her not to have any opportunities to do something like that with her own life.

Last night, she went to bed early so I came downstairs and turned on the television. I ended up watching this documentary called 'The Forest Monks of Sri Lanka'. It was full of all these scratchy black-and-white images of the monks – walking in solemn lines, sitting cross-legged under scrawny trees, holding out a bowl, cooking over a small open fire on the forest floor. Theirs is an ascetic lifestyle, said the narrator. The forest monks do not care about anything except enlightenment. Living in single huts in the forests, they meditate alone. Some go begging for food. In the evening, they chant hymns to the Buddha. Their entire lives are devoted to following the Four Noble Truths. All about how life *is* suffering because we always want things to be different from how they are. And how you can escape suffering by following something called the Middle Way. All to do with being mindful in everything you do and meditating.

I looked up 'ascetic lifestyle' on my phone. 'Characterised by abstinence from sensual pleasures,' it said, 'often for the purpose of pursuing spiritual goals.'

There was one time Mum showed some concern. Or it's probably more accurate to say she bothered to go through the motions of showing concern. I had been back here about two weeks. Back then, I was not in a good way. The bad feeling was at its worst. Like the blood in my veins was getting heavier, like any second it might set like concrete. I was lying in bed when she came into this room and said, in that short snippy way she has of speaking to me without looking at me, that I should probably go to a therapist or something. Or at least a doctor. She said it in that way of hers that implies it's irritating for her to have to point this out to me. That, somehow, my feeling bad is an embarrassment. Bad manners almost.

She hasn't once asked me anything about what happened. Not once has she said if I need to talk she's here. Which is to be expected. I don't know why I feel let down, again. It's as though, when it comes to my mother, there is no learning curve. I have to remind myself this is true to form. That in fact it suits my purposes because it lets me get on with this.

Anyway, going to a therapist is a terrible idea. All they ever want is for you to talk about your childhood, then try to let you off the hook for anything you might have done. As if anything that happened on the estate had anything to do with my childhood.

No, the only thing that can help me is doing this – writing it all down. As objectively as possible. It's the only chance I stand of being able to believe what that nice guard said.

'You have nothing to feel bad about, Beth. If anything, you're a victim.'

If I hadn't had the idea of doing this, I don't know what would have happened. It feels like this grim little routine is saving me from that awful feeling coming back.

God, it is grim, though. Every morning, waiting until the front door clicks shut, which tells me she's gone to work. Going downstairs to make myself coffee and toast, then back up here to sit in bed for the entire morning. Typing, typing, typing. After a sandwich at lunchtime, a quick walk around the block, if I manage to force myself to do it, before coming back here, to this awful little room, always cold, on account of it being north-facing, and so sparsely furnished – just this single bed, a skinny built-in wardrobe and a chest of drawers. (I use the wardrobe for my clothes. Everything else goes in the chest of drawers. In the bottom drawer, I stash my bottles of wine. In the middle one I stash the empty bottles. In the top one, I put my other stuff – toiletries, hairbrush, the jar of sleeping tablets the doctor prescribed to me, stuff like that.) In the late afternoon, I come back downstairs to make dinner for me and Mum. Only then do I allow myself my first glass of wine of the day, taking care to wash the glass before Mum gets home. After dinner, as soon as I've loaded the dishwasher, I'm straight back up here, where I finish my daily bottle of wine. Only one bottle a day. I've found that's all I need so that has become the rule.

I got off to a good start with this, typing away every morning last week. But the past couple of days have been disheartening. Yesterday I just did pointless things, like messing around with the font or looking at photos of the girls on Facebook, Alice and Sarah in Australia, Jane with her new boyfriend. It was like I didn't want to get on to the next bit, that first night when Jason and I arrived at the estate. And today, after reading Mum's thing, I must have spent about an hour just staring out the window. A couple of grey squirrels were darting about among the branches of the horse chestnut. Leaping from one branch to another. Changing their course just like that, because they wanted to.

As though that is the easiest thing in the world to do.

Eileen Sheehan
Creative writing class.
Assignment 3: Memoir.
I was born in 1949. I was born in Dublin. Our small terraced house, where I was born, was one of many like it, on a neat little square, just by where the cattle mart used to be, in Smithfield. There were ten of us in that little two-bed house – my parents, my five brothers and my two sisters and me. It was the same in all the other houses, more or less. That square is still there. There's a playground on its green now, where we grew our vegetables. People are paying God knows what to buy one of those houses. But back then no one living on it had any money.

I was the youngest, so I got the worst clothes. By the time they reached me, they'd not be falling apart because my mother was good at sewing, but they would look terrible. The fabric all shiny and thin, patches on every knee and elbow. But I also was the only one who got to stay on in school. Right up to the final exams and then on to a secretarial course. The others were all working by the time they hit their teens – the boys on the building sites with my father and the girls married jobs in factories. That is why I got all the schooling. By the time it came to me, there was money to spare for it. They said I had the brains, but the truth was I had no more brains than any of them. I was just lucky where I came.

Another thing that was lucky for me was that my father did not drink; otherwise, there probably wouldn't have been enough money for me to go to school. He rarely went to the pub at all – he said he did not like the pressure from the other men, his workmates, to drink. They could not tolerate the sight of him sipping a lemonade, he said. Another thing he said was that they would always remember exactly what each of them had drunk the night before. 'You had two Harps,' one would say to the other, 'before you went on to the Guinness.'

I found the secretarial course very dull, mostly because I had no money to spend at that time, and also because none of my school friends were there, and the other girls looked down on me because of my clothes. I don't mean to spin some kind of a sob story, that was just the way it was. I would have been surprised if they hadn't. Anyway, I kept my head down and passed all my exams, and before I had even graduated, I had got myself a job as a clerk in a small insurance company.

Not that it seemed a small operation to me when I first started. I had never seen anything like that place before. It was on the third floor of an old building along the quays, and looked right across the river to the Four Courts. The other clerks were older than me, but they were still young. Two of them were women, and single like me. Well, we hit it off straight away. They took me under their wing and soon I was having the time of my life with them.

You're probably thinking this is full of clichés but sometimes I think that clichés are clichés because there is truth in them. Anyway, all of this is the truth.

We used to go out together to dances. The pictures. Shopping. To pubs, even. Of course, my parents knew nothing about that. Back in those days, half of them still wouldn't admit women. You weren't allowed order a pint of beer, if you were a woman, unless you were accompanied by a man. But there were places we could go. One was on Leeson Street, a big place that students over from Earlsfort Terrace used to drink in. They were fascinating to us, the students. Especially the women. The way they dressed. The way they spoke. Full of confidence.

One evening, we got chatting to some of those students. It was a Friday night and we'd had a bit to drink. They were taking part in a student protest, they said, over in the university. A sit-down in the great hall, they called it. The three of us ended up sitting in this huge hall with all these students. There must have been hundreds of them in there. Someone was shouting a chant out, the others following. It is the National Concert Hall now but then that was where the university was. They were protesting the way the place was being run, or something like that. I couldn't really understand all the indignation. I must have got very drunk because I only found out the following Monday that the girls had left before I did. And I can't remember how I ended up in this small classroom with the man whose face I cannot remember, who I never saw again. Not that I didn't try, when two months later, I couldn't ignore it any more. The fact that I was pregnant, I mean. I used to stand outside the university after work, hoping to catch sight of him.

I was nineteen. The year was 1968. My parents were very religious. The whole country was very religious in those days. Then there was all the sacrifice everyone in my family had made for me. They would never forgive me. That was clear as day.

I tried all the usual methods – drinking gin, lifting heavy things, even once throwing myself down the stairs. Except you don't actually throw yourself. You make yourself jump forward, over the stairs. It takes an amount of courage. It took me a long time, one Sunday morning when I had cried off Mass saying I had a headache. Nothing worked. The months passed.

I pretended to the other girls to be annoyed about putting on weight. I wonder now did they guess. Occasionally, ending it all flickered as an easier thing. Maybe I would have gone through with that had my mother not walked into my room one morning as I was dressing for work and caught sight of my stomach.

They sent me to live with my Aunt Bríd in Brighton until after the baby was born. She had me work for her – cleaning the place and cooking. When I wasn't doing that, she made me stay in a tiny bedroom on the top floor of her narrow little house. She told me I should spend the time praying for God's forgiveness. All the weeks I was with her, my parents never sent a reply to any of the letters I wrote them. Or perhaps she never posted them for me. I never learned which it was.

The plan was that when the labour started, a friend of hers, a midwife, was going to come to the house and deliver the baby. Then they were going to give the baby to an orphanage, there in Brighton.

They didn't know about my savings – a small fraction of my weekly pay that I'd been putting aside ever since I had suspected the worst. Money that before I would have spent on clothes or going out. I had brought it with me to Brighton, and I kept it and my passport in my suitcase under my bed. It had never occurred to Aunt Bríd to take my passport off me. It would have made no sense to her – the idea that I might want to run away. Wherever would I run to?

I would run home. That was what I had decided. My

parents would see me and the baby and they would forgive me. And somehow we would manage.

The night the labour pains started, I left the house as easily as anything, with my money and passport carefully stored in the inside pocket of my coat. It was about two in the morning. Of course it was dark and before long it seemed my plan was hopeless. If it wasn't for a passing policeman, who I never saw before and have never seen since, I would probably have given birth there on the street. He got me safely to the hospital. Only a couple of hours after I arrived there, the baby was born. The year was still 1968. It was half five in the morning.

'Eight pounds two ounces,' said the nurse, handing her to me. 'That's a healthy weight.' I looked down at this new human being who was mine and no one else's, nuzzling at me like we had always been together and I knew no one was ever taking her from me and that I had done the right thing.

'She's a lively one,' said the nurse, as the baby latched on and began to feed straight away, urgently, little eyes closed tight. 'No flies on her, are there?'

'No.'

She looked at me. 'Wandering the streets in labour. All on your own, too. How did that come about, if you don't mind me asking?'

'I was staying with my aunt,' I said. 'I thought the pains were just – I thought it would take much longer. I thought a walk might help.'

'The dad?'

'My husband is in Ireland,' I said quickly. I had a whole story ready, about him working there and my aunt needed help, but the nurse just nodded in a brisk, no-nonsense kind of way and I realised she didn't give two damns whether or not there was a husband. The idea was startling – that someone might simply not care.

'Give us your aunt's number and I'll get one of the girls to call her for you,' was all she said.

'She's very old,' I said. 'I don't want to wake her. I'll call her first thing.'

'You're sure?'

I nodded.

'Well, you could certainly do with a rest.'

They wheeled me to a ward, where I fell into a deep sleep before waking with an awful start. I was in the semi-dark. Around me were the sounds of people sleeping, a baby crying. Not my baby. She was fast asleep in the cot beside my bed. Then I heard what must have woken me so suddenly. It was Aunt Bríd's voice, coming from the nurse's station.

'It is a matter of urgency that I see her,' she was saying. 'Her parents are out of their minds with worry.'

'I'll check if she's awake,' said a nurse. 'But can we keep our voice down, please? This is a maternity ward. As I said, visiting hours are not until eleven thirty.'

I half sat up. Pulled the cot closer to my bed. Then the curtain swished back. It was the same nurse from earlier.

'Eileen, isn't it? There's a woman here says she's your aunt.'

I just stared back at her.

The nurse walked up to me. 'Do you want to see her?' she whispered.

I still didn't know what to say. I suppose I was surprised at that question. The nurse looked at me, waiting for an answer. Something about her expression told me I maybe had more power in that situation than I thought I had.

'No,' I whispered back.

'That's all right,' she said.

Aunt Bríd appeared then, at the end of my bed. 'This girl has been put under my care by her parents,' she hissed at the nurse.

I lifted my baby out of the cot. Held her to me. She slept on.

'This woman,' said the nurse, 'is nineteen years of age and therefore free to make decisions for herself. She is not under anyone's care.'

I could not believe the calm authority of that nurse. What would have happened if I had been in a hospital in Ireland, I wondered. With the nuns running half of them. I still wonder that sometimes.

Aunt Bríd moved towards me then, pushed past the nurse. She almost had her hands on my baby, who woke and began to cry, nuzzling around for my breast. There was an awful minute when the nurse, and then another *nurse, had to hold her back, before the security guard appeared. But he put a firm hand on her shoulder, and that was the last I saw of her – being led off by this thick-set, stony-faced man, her face all indignation.*

'Now,' said the nurse, who was back by my side, 'you must be famished. How about some tea and toast?'

I could not believe the nerve of her.

Later, I called my parents, from a payphone there in the hospital. But when my mother heard my voice, she just hung up. The same thing happened the next two times I rang. Only the fourth time, did she speak.

'You listen to me,' she said, her voice hoarse and strange. 'We're finished with you. There is no point coming back here because we're finished with you.'

'What will I do?' I said.

'You needn't bother contacting any of your brothers or sisters. They're finished with you too.' She hung up.

I survived, because I had to. Got a place, got a job. Not that it was easy. I think nowadays they would say I was depressed. Post-partum depression, isn't that what they call it? They definitely would say I was poor. There were weeks we lived on tinned soup and cheap bread. Winters when I could only put the heat on for one hour in the evening. But I'm not complaining about Brighton. Eventually, things did get easier. And it was better to me than Dublin would have been in those days. It was my home for sixteen years. It is where Helen grew up, where she did most of her schooling.

Her first name is actually Eileen. That's right. I

named her after myself. Well, I wasn't going to name her after my mother or any of my sisters, was I? Despite what my mother had said, I contacted them – all of them – and my brothers and all of them hung up on me. Not one sent a reply to any of my letters. But after a while, I stopped calling her Eileen and started using her second name instead. Helen. After that woman in history who was a warrior. It felt almost like a curse on her, naming her after myself, given how things had worked out for me. Anyway, I wanted her to have a strong name. I figured she needed all the strength she could get.

4

The next morning, Jason suggested he drive us down to the estate, where the rent-free house was. He wanted me to see it for myself, before we committed to it. The owner might be able to meet us there, he said. Maybe we could even seal the deal today.

In the car, my headache got worse and I felt queasy as Jason switched lanes and speeded up and slowed down through the Saturday-morning traffic of the city. On the motorway I felt even worse, as we rushed along the straight unchanging road, passed through the road tolls, then descended into this sudden landscape of fields and trees, some of them already turning yellow. On and on we went for ages, it seemed, fields on either side of us, then a kind of bogland, a strange sculpture of moons.

The whole way, neither of us spoke. We hadn't spoken much before we got into the car. Ever since I had woken to find he was ready to go, had even had his breakfast, I had known instinctively not to say anything – that if I did, there was a good chance of it being the wrong thing. Anyway, I was horribly hung-over. Doing or saying anything involved effort, my stomach lurching.

At some point on the motorway, I fell asleep. When I woke, we weren't on it any more. We were bombing along, it seemed to me, a narrow, winding country road, past knobbly hills covered with bright yellow furze, the occasional farmhouse. My headache was gone. I was really hungry.

Jason glanced at me. 'Nice sleep?'

'Sorry. Where are we?'

Just then we passed a sign that said, 'Welcome to Ceanna'.

'Is this the village?' I said.

'This is it.'

He slowed down a bit as we came to a sort of main street, I suppose – on one side, a pub with what looked like a restaurant beside it, a shop, a couple of houses, on the other a church and a primary school. Right after the street there was an entrance to a golf course and past that a second driveway, which Jason turned into. At first I thought it was another entrance to the golf course and I hoped we were going to the club to eat first. But then I saw the houses below us, and I realised that the driveway was for the estate, which sort of nestled into the course.

Halfway down, he pulled in.

'That's it,' he said. 'That's the estate.'

It was in a sort of hollow. Seven large houses in a semi-circle, all facing onto what I suppose was meant to be a green but was really just mud and rocks and concrete blocks. Three of the houses looked normal, finished, walls painted, everything. Another three didn't even have windows or doors fitted. Then there was one, at the start of the driveway, with its windows and doors in place but the walls bare brick. All of them had the same gable-front design. There was no wall or fence between any of the gardens, front or back, except for one of the finished ones, which had its entire back garden cordoned off by a kind of makeshift fence. To the left of that house sat a small grey Portakabin.

On both sides of the estate, the golf course was visible, a lone golfer making his way up a steep slope. Everything was bright in the morning sun – the course, the finished houses, which were painted a bright white, their red doors, the dark slate tiles glossy in the sunshine.

'Well?' said Jason. 'What do you think?'

'Pretty,' I said. 'Have you already been here?'

'Just a quick visit yesterday,' he said. 'Paul wanted to say hello. It didn't seem to mean much at the time.'

'Paul?'

'The developer. Actually, I think that might be his car. See, the silver one?' It was parked beside the house, which was to the left of the Portakabin, across the green from the one with the fence.

'Wow.'

'It's *really* pretty,' he said.

Pretty was not a word I had heard him use before. It almost made me laugh.

He drove down into the estate and parked behind the silver car. Paul was inside it talking on a phone. He raised his hand to us and smiled, and soon he ended the call and emerged from the car.

Jason opened his door and got out. I followed.

'Paul,' he said, smiling at the man.

'There he is. Bang on time.'

'This is Beth,' said Jason.

'This is the lady,' said the man, and he extended his hand to me. 'Paul Gilroy.'

Everything about him suggested wealth – the tweed overcoat, the leather briefcase, the smell of his cologne, the way his grey hair was styled, his voice.

'Beth,' I said, shaking his hand. His skin was soft.

'Pleasure to meet you, Beth.'

'You too.'

'Our good man here has told you the story.'

'He has.'

'Well. Here it is.'

We all looked up at the house. In the sunlight, the white walls glared, and the windows shone.

'They remind me,' I said, 'of houses you see on TV. You know. American houses.' I looked at Jason. 'That's probably stupid.'

'Dead on, Beth,' said Paul. 'Well spotted. It's the gable-front design. Based on Greek temples, would you believe?' He held my gaze as he spoke.

'Oh.'

'Very popular in the States, as you say. I've always liked it. It's a classic style. You either get it or you don't. Will we go in?'

We followed him into a wide hallway with a wooden staircase, then on into a large, open-plan living room and kitchen. All the furniture looked expensive and new. Paul opened kitchen cabinets to reveal lights coming on inside them automatically. He showed us the ice-maker on the fridge, the deep drawers that held crockery and glasses. He pointed to a heavy double pendant light hanging from the ceiling over the dining table. He rapped his knuckles on the granite top of the vast kitchen island. He nodded at the fake wooden beams above his head, spotlights embedded in them. He looked at me.

'Very nice,' I said.

'All top of the range. You won't get better.'

Then he led us upstairs, showed us the large master bedroom, with an en-suite, the two smaller bedrooms, the bathroom with a standalone bath.

'Well?' said Jason, when we were back in the living room. 'What do you think?'

'It's gorgeous,' I said.

'Isn't it?'

'Big utility room in there, washer, tumble-dryer,' said Paul, indicating a door off the kitchen. 'And the light just pours into the place. You can see that for yourselves.'

I walked to the front window, by the sofa, and peered out. Across the way, at the house with the fence around its garden, a man stood in the doorway. He was wearing a thick jumper and a wool hat. He seemed to be staring right at us, even though he couldn't have seen us through the windows reflecting the sunlight.

'Who's that?' I said.

Paul walked up to me, looked out. 'That would be Mr Doran,' he said. 'Lives there with his wife. They have a little baby,' he added brightly. 'And you have a lovely lady next door. Claire Walsh. You couldn't meet nicer. Now, this garden is south-facing,' he said, walking across the room, to the French doors. 'And you couldn't get a better view.'

We followed him and gazed out at the golf course beyond the garden, its soft hills and copse of trees on the horizon, the manicured lawn and little flags.

'Didn't someone once say,' I said, and they turned to me expectantly, 'that every time they saw a golf course they saw a ruined view? Who said that?' I folded my arms. 'Only joking,' I said. 'It's lovely.'

'It is lovely,' said Jason. He looked at me then, and I immediately regretted the comment.

'Gorgeous,' I said. 'It really is.'

'You're not the golfing type. No offence taken,' said Paul. To Jason, he added, 'The place is yours if you want it. Terms as we discussed – you pay a nominal rent of fifty euro a month to cover the insurance; you commit to a two-year contract. But I'll need to know by tomorrow morning.' He smiled at me. 'I've a few other potential takers.'

I looked at the dining table. I supposed that was where I would work, alone, every weekday until Christmas. I tried to imagine it. I already worked alone. Once I was working, what did it matter where I was? This was what I told myself.

'It does feel a bit – quiet.' I smiled at them. I wanted to cry, I was so hungry.

'You're always complaining about the noise in your own place!' said Jason.

'I know.'

'Twelve weeks until I'm down, remember?' he said. 'And I'll be here every weekend between now and then.'

There was a moment when I almost said, no, I was so sorry for wasting everyone's time, but I didn't think I could do it. I don't think I'm imagining I almost said that. But then Jason's face, somehow it brought it all back, all we had talked about. The bright future ahead if we did this. And if I didn't move down – if I stayed in Dublin – how empty my life would be. Living and working in a house full of strangers.

I only make sense with him, I reminded myself.

'It's entirely up to you,' said Jason.

'It's great,' I said. 'Really. It's a great opportunity for us.'

'We'll take it,' said Jason.

5

I first drove to the estate myself on a Sunday evening. I can
even remember the date: 5 October. Just over a week after
Jason and I had met Paul there. It's a westward journey,
from Dublin to Ceanna. All the way down, the sun moved
closer and closer to the horizon ahead, until the sky turned
into a sunset – fat cumulus clouds burning a sharp orange
against the pale blue, the sun growing bigger and bigger
until I could look straight at it. By the time I had reached the
estate, the sun had disappeared. All that was left was a deep
pink silhouetting black trees on the golf course. There was no
moon in the sky, but already some stars had appeared.

I had not expected to be moving in so quickly, but of course
that was the whole point. It just hadn't sunk in until after

we met Paul, and Jason asked if I thought I'd have my room rented out by the end of the week. After that, the days went by in a blur – what with clearing out my room and getting someone to take it and trying to keep up with my work. I barely had any time to reflect on what was happening. I think that was why, when I turned the key in the lock that evening, and stepped back into that hallway with its wooden staircase, I felt like I was breaking into someone else's house.

It was freezing in there. It seemed even colder than outside. The first thing I did was get the heating on. Then I brought all my things inside. There wasn't that much – a couple of bags of clothes, my laptop and all my work stuff, and then, of course, my books, which I piled up in towers, against the wall by the fireplace. Having done that, I made myself toast and tea. I must have eaten about ten slices of toast at that dining table, still in my coat. When it grew so dark that I could see my reflection in the glass, I drew all the curtains.

Originally, Jason was supposed to come down that Sunday and help me get settled in. But this big meeting had come up for him on the Monday. In the end, I told him I'd be fine, moving in on my own. It wasn't as though there was that much unpacking to do. It wasn't as though the house was not already sparkling clean. It would be nice, I told him, to settle in by myself, seeing as it was to be my home for the next while. And then, by the time Friday came around, I would be used to it, ready to welcome him. And already one week down. I told him I was looking forward to it.

After unpacking my clothes, making sure to leave space in the wardrobe and bathroom cabinet for Jason's stuff – I decided it made sense for me not to get used to having all that space to myself when he'd be moving down in a couple of months – I went and stood at the front door. I remember thinking vaguely it would be nice if there was another house to my left, instead of the Portakabin, with all its windows, I noticed then, painted black. Every now and then, a sudden sharp breeze shook the wild grass in the green, and the hedge that separated the estate from the golf course. I saw now there were no streetlamps on the estate. Soon the place would be in complete darkness. The only light I could see was in the downstairs window of the Dorans' house opposite.

I'm not sure what I was thinking as I walked across, my arms folded against the cold, and rang the Dorans' doorbell. Immediately, a dog began growling from behind the fence. Then a thud sounded against it and there was a flash of paws. He barked. I took a step back and was about to retreat completely when the front door opened, and a woman in a dressing gown was standing there, holding to her chest a sleeping baby. She had a pale face, her hair bleached and pulled off her face into a high ponytail.

'Shut up, you,' she shouted, stepping out beside me and banging on the fence with her fist until the barking stopped. She had to shift the baby a little to do so. Then she looked at me.

'Hi,' I said. 'I'm Beth. I've just moved in across the way.' I pointed to my house. 'I came around to say hello.' I extended my hand. It was shaking.

'Oh,' she said. Her eyes seemed to widen a little. But after a moment, she shook my hand.

'Sorry,' I said. 'I probably shouldn't have come over like this. I literally just wanted to say hi.'

'I thought you were selling something,' she said.

'God, no,' I said.

'Well, it's nice to meet you. What did you say your name was?'

'Beth.'

'Beth. I'm Frances.'

There was a pause. I thought she might invite me in then, and she glanced for a second behind her.

'And tell us,' she said, 'did you buy the place or . . .?'

'Oh, no.' I laughed.

'You're renting.'

'That's right.'

'Off Paul Gilroy, is it?'

'Yes.'

'And, where are you from Beth, if you don't mind me asking?'

'Dublin.'

'Dublin. And do you mind me asking, how much are you paying him?'

'Paying him?' I said. 'Eight hundred a month,' I lied.

'Eight hundred.' She frowned, her gaze still on me, as though she expected me to say something else that would explain things better to her.

'That includes utility bills and stuff.'

'Eight hundred a month.' Again the stare, as though that made no sense to her at all. I should, I realised, have given a lower figure. Maybe six hundred? Four?

'Sorry now,' she said. 'I'd ask you in but the place is in an awful mess. And when this fella wakes, he'll be looking to be fed. He's only a few weeks old.'

'I shouldn't have called over like this,' I said again. 'I really just wanted to say hi. He's lovely,' I added, nodding at the baby.

'A little handful, is what he is,' she said. 'I can't put him down or he'll wake. No. It's nice to meet you. And – have you family local?'

'Oh, no. My boyfriend starts a new job in a few weeks, in Dunlone. I work from home. I came down to – settle us in first.'

'On your own?'

'Yeah.'

'And you don't know a soul around here.'

'No.'

She shook her head. 'Ye must be very fond of the place.'

'We are,' I said. 'Jason plays golf, so.' Another lie. I gestured at the course, now hidden by the night.

'There mustn't be any golf courses in Dublin.' She smiled.

'Well. You know. It's a good job. For him. He really wanted it. Anyway, it was nice to meet you. You won't want him getting cold.'

'No. Goodnight now. Hang on till I get the porch-light on. Give you a bit of light anyway. You could trip on one of them damn potholes in this dark.'

Back inside, I sat at the dining table again. I poured myself a glass of wine. It would have been much better, that first evening, if I had brought a radio. It was a stupid oversight. Especially as the internet guy wasn't due out until the Thursday, which meant no TV until then. But, of course, I'd been so busy.

Then I had an idea. I opened a large notebook, one I used for making notes on a work project, and tore out a page. On it, I drew up a schedule.

Morning: Walk, shower, breakfast. Three hours' work. Lunch.

Afternoon: Four hours' work. Walk. Dinner.

Evening: TV, Facebook, bed.

Then I tore out another page, on which I drew a table, with thirteen rows, eight columns. In the box at the top of the first column, I wrote 'Week'. Then in the other boxes in that top row, I wrote the days of the week. Monday, Tuesday, Wednesday and so on. And then, in the boxes at the start of the remaining twelve rows, I wrote Week 1, Week 2, all the way down to Week 12. Then I drew a large X in the boxes of every Saturday and Sunday, and the October bank holiday, because Jason would be with me on those days. And then I counted all the days when I would be on my own. There were fifty-nine.

I stuck both that table and the timetable on the fridge. I told myself that that first day was going to be the worst. I just had to follow the timetable for fifty-nine days. How hard could that be?

Then I took painkillers. Strong ones, with codeine. I sometimes take them if I've trouble sleeping. Then I poured myself a second glass of wine, which I also drank at the dining table of that vast room.

All the time I was sitting there, I felt as though I was being watched. As though the room itself was watching me. That still makes no sense, because a few weeks were to pass before the attacks began.

6

That first week wasn't too bad, mainly because I had another deadline that Friday, which meant working long days all week. I began early every morning and didn't stop, except for a quick lunch, until late in the evening. By then I would be so tired that, after a couple of glasses of wine, I would be ready to sleep. And then the internet guy came and that night I had dinner on the sofa watching TV.

A couple of times, I heard a car pull up but when I went to the window, it was a visitor for the house next door.

In the end, I never went for a walk that first week. I never spoke to anyone. I was just really focused on getting the report in by lunchtime on the Friday, so I would have time to clean the place, buy food and make dinner before Jason arrived. I managed it too. I did all those things and was sitting by the table at seven, when he was due, showered, hair blow-dried and make-up on, for the first time all week.

In the three months that had passed since our last night out, I hadn't once heard from any of the girls. I hadn't contacted any of them either. That, I told myself, sitting at the dining table and sipping my wine, was a reflection of how close Jason and I had grown. I thought of all the things about him that had attracted me at the start. Broad shoulders. Steady gaze. That smile. The confident face he showed to the world. And, beneath it, his vulnerable side. All the things he had confided to me.

Eight o'clock came, then nine, and there was still no sign of him. I called his phone but it went straight to voicemail. Around then I started helping myself to thin slivers of the lasagne I had cooked. I couldn't help it, I was so hungry. I poured myself a second glass of wine.

'I've earned this,' I said aloud. My voice came out all high and reedy. Besides Mrs Doran on the Sunday evening, and the internet guy, and one shopping trip, I had not been in the company of anyone all week. I'd spoken to Jason on the phone, of course, a couple of times. But his work was super-busy, as he had warned me it would be, as the end of this big project drew near.

I tried his phone. It went to voicemail again. I started leaving a message. 'Hey, honey. How are you getting on?' But just then I heard a car pulling up outside and headlights lit the curtains, the sofa. Quickly, I finished my drink and rinsed the glass. I put the bottle on the worktop by the hob. I wiped the surface of the table. I checked myself in the mirror by the door, rubbed off the wine stains above my mouth. I opened the door before he had a chance to ring the doorbell.

'Welcome,' I said. 'Stranger.' I put my arms around his neck, kissed him.

'Were you drinking?'

'Just a glass. Not even a glass. More like half a glass. While I was cooking. I was using it for the sauce.'

I don't know why I lied like that. It wasn't as though we hadn't drunk plenty together over the summer. I suppose things felt different, now that I'd moved down and we were doing the Plan, on that tiny budget. It felt like now we had to be more grown-up, more sensible. Even though Jason had never said any of that to me, I knew that was what he wanted.

'Can I come in?'

'Of course, of course.'

He dropped his bag by the stairs and looked at me.

'I've made lasagne. It won't take long to heat up. The oven is probably still warm.'

'I need a shower.'

'God, yeah. Did you come straight from work?'

'Towels?'

I got him towels, then waited until he came down in a sweater and jeans. 'Better?'

He nodded. I went to him, put my arms around his neck and kissed him again. This time he put his arms around my waist, kissed me back. Only for a second, though.

'Where's this dinner?' he said.

About two-thirds of the lasagne was left and he ate it without speaking. I refilled his glass when it grew low, only then pouring myself some.

'Bad day?' I said.

He closed his eyes, shook his head.

'What happened?'

'Nothing in particular. The usual.' He rubbed his face. 'I don't want to talk about it. Anyway, I'm here.'

'It wasn't easy,' I said. 'To get here.'

'Not exactly, no.'

He glanced around the room, his gaze falling on the bowl of fruit on the island, fruit I had bought only that day, really because it would look nice after all the cleaning.

'You're sticking to budget?'

'Without a problem,' I said. At that point, we still hadn't fully sorted out all the stuff we'd agreed to do, to help us keep to budget, like my work payments going into Jason's account, which he was going to change to a joint account, and weekly pocket money being paid into my personal account. That way, I wouldn't be tempted to spend more than we'd budgeted for. Until that was all sorted, it was up to me to keep to budget by myself. So I told him about my one shopping trip to a supermarket – besides that I had barely left the house. I told him the week had flown by, I'd been so busy with work.

'We're doing it,' I said. 'The Plan is happening.'

He looked at me.

'You can trust me, Jason. Remember?' I put my hand on his.

He drained his glass, closed his eyes, nodded.

'Let me get you another glass,' I said, opening a second bottle.

After he had eaten, we went to the sofa and watched TV. He didn't seem to mind when I let my head rest on his shoulder, but I knew not to start talking when he was so stressed out. After a while, he began to snore. I had forgotten he snored. He seemed so tired.

'I love you,' I said, to his sleeping face. He didn't wake up. 'I love this man,' I said to myself, out loud.

The next morning, we had sex first thing. It had taken me much longer to get to sleep, and I still felt tired when I woke to him kissing me. But I decided there and then that it was best to go along with it and have it out of the way. I knew, of course, that this was a less than ideal way to feel about sleeping with my boyfriend, but I told myself we were both still adjusting to everything. I wanted so much for him to be in a good mood for the rest of the weekend.

Afterwards, I cooked us breakfast, and then we drove to his new workplace, because he wanted to check again how long the journey took. It was in a business park on the outskirts of Dunlone, a vast modern set of buildings with a shiny sculpture in front of the main entrance. I suggested we go into Dunlone and walk around, but there was a football match on TV he wanted to watch and, anyway, we weren't supposed to be spending much money. He just needed to chill out for the day, he said. I don't mind what we do, I told him, as long as we're together. So we went back to the house and watched the match. The day trickled by. In the late afternoon, we went for a walk through the village, before returning to the house.

'Next weekend's looking tricky,' he said, just as I'd started making dinner. He said it in a casual voice, almost sounding cheery.

'What do you mean?'

'Work. What do you think? Nightmare.'

'That's okay,' I said. 'I can just drive up to you instead. I can amuse myself when you're working.'

He made a face.

'What?'

'What do you mean "what"? You can't have forgotten?'

I didn't know what he was talking about.

'My new landlord doesn't allow stayover guests.' He had moved into a house share to save money.

'You never told me that.'

He rolled his eyes. 'I told you at least twice. Honestly. Half the time I don't think you're even listening to me.'

'When?'

'When? I don't know.'

I couldn't remember. I wanted to ask him when exactly he'd told me. Like, were we out, or in bed, or whatever? But I knew if I did, I'd only annoy him further. In the end, I just shook my head.

'I'll be down the weekend after,' he said.

'Shit,' I said. I had said it quietly. Not quietly enough, though.

'Shit?'

'It's just – disappointing. That's all.'

'Have you changed your mind?'

I looked at him. He was serious. 'About the Plan? Of course not.'

'I can't hear you.'

'I haven't changed my mind.'

'Jesus Christ.' He ran his hands through his hair. 'What am I supposed to do?'

'Nothing. It's fine. It just feels – a bit of a lonely prospect. Two whole weeks here on my own.'

'A lonely prospect. We're planning to have a mortgage-free home in fifteen years. What part of you thought this would be easy?'

'You're right. It's fine, honestly.'

'It's not like I'll be enjoying myself. How hard is it for you to live in a nice house for a couple of weeks on your own, anyway?'

'I suppose we could talk on the phone. Maybe Skype.' I put my hand on his arm but it stayed tense.

'I need some air,' he said, and walked out of the house.

He did not come back for over an hour. When he did, it took the whole evening to get him back into good form. I knew better than to argue when he told me over dinner he would have to leave after breakfast the next day.

Standing at the doorstep the following morning, watching him put his bag into the boot, it struck me how tired he looked. I walked towards him, even though it was a cold morning and I was just wearing a light cardigan over my T-shirt. I put my hand on his arm. 'I'll be fine,' I said. 'I'm sorry.'

'You don't need to keep saying it.' But that time he didn't turn away, or shrug my hand off.

'It's just been so nice having you here.'

'Two weeks is nothing.'

'I could maybe call Jane. Maybe she could come down.'

'Jane?'

'I know.'

'You're tougher than that.'

'You're right.'

'Every week gets us closer to Christmas. This is the hardest it's going to be.'

'It can only get better.'

'Exactly.'

I shivered, folded my arms.

'I'd better get going,' he said. He kissed me lightly on the lips.

'I love you,' I said.

'I love you too,' he said.

I stayed standing there until his car had rounded the curve on the driveway and disappeared. Then I looked at the house next door. For a second, I seemed to make out a woman standing at an upstairs window, watching me. I say 'seemed', because as soon as I saw her, she disappeared.

I had been about to wave up at her. My next-door neighbour whom I had yet to meet. All week, I'd been hoping to bump into her. Paul Gilroy had said she was nice.

I stood there for another moment or two, squinting and seeing no one, before I went back inside.

7

At the table, I opened my laptop and sent a message on Facebook to Emily and Jane, in which I told them about my move:

It's amazing down here. The countryside is so beautiful. And this house is like something out of a magazine. But I need help sussing out the local nightlife! It would be so great to see you guys – it feels like ages. Any chance you could make it down next weekend? Get back to me as soon as you can – there is this amazing restaurant I want to bring you to, and it's always booked up.

Jane replied almost straight away: *No can do. Catch you*

next time x. It was almost midnight when Emily's text came: *Away next weekend. Have fun!*

That was when I texted my sister, Helen. I hadn't spoken to her since she'd moved to London. The last time I'd seen her was back in the spring, and we'd had this huge row. Usually when that happened, she would call me sooner or later and things would go back to normal. But this time she hadn't called. Not once. I suppose I should have called her and apologised. But for one thing, I'd been so busy. And for another, I had a feeling something was brewing with her. That she was going to take me to task for whatever I'd said to her that night. So, when I texted her, I suppose I just wanted a reply. It never occurred to me that she might decide to come home just to see me.

Don't know if Mum mentioned it, I wrote, *but I've moved! To the heart of the midlands . . .*

She replied minutes later: *She did not mention it! When did this happen?! Why?!*

A couple of weeks ago. It's a long story.

There was a pause then, but just for a few minutes.

Can I come visit?

Of course! Are you not still in London, though?

I have this weekend off. I could probably get there for Saturday afternoon, if that works? Just send on address.

All that week, I did not see or speak to anyone on the estate. There just never seemed to be anyone about. I considered calling in to the woman next door, but I lost my nerve. By the time I saw Helen arrive, in a car she had rented at the airport, I had spent so much time on my own that I felt like I hated my neighbours. As I went out to greet her, I hoped the Dorans heard her arrive, with their stupid fence. I hoped the woman next door heard her, with her dumb little back-room light always on, her visitors coming and going.

'Hey! Over here.' I waved crazily, until she was waving back and smiling, as she parked behind my car. For a moment then I felt so happy. Not just because I had company at last but because it was Helen. It was just like when I was a child, and she would show up out of the blue.

She got out of her car. 'Hey,' she said, still smiling.

'Hey!' I said again. And I walked down to her and we hugged. That isn't something we normally do. I think we were both surprised. But it had been so long since I'd seen her. It was all that time on my own, I think. It makes you over-sensitive. I had to pull away quickly, before I started crying.

'Do you need a hand?' I said.

'You're all right.' She looked around the estate. 'Some place,' she said.

'I know. It's a bit weird. Come on in. It's cold out here.'

Inside, I took her coat. I led her into the living room. 'How was the flight?'

'Fine,' she said, looking around her again. 'Holy shit,' she said.

I had been cleaning all morning. The place was gleaming. There were fresh apples in the bowl on the island.

'I know,' I said again. 'It's crazy, isn't it? So, I'm guessing you must be thirsty after all that travelling?' I took the bottle of sparkling wine I had bought that morning out of the fridge. It was nicely chilled. I dangled it.

'Actually, I'd love a cup of tea,' she said. 'And one of those apples. They look really good.'

'Go for it. That's what they're there for.' I put the wine back in the fridge and switched on the kettle.

'I'm guessing Mum's filled you in by now,' I said.

'Well. Kind of. You know her.'

So, I told her the story, as briefly as I could. Me and Jason. Jason's new job in Dunlone, and him finding out about the house. Why I'd had to move down straight away, even though he wouldn't be down until Christmas.

'You've been busy since I saw you last,' she said.

'Yep.'

'I'll have to meet this guy, Jason.'

'I'm sure you will.'

'How are all the girls?'

'Oh. I wouldn't know.'

'What does that mean? Sarah, and those girls. Don't tell me you've fallen out with them?'

'Sarah and Alice are in Australia. So it's a moot point, really, as far as they're concerned.'

She was staring at me. It made me feel restless or something.

'What about Emily and Jane?'

I shrugged. 'Emily's in Galway now. Jane moved in with her boyfriend.'

'I see.'

'What does that mean?'

'Did you have a falling-out?'

I didn't want to tell her about it. I knew what she would think. She would think it was my fault. 'Not really,' I said. 'We've just gone our separate ways for a bit.'

She didn't say anything.

'What?' I said. 'There's no problem, honestly!'

'Do you really like it here?'

'I love it,' I said. 'Why wouldn't I? The countryside is beautiful.'

'I actually think I prefer a good park.'

'Really?'

'They have footpaths. No one is driving past like a lunatic. There aren't any ugly houses in the park.'

'This one excepted, I hope.'

'Oh, of course, yeah. But why do they need them so huge? And in a park, you're never far from decent coffee.'

'Would you prefer coffee?'

'What? No, no. Tea is great. So you're basically here rent-free?'

'Nearly. We cover the insurance.'

'And you're not, like, lonely down here on your own?'

'How do you mean?'

She just looked at me.

'Well, Jason was down last weekend. And there are other people living here too.'

'In this house?'

'On the estate.'

'And – have you met them?'

'Yes,' I said, deciding I was going to get very drunk, as soon as I could. 'They're very nice.'

Helen wanted to watch the news channel. Campaigning for the US election was going on, Barack Obama against John McCain. She was interested in that. She had wanted Hillary Clinton to get the Democratic nomination, she said. Obama seemed too young, too inexperienced. But, of course, now she wanted him to win.

We sat side by side on the sofa, not talking, watching BBC News, sipping our tea. Every now and then, I felt her glance at me, but she never said anything. She might as well have been a stranger. Actually, it was worse than that. It can be easy to make conversation with a stranger, or ignore them if that doesn't work.

'How about a walk?' she said suddenly. 'In the beautiful countryside.'

We went along a narrow, curving road that took us past fields full of small round hills, here and there a scrubby fairy fort. It was already the middle of October. Swallows swooped low on the fields, and gathered on telephone wires. A sharp breeze cut through my light jacket. Every now and then, we had to stand almost in the ditch, single file, as a car or tractor roared past. It was a relief, when that happened, a break from trying to talk to each other. Usually, she would make more of an effort to keep a conversation going, but she seemed different this time. More pensive or something. Helen is in her early forties but that was the first time I really noticed that she'd aged at all, from when I was a child. A couple of lines at the side of her eyes. A very slight slackness to her chin I hadn't noticed before. It occurred to me I didn't know how the acting was going for her, besides this play. Was she getting by okay? Did she still temp between plays? It's not as though she's had no success at acting – she's been in a few plays that got good reviews, and when she was in LA that time, she'd even had a small role in some sitcom. Still, though, that would hardly be enough to make a living.

'I'm sorry I wasn't in touch this summer,' she said suddenly. It seemed to come from nowhere.

'Oh. That's okay. I wasn't either, I suppose.'

'That's true.'

She seemed so serious.

'I was a bit out of it the last time,' I admitted.

'You were.'

For some reason, I didn't want to apologise. I couldn't remember why, but it felt like, even though I was drunk, I had had good reason to get annoyed with her. Then again, it always felt like that.

'Beth, do you remember when you were young, and I would take you to the cinema?'

'I used to love it.'

'You really did.' She smiled.

'You used to show up out of the blue. I remember one time, you showed up after Mum and I had moved, and I couldn't believe it. I think I thought when we moved that time I'd never see you again.'

'You didn't. Why?'

I thought about it. 'Maybe you and Mum had had a row or something. I can't remember. Maybe it just seemed so sudden.'

'How many moves were there?'

'God.' I tried to count them all. 'I think four in total,' I said.

'Well, we were in Dublin when I was born. Then I was five, maybe six, when we went to the countryside. That was to move in with the solicitor. Then back to Dublin when I was nine. Then to another part of Dublin when I started secondary school. Into the flat. When she broke up with whatshisname. Patrick. That's three. And then out to her house now, when she bought it. Remember that?'

'The year before you did the Leaving Cert, wasn't it? You had to switch schools.'

'Yeah. What's wrong?'

'Nothing's wrong. I just . . .' She glanced at me. 'Sometimes I wonder if I shouldn't have gone to LA that time.'

'Don't be daft. Why would you not have gone? Because of me?'

She didn't say anything. She was frowning.

'I was fine.'

'Once,' she said, 'you told me that Mum used to leave you in the car when she went to the pub with whatever guy she was with. Remember, when she was with the solicitor.'

'Oh, yeah.'

'Do you remember that?'

'She used always bring me out crisps and a bottle of Coke. Coca-Cola in a bottle with a straw. That's what I'd ask for.'

'She's unbelievable.'

'It was fine. I preferred being in the car. Anyway, everyone did stuff like that back then.'

'I don't know about that.'

'They did.'

We walked on in silence for a while.

'Do you see much of her now?' she said.

'Mum? No. I mean, sometimes. She keeps herself really busy. Which is good. I hope I'm like that when I'm retired.'

She said nothing.

'Do you see much of her?' I asked.

She shook her head. 'The odd time. We don't have the most amicable of relationships, as you know.'

Then she stopped walking. She put her hand on my arm so I would stop too.

'What?' I said.

'Nothing.'

'What is it?'

She kept looking at me in this weird, desperate kind of way. 'You know I'm always here for you, don't you?' she said finally.

'I suppose so.'

'Mum. She does her best. But, as you say, she's very busy. She's always been very busy.'

'What's wrong with that?'

'Nothing, I suppose. She does her best,' she said again. 'Life dealt her a few blows.'

'I know all that.'

'You know you can come to me any time?' she said. 'It doesn't matter I'm in London. Look how easy it was for me to get over this time.'

I wanted to pull my arm away. She was staring at me so intensely. 'Seriously, Helen, I'm fine. I don't need help.'

'Don't you?'

'No! I've never been better.' I paused, then said brightly,

'So, what's Mum doing for her fancy dress this year? Has she told you?'

'God knows,' she said.

'Last year, it was Marvel superheroes.'

To my relief, she smiled – barely, but enough for me to start walking on so she had to let go of my arm.

'Were you there?' she asked.

'No, but I saw the photos.'

For the rest of the walk, we talked about Mum. The finger food she puts on for visitors – devilled eggs, cheese cubes and olives on toothpicks, that kind of thing. The way she's always doing some course or other. Photography, sewing, creative writing. Her bridge. How dressed up she gets on nights out. Her string of boyfriends. That way, the road had looped us back to the village, where we made straight for the golf club, without any more awkwardness.

When she was in the bathroom, I ordered two gin and tonics, then took a table overlooking the course. The sun was already low, shining weakly through the black silhouette of trees on a hill. To the right, two chimneys were just visible. One, I realised, was mine. The estate would already be in shadow, the houses soon to disappear into the darkness.

I went to the bar, ordered a second gin, which I poured into my glass, then took it back to the table. The place was quite busy, with golfers and families. It was strange to realise that all this activity was taking place so close to the estate. I looked out the window. I started thinking about the budget

Jason and I had agreed to. My weekly allowance definitely didn't allow for an occasional gin and tonic. But for that night I didn't have to worry about it, as I still had some money left in my personal account. I would just spend that, I decided. The following day I would start the budget for real.

Helen came back, sat down opposite me.

'What's this? Gin?'

'Just a little aperitif.'

She took a sip. 'Mm,' she said, picking up a menu. 'I'm starving.'

We ordered steak sandwiches and a bottle of wine.

'So has Jason been down much?' said Helen.

'Last weekend. He'll be here next weekend too.'

'That's not so bad, I suppose.'

'He's crazy busy at work. He has to finish this massive project by Christmas.'

She said nothing.

'You sound as if you already don't like him.' I wanted it to seem like it was a matter of complete indifference to me but it came out whiny.

'I've never met him.'

I thought about it. 'You don't like the idea of him,' I said.

'I'll reserve my opinion on Jason until I've met him,' she said. 'If that's okay.'

The waiter came then with our food. For a while, we ate and drank in silence.

'It does seem a bit weird, though,' she said, as I refilled our glasses. She flashed me a nervous look.

'What does?'

'Your set-up. You being down here on your own.'

'I've explained it all. This is the only way we could do it.'

'I know, but . . . why would you want a mortgage at your age?'

'Well, because it's an opportunity.'

'For what?'

'To be set up for the rest of my life. To be sorted financially, you know, when I get older.'

She smiled. '*Touché*, I guess.'

'You know what seems weird to me? You acting like you're worried about me. Yet, let's face it, you hardly know me.' I drained my glass and refilled it. Then I looked around for the waiter. When he came over, I ordered another bottle. I knew at that moment she wouldn't dare argue.

'I wouldn't say that.'

'Jason is my best friend,' I told her. 'He looks after me.'

'Okay. Okay.' She held her hands up.

'He's always there for me,' I said. 'He understands me.'

'Right.'

'Right. You don't understand everything, Helen.'

'I understand some things.'

'Well, I'm sure you do,' I said. 'But that doesn't mean you understand everything. You definitely don't understand me.'

The waiter came with the second bottle. He showed me the label and I nodded. He pulled the cork, poured a small amount. I tasted and nodded again. It felt like a victory when he filled our two glasses and Helen didn't say anything.

'Wasn't all that a bit fancy for a golf club?' I said, when he was gone.

She shrugged. 'I don't really feel like drinking any more.'

'Do you want a nice cup of tea?' I said. 'I suppose you can't put away as much as you used to.'

'I do, actually. Want a nice cup of tea.' She looked at me, as though trying to decide what to say next. What to do next. I had seen that look before. It was like she wanted to say something, but couldn't quite bring herself to do so.

'It's two glasses each,' I said. 'It's nothing. Why is that guy at the bar staring at me? Do you see him? The big head on him.'

'Will you calm down,' she said. 'Look. I didn't mean . . . it's just – we were talking about you the other day.'

'Who's we?'

'Me and Mum.'

'You and Mum.'

'Just on the phone.'

'You were talking to her earlier, weren't you?' I asked.

'Who?'

'Mum. That's why you were so long in the loo.'

I realised, to my surprise, that I had guessed right.

'I did happen to chat to her for two minutes.'

'What's going on?'

'Nothing!' She looked out the window. 'Is your house over there?' She was nervous, I saw.

'What the hell are you doing talking to Mum about me?'

'I'm worried about you, Beth. I'm always worried about you, if you want to know the truth.'

'That's hilarious.'

'It's not healthy, living down here on your own in that spooky estate.'

'Wooooooo. Spooky.'

'And you're still drinking a lot.'

'It only seems a lot to you because you're ancient.'

'Funny.' She wasn't smiling, though. She was studying me, in the weird, inscrutable way she does sometimes.

'You're always saying we need to get to know each other better. You know what I think we should do?'

'What do you think we should do?'

'I think we should get a taxi into Dunlone and go to a nightclub.'

'That's a terrible idea.'

'They're the best ones.'

She smiled, despite herself. 'If I go to some god-awful nightclub with you,' she said, 'do you promise to introduce me to Jason? Like, soon.'

'Absolutely,' I said.

'Okay, then.'

We finished our wine, paid up. The barman called a taxi for us and soon we were zipping along a curved road in the dark, and then along the main street of Dunlone, its narrow pavements busy with people.

The next thing I remember is being on the dance-floor of some nightclub, full of dancing bodies that bumped up against me, spilling my drink. I was angry – furious – about something. Something Helen had said, or hadn't said. I had stopped dancing. She had too. She was staring at me, all wary and tired-looking.

I didn't mean to push her. At least, I don't remember meaning to. Certainly not so hard that someone had to catch her arm to prevent her from falling back onto the floor.

The next thing I remember is us on the street and me screaming at her. I don't even remember what I was saying. But I do remember the expression on her face.

I think I told her I hated her. I think I said I wished she'd leave me alone. That I wanted her gone when I woke.

Frightened. She looked frightened.

I suppose we got a taxi home, I don't remember. When I woke early the next morning, I knew straight away that she was gone. Sure enough, from my bedroom window I saw her car was not there, just a dry patch of ground behind mine. Downstairs, on the kitchen island was a note. There were three black marks, like words had been written and then scribbled out. Beside them it read, 'Call me when you calm down. H.'

I tried to drink tea but it made me sick. In the end, I went back to bed and managed to fall back to sleep. When I woke again, it was midday. I showered and dressed. Unable to face eating, I went for a walk. But it was cold and I still felt awful. I got as far as the primary school and then I turned back.

I spent the next few hours watching television and eating toast. As the afternoon melded into evening, my anxiety, which had been hanging around me all day, sharpened. The room was so quiet. I had that feeling again, like I was being observed. The only sound was the quiet droning of the fridge. At one point, a car pulled up and I thought for a second it was Helen, but it had parked outside the house next door.

I rang Jason, but his phone went straight to voicemail. I poured myself a glass of wine. When I had finished it, I picked up my phone again. I called my mother.

8

'Hi, Mum.'

'Beth.'

'How are you?'

'Oh, out the door as usual. I have my bridge tonight.'

'Oh, it's Sunday. I forgot.'

'What's up?' she said.

'Nothing. I just thought I'd give you a ring for a chat. Nothing major.'

'Right.'

There was a pause.

'Helen was down last night.'

'Yes.'

'We had a stupid row.' My voice quivered.

'I know.'

'Did she tell you?'

'She called earlier.'

I was surprised. Mum and Helen rarely spoke. That was how it had been since I was a child. Even back then, whenever Helen visited, she would give all her attention to me. When they did speak, they always seemed to argue.

Then I remembered how Helen had called Mum in the golf club. Her saying they were worried about me.

'Well, what did she say?' I said.

'She was very upset.'

There was another pause. I could almost hear her looking at her watch.

'I just had too much to drink.'

'Beth, what in the name of God are you doing drinking like that?'

'I don't know.' I wiped my cheeks. I tried to blow my nose without making a sound. 'It was stupid. I'll call her and apologise. It'll be fine. So, how are the Halloween party preparations going?'

'Oh, I don't know why I bother,' she said, but her voice had brightened.

'What's the theme this year again?'

'Moulin Rouge.'

'That's it. Brilliant.'

'My costume's been delayed. I was supposed to get it last week. There'll be hardly any time for alterations. If it comes at all.'

'Mam, I was thinking. What if I came down for it?'

Silence.

'I bet I could get a costume here. I could stay for the weekend.'

I'd been thinking about it. There was still some money left over in my personal account. If I filled the car with petrol that evening, Jason wouldn't even have to know I'd gone anywhere, or spent anything.

'You wouldn't enjoy yourself,' she said. 'They'll all be twice your age. And a lot of people are staying over. You'd just feel in the way.'

'I don't mind. I'll sleep on the sofa.'

'The sofa is taken. So is the floor.' She laughed unconvincingly.

'What about the table?'

'Beth, you're a grown woman now. Do you not have parties of your own to be going to?'

'Of course.'

'Well, then.'

'No, you're right. It was a stupid idea. Maybe we could just get lunch some Saturday or something.'

'Well, I'd need my diary. You have no idea how crazy things are between now and Christmas. I think literally every weekend I've something on. And I'm flying out to Spain on the fourth of December.'

'That's early.'

'The girls and I are going for a full month this year. We decided to make the most of it.'

'That sounds like a good plan.'

'Well, I'd better be going or they'll have given me up.'

'Okay. Bye, Mum. I'll call next week and maybe we'll find a date between us.'

'We can try. Bye-bye now.'

When the doorbell rang a little later that evening, for some reason I imagined it might be my mother. But it wasn't. It was a woman I didn't know.

I thought maybe she was a Jehovah's Witness. For the first time in my life, I understood why sometimes people actually let them in.

'You're wondering who is this crazy woman knocking on your door at this hour,' she said, smiling. 'I'm your next-door neighbour.' And she nodded towards her house.

She looked anything but crazy. My first impression of her was that she was beautiful. I suppose she was what they call preppy, in skinny jeans and a grey sweatshirt, her straight, shiny dark hair pulled back in a high ponytail. The kind of person who has a gym membership, who does Pilates every Thursday. Who drives her kids around in a shiny new Range Rover.

'Oh. Hi.'

'I thought I'd come by and say hello.'

'Of course. It's nice to meet you. I'm Beth.' I may have slurred a little. We shook hands, and laughed as we did so – at the formality of the gesture, I suppose.

'Claire,' she said brightly.

'Come in,' I said, opening the door wider and leading her

to the dining table, where I pulled out a chair. 'Sit down. I'll put on the kettle.'

'Oh, I won't stay,' she said, putting a dish covered with tinfoil on the table. 'I just wanted to pop by and introduce myself. I've been meaning to come around ever since you moved in. I wanted to tell you how delighted I am to have a new neighbour.'

'It's great to meet you.'

'Two women on our own. We should look out for each other.' She smiled. In the light of the kitchen, I could see that she was wearing a lot of make-up. Nothing garish or anything, it was very natural, but foundation, even some blusher, and subtle eye make-up too. It occurred to me then that she might be a little older than she'd initially seemed.

'Oh. Yes,' I said, wondering if I had misheard her. It seemed incongruous, the idea that someone like her was living all alone in that big house. But she just continued to smile, in an expectant sort of way.

'Have you met any of our other neighbours?' She raised her eyebrows comically.

'I met Frances Doran.'

'Did you? God.' Her face grew serious. 'But, tell me, have you bought this place?'

'No, no. Just renting for a while.'

The way she was watching me reminded me of Mrs Doran's reaction, that first night on the estate.

'My boyfriend is starting a new job in Dunlone in the new year.'

'Aha.'

'I'm just holding the fort until he moves down then.'

'Well, look, I won't keep you.'

'Are you sure you won't stay for a bit?' I lifted the kettle.

'I won't. Honestly. You're very good. But I hope you'll come over for dinner one of these nights.'

'I'd love to,' I said.

'When would suit?'

'Any night, really, except the weekend. My boyfriend will be down then.'

'The boyfriend will be down. Well, now, let me see. I've the book club tomorrow night. Then Tuesday, I'll be in with Mam. Will we say Wednesday?'

'Perfect.'

'Now, if you ever need anything, you're to call on me. Okay?'

'Okay. Thank you.'

She glanced at the sofa, where I had been sitting. There was a half-empty bottle of wine on the table. A property programme on the television. 'It can be awful on your own here, can't it? All the windows and the space.'

'Yes.'

She nodded, smiling. 'I know all about it. It's easier in the summer.' Then she opened the door. 'Night-night.'

'Good night,' I said.

It was an apple tart, still warm. I ate all of it, slice by slice, standing at the island. Then I went to bed. Before I turned out the light, I texted Jason. *I love you* it read. *I miss you. Can't wait to have you down again. Xxx.*

*

I went to this mindfulness class yesterday evening. Just a weekly drop-in session, run by a Buddhist organisation. It was in town – I had to take a bus to get there. It felt like going back in time, doing that. The last time I took a bus into town I'd been living with the girls. It felt like a lifetime away.

There were about thirty people, sitting on hard cushions in a room with white walls and big windows, blinds drawn against the night. At the top of the room a woman with silver hair cut tight to her skull, wearing a long, maroon robe, her face clear and open, introduced herself as Chenda, welcoming the regulars and newcomers alike. Then she talked a little about meditation. She said it's not about escaping your problems. It's not about escaping anything. It's about accepting the unacceptable. And it's not a religion. Instead, it's about learning to face yourself with honesty and compassion. It's about watching your thoughts come and go, like soap bubbles forming and bursting. It's about learning to treat your feelings as something that happens to you, that is separate from you. Learning to see yourself. This is what makes the difference, she said. This is what enables us to gain true inner peace. She said meditation is beautifully simple, but that doesn't make it easy. She smiled when she said that last bit.

She reminded me of the monks in the documentary and I started wondering where she lived. If maybe there was a Buddhist monastery in Ireland that anyone could join.

The practice was more tiring than I'd expected it to be. All that sitting still, trying to focus on your breathing until your thoughts draw you away, then remembering to return to your breathing. I would manage about five seconds before I started thinking about something. Like the person beside me. What had brought them there? Like what I was going to eat when I got home. And so on. Then I would remember what I was supposed to be doing, and draw my focus back to my breathing.

It wasn't long, of course, before my thoughts brought me back to the estate. Specifically, I started thinking about that first evening in Claire's house. The intimacy of it came so vividly, like in a nightmare.

When that happened, I stopped even trying to meditate.

Afterwards, Chenda said there was going to be a 'sutta hour', which everyone was welcome to stay for. It would consist of someone reading a sutta, or reading, from the Buddha's teachings, and then a discussion. I hung around for it, even though I was hungry. A guy stood and read a sutta called 'The Fullness of Emptiness'. It was very complicated. All this technical detail. But I wrote down some phrases I liked, even if I didn't understand them.

> *Paying attention only to perception of the forest, perception of the earth.*
> *He cleans out, tidies up and liberates his mind.*
> *A sitting down to empty out that results in surpassing purity.*
> *[And my favourite:] All those shamans or Brahmans of the long-distant past who attained the highest surpassing purity of emptiness and made it a*

habitat, all of them did so by attaining this same highest surpassing purity of emptiness and making it a habitat.

A habitat of emptiness. There's something about how that sounds. I keep saying it to myself, over and over.

9

Wednesday evening, I walked around to Claire's house, carrying a bottle of wine and a small box of chocolates. It was a cold night, the sharp wind carrying icy drops of rain. It was dark too; of the golf course, all I could see was a small copse of trees on the horizon, its silhouette lit by the hidden club beyond. In the estate, the only lights were the one that was always on, dimmed by curtains, in the front window of the Dorans' house, and Claire's porch-light, which I suppose she had left on for my sake.

I hadn't seen her since she had called over. I'd kept thinking about her, though. She was an enigma. I guessed she was at least in her thirties. Why was she single? I wondered. Or, at least, not living with anyone. Lots of people are, of course. And lots of people don't have children. But they tend not to live in a big house on their own in the middle of the countryside.

She had seemed happy, though. In fact, she had acted as though there was nothing unusual about her circumstances at all. Maybe she was happy, I thought. I once read that a person's disposition decides how happy they are, more than their circumstances. For all I knew, she could be the happiest person in the world.

She answered almost as soon as I rang the bell, as though she'd been waiting by the door, and beamed her big smile at me. For a second time, I was struck by her beauty. And how young she looked. In jeans and a dark pink hoodie, a pair of Converse, her shiny hair bone-straight, she might have been my age.

'I hope you're hungry,' she said.

'Starved.'

'That's what I like to hear.'

Her dining room had the same layout as mine, but in place of light linen curtains there were thick dark grey velvet ones, over all of the windows, and even over the door to the hallway. There were candles everywhere – on the mantelpiece, the coffee-table, the island, the dining table – all lit. There was a portable gas heater beside the dining table. Classical music was playing at a low volume.

'I thought of walling off the sitting-room bit,' she said, when I commented on how lovely it was. 'This room is impossible to keep warm without racking up huge bills. You'll know all about that.'

I had started leaving the heat on all day in my house. Otherwise, I found it grew so cold I couldn't concentrate on work. 'Is it that expensive?'

'Last January,' she said, 'I paid three hundred euro for a single bill.'

'Three hundred.'

'You need to get one of these,' she said, nodding at the gas cylinder. 'Much cheaper.'

She had made a kind of spicy fish stew, with rice. Nothing fancy. But I had got into the habit of eating cheap processed stuff – frozen pizza, that kind of thing. I was finding it hard to cook proper meals when it was only for me. So Claire's stew seemed amazing. I don't think I said anything until I had cleared my plate and was sure my voice would come out okay. It sounds ridiculous, but I felt a bit emotional, eating it. I think I was just so tired from work and everything.

'That was gorgeous,' I said.

'It has a bit of a kick, hasn't it?'

She was up with my plate before I had a chance to answer, ladling out more stew. She didn't have a second helping. Her plate was almost untouched.

'Thanks.'

'You look famished, do you know that? Honestly, it's nice to feed you.' She was laughing, but I couldn't help thinking what a pity it was that she didn't have children. She was being so kind, so maternal, I suppose. I wondered about her age. In the candlelight, she really did look very young. But she was wearing lots of make-up again.

'So, I noticed you're a bookworm,' she said, back at the table.

At first, I didn't know what she was referring to.

'The big stack of them by the fireplace,' she said.

'Oh, yeah. I need to get a bookshelf.'

'Not at all, they look cool there. They were the first thing I noticed in your house.'

'Really?'

'I love reading too,' she said. 'I can never find the time any more, but there's nothing nicer than curling up with a good book.'

'What do you read?'

'Oh, all sorts. Anything. Novels. Biographies. Some self-help stuff. You know. A lot of that's pure rubbish but some of it's good.'

'Ah, yeah.'

'Like whatshisname. Really spiritual.'

'Oh. I think I know who you mean.'

'Deepak Chopra. He's good. Makes you think. All that stuff about mind over matter. How what happens in your life reflects how you feel. What you expect to happen.'

'I must try him.'

'And tell me, you probably love the theatre as well.'

'Not really. I mean, I don't not like it. I don't go that much.'

'Oh, I love the theatre.'

'Is there one in Dunlone?'

She frowned. 'In Dunlone? Not that I know of,' she said.

'Maybe a small community one.'

'There might be something like that. There probably is, I'd say. No, I was thinking of when I lived in Dublin. I used to go the whole time. The Abbey. What's the other one? The Gaiety. I loved that one too.'

'I should have gone more.'

'Well, you'll get a chance again. You're only a whipper-snapper. What age are you? Twenty-three, twenty-four?'

'Twenty-four.'

'Twenty-four. The same age I was when I came back down here. I turn thirty-nine this year.'

'Stop it. You look half that.'

'Ah, the tell-tale signs are creeping in. Well, thank you, you're very good. No, I'm beginning to think my theatre-going days are gone for ever.' She laughed. 'That's very melodramatic, isn't it?'

'Not true, I hope.'

She laughed again. Then she looked at my plate. 'Better?' she said.

'Better. Thanks.'

'Good,' she said. 'Now don't move.' She took our plates, went to the kitchen and opened a second bottle of wine.

'Maybe you're right,' she said, back at the table. 'Let's just say things have been a bit different, these past couple of years.' She poured us each a fat glass. She opened the chocolates I had brought. 'A rare treat for me,' she said.

'Really?'

'I'm type-one diabetic. Not a big deal, I've had it since I was born. Now,' she said, 'I have a proposal to make. You're probably wondering what landed me here, and I'm wondering the same about you. Am I right?'

I couldn't help smiling.

'So here's my idea. I tell you my story, and then you tell me yours. And then we'll have it out of the way. And if we decide we don't like the sound of each other, fair enough. And if we do like the sound of each other, so much the better. Are we agreed?'

'Why not?'

'I'll start. Okay?'

'Yeah.'

And she did. In my whole life, I don't think I've ever heard anyone talk for so long as Claire did that night. I'll try to get it all down here – every word of that conversation. I don't think it will be difficult. I remember it so vividly.

'I actually grew up not too far from here,' she began. 'I moved to Dublin when I was nineteen. A year after I did the Leaving Cert. My parents wanted me to go to college, of course – that's what most of my friends were doing. But I wanted to work in childcare. I didn't need to move to Dublin for that but I was sick of my hometown. I wanted a go at living in the city. You know?'

'Yeah.'

'All went fine. I finished the childcare course with flying colours. Spent a few years after that working in a crèche. A nice place. I loved working there. Then one day one of the mothers told me she had heard I was from down here, and that she and her husband were going to move to this area themselves. And would I consider moving with them to look after their two children? The little boy in the crèche and his older sister. And the mother was expecting a third that summer. A live-in nanny job, you know.

'So down I came. I was twenty-four. I'd just had my heart broken. If that hadn't happened, I think I would have said no. But this fella had got engaged to someone else and I was just in bits. It was appealing, you know, being back so close to home after that. Dublin had started to feel unfriendly. Not the crèche, but the city. They promised me a room and bathroom of my own. And the salary they offered was twice what I'd been getting in the crèche.'

'You took it.'

'I took it. And for a while it was grand. Looking after the kids while the mother worked.'

'Why were they moving?'

'Her husband was a consultant. Neurologist, I think. The move was for him – he was starting in the hospital there in Dunlone. She brought in a fair bit too, I'd say, though. She was an antiques dealer. She had this massive room that was always under lock and key. You should have seen the house. A mansion. It literally was a mansion.'

'Wow,' I said.

'Yeah. To be honest, I think half her dealings weren't above board, if you know what I mean.'

'She stole them?'

'No, she didn't steal them! You're hilarious. I mean, not telling the taxman. Selling stuff for cash.'

'Oh.'

'Whatever way she was selling them, she was doing something right. There was always stuff coming and going from that place. Anyway, I used to drop the girl off at school, and then I'd spend the rest of the day with the little boy. And the baby, when she came along. I'd make their dinners. A bit of housework. I'd call out to Mam and Dad at least once a week. For a while it was grand. But it wasn't long before I was bored out of my skull. I mean, all my old friends from school had moved away. The odd one would come back at Christmas or whatever, but generally there was no one to go out with. And it can be tedious, looking after young children all day. Have you ever done it?'

'No.'

'No. Well, it can be very boring, let me tell you. Three-year-olds don't stop talking. Most of it rubbish. I don't mean that in a nasty way. It's the truth. And the parents were always busy with work. They were nice enough, I suppose. They weren't horrible. But they weren't friendly either. Like in the evenings, I used to eat on my own in the kitchen. I hated that.'

'God.'

She smiled. 'You reminded me of myself, the first time I saw you.'

'Did I?'

'You did. You were walking across the green in the evening. I suppose you'd gone for a walk, to get out for a while. Anyway, where was I?'

'You were getting bored. Of your job.'

'That's it. And you know the worst bit? Before I left the crèche, the manager there had offered me assistant manager. I was a bit older than the other girls and sometimes when she was away she'd leave me in charge. So it made sense, you know. The place was doing well. A few months into the nannying I was kicking myself I hadn't taken it. I even thought of writing to my old boss, to see it was still available. But then I met Andrew.'

'Andrew.'

'Now it's getting interesting, isn't it? Yes. Andrew. I was nearly a year into the job by then. I met him in this poky little café. I used to go there on my own every Monday, after dropping off the dry cleaning. The mother would nearly always be home Mondays and she would look after the boy until I came back. How I loved my Monday trip to Dunlone. That probably tells you everything. Pathetic, is what it was. But afterwards, you see, I'd go to the café and have a coffee and a sticky bun. You might find this hard to believe, but Dunlone twelve years ago was a much different place. We'd be talking – let's see – 1996. No fancy barista coffees or the like then, I can tell you. I'm sure the coffee they made in that place was the instant stuff. And it was always raining. At least, that's how I remember it. But it was a break. Time to finish a thought or two.

'Anyway, a couple of times, I saw this man in the café. He was good-looking. Very good-looking. A bit like Richard Gere. Richard Gere! That's probably me showing my age. You probably don't even know him. Anyway, he was a bit older than me, but not too much. The first time, he just happened to be there himself. But he showed up the next time and he glanced at me a couple of times. And the third time, didn't he smile at me on his way out? Not just a small smile, I mean a big grin. Like he knew I was skiving. And then the following Monday, didn't he sit down beside me? I was lost in my thoughts. I didn't know where he came from – he seemed to come from nowhere. I let a scream out of me and he laughed his head off.

'Well. It was like my life transformed in that second. I was going out with him, to his nightclub, every Saturday night. He owned it – it was just outside town, and we would go for dinner and end the night there. Drinking champagne in the VIP section. As if Dunlone has any VIPs. This was all before the boom started. Or just when it started. Maybe we started the boom. I was having the time of my life. I was changing and the world was changing. Those fancy coffee shops were popping up. Everyone had a mobile phone all of a sudden. Andrew had these minibuses running in and out of his nightclub, and the drivers would play music loud and everyone loved it. They would bring drink on board and Andrew pretended not to know anything about it. We would always get a taxi. Arrive when the place was hopping. I must have spent a small fortune on clothes and jewellery.'

She took a drink.

'The nightclub kept turning in huge profits. One day he asked me to do his admin work for him. By that stage, the people I was nannying for were pretty sick of me. I was hungover half the week, sleeping in, sneaking out and all sorts. I'd say they were as happy as I was when I handed in my notice. I moved in with Andrew – he had a lovely apartment on the river in the middle of Dunlone. Every day I would work away in his office. Things got busier and busier. He started investing in property. Rental properties in Dublin, and then holiday apartments in eastern Europe and Spain.

'We were three years together before we married. You

should have seen the wedding. It was in that place Paul McCartney and Heather Mills had their wedding, Castle Leslie. My dress cost thousands. Literally. I think it was just over two thousand.'

'That's insane.'

'I know! Insane. The guest list had over two hundred people. Most of them were on Andrew's side – business people and his huge family. I had a few of the school friends, a couple of the girls from the crèche. My parents. They were shocked by the expense of the whole thing. I can't remember a single thing either of them said on the day – just their faces, trying to take it all in. I didn't care. That was what I told myself, anyway. We had a goal, Andrew and I – for Andrew to end up on the list of the top one hundred wealthiest people in Ireland. It sounds crazy now, God knows.'

She glanced at me. I just shook my head.

'We went to Costa Rica for our honeymoon. I loved that place, so I did. The Pacific. Nothing like it. Well, anyway, you can see where this is headed. Not long after our wedding, there was a period when things seemed a little shaky. That might be too strong a word for it, but the growth in the value of Andrew's property slowed a bit. Figures for the nightclub fell a little bit. It was still doing great, just not as great as it had been. Then that seemed to pass. The value of the property started to rise again. So, he bought more.'

She refilled our glasses, gave the bottle a little shake for the last drop to fall out.

'We started trying for a family. By then I was nearly thirty. Nothing happened for a year. We were about to go to a fertility clinic when I got pregnant. I was so happy. I realised I wanted a child more than anything else. And then I miscarried.'

She said it matter-of-factly, like it was just another detail in her story.

'I'm so sorry.'

'It happens. We started on the IVF then, and I got pregnant again, and I miscarried again. And then my father died.'

'Oh. I'm sorry,' I said again.

'A heart attack.'

'That's awful.'

She nodded. 'That was when Andrew decided we needed to move. He got it into his head that it would be good for me to be in the countryside. I needed rest and fresh air, he said. He wouldn't have me work for him any more. So we bought this place. He knew the developer.'

'Paul Gilroy.'

Her lips pursed in a thin line. 'That's him. That was in 2006, just before Christmas. We did a second round of IVF around then, which didn't work. But the doctor in the clinic said she was optimistic for us. She said most people have to do it three times before it works. We decided to take a break for six months and if nothing happened we'd go back for a third round. That was when the prices started to fall again. We told everyone who asked that we were confident they'd creep back up again. The market was like that, ups and downs, but Ireland was on an upward path and it was taking us with it. What did we know about the market? We wouldn't have dreamed of selling anything. Cutting our losses was not part of the plan.

'And then – they kept falling. And falling. I stopped turning the radio on in the morning, you know.

'The third round of IVF never happened. Even before everything went completely belly-up with the property and the nightclub, things had changed between us. And then it happened.' She looked at me. Raised her eyebrows. 'Can you guess?' she said.

'I – don't think so.'

'You can't. It seems blindingly obvious to me now. Benefit of hindsight and all that. Didn't I get up one morning to find him gone? All his clothes gone, and his iPad and laptop. He'd taken his games console. And all his games. He used to disappear into those games for hours, so I suppose that wasn't surprising. Microwave gone, and the luggage. It was nice luggage. Expensive. I'd bought it for our honeymoon. Television gone.'

'That's terrible.'

'One of the women at work gave me that old thing there in the corner,' she added, waving at the set, 'or I wouldn't have any at all. He'd even tried to take the wine humidifier but he hadn't been able to fit it in, I suppose. I found it there on the front lawn.'

'Oh, my God,' I said.

Silence filled the room.

'Where did he go?' I said, finally.

'London. To declare bankruptcy, I found out later. And to start a new life with a woman he'd been seeing. I only know because his old accountant told me. After I threatened to burn his office down.' She sipped her wine.

'Can he do that?'

'Apparently he can.'

'But if he declares bankruptcy, does that mean the mortgage on this place is gone?'

She looked at me. 'You know, there was a day when I thought that was the case. I mean, one actual day. You would think, wouldn't you? So I rang the bank and asked. Got this young fella. Real pompous-sounding, you know? Like he thought I was a complete idiot for even asking. It would have to be repossessed by the bank first, he said, before it could be seen as debt. Unsecured debt, it's called. This is secured debt. Doesn't that sound wrong? Secured debt. Like it's something you'd want for yourself.'

'So.'

'So, I managed to get hold of a waitressing gig in a café in Dunlone. Doesn't sound like much but there weren't many jobs of any description going, I can tell you. Since Andrew left, I've been paying the mortgage on my own. And if he comes back in thirty years' time and I have it paid off, he's as much entitlement to the place as I do.'

'That can't be right.'

'I can try for a thing called judicial separation, where a judge transfers it just to me. But the bank would have to agree to that. Can you imagine? Woman in her late thirties, just about holding down a waitressing job.'

'Could you go bankrupt?'

She frowned. Didn't say anything.

'Sorry for all the questions. It just seems so unfair.'

'I did consider that. I could, if I really wanted to. But I'd have to move to the UK. I don't know anyone there. And it can take years. What would I live on? And then there's poor Mam. She has dementia. Fairly advanced at this stage. She's in a nursing home in Dunlone. I call into her most days after work. Last year I had her house sold, to pay for the nursing home. Got a pittance for it and that place eats up money. God, this is an awful story. You must be sorry you came over.' She laughed.

'But – what's going to happen?'

'I've the mortgage down to interest-only until the end of this year. The bank found it in its kind heart to give me that. Then I imagine this place will be repossessed.'

'And sold by the bank?'

'And sold by the bank.'

'And then will you be left with the debt?'

'We just have to get on, don't we? Life throws shit at us.' She looked at me, not quite smiling.

'But where will you live?'

'Some shithole in Dunlone probably. Back to renting.'

I thought, if she could meet someone who had a decent income it isn't too late for her to start a family.

It was as if she read my mind.

'I can't imagine anyone coming near me now, can you? With this place as a millstone around my neck. Anyway, it's slim pickings around here, I'm afraid. You're lucky you came with a fella. I had a look on one of those dating websites. You know. If you put in Dublin, the world's your oyster. Hundreds of guys. All ages and sizes. Around here they were all farmers in their fifties, if not older. Big, hungry-looking ould lads wanting someone to make their dinner, like. I couldn't stop laughing.'

She examined the remaining chocolates. 'Now,' she said. 'Your turn.'

I looked at her blankly.

'What's your story?'

'Well . . .' I began, trying to think '. . . I have a mother.' I laughed at the stupidity of what I'd just said.

'That's a start,' she said. 'Go on.'

'And a sister. She's a lot older than me. Like, a lot. She was down at the weekend.'

'Not much sisterly love there, am I right?'

I was surprised she had picked that up. From what – my expression? My tone of voice? But it wasn't as though she was wrong. I don't know why it bothered me.

'No.'

'That's a pity.'

I didn't know what to say. I suppose I felt embarrassed. 'We just don't click.'

'Dad?'

'I never knew my father, actually.'

She frowned, as though confused.

'I've asked Mum, but she knows hardly anything about him herself.'

'That was hard, I imagine. Not knowing your father.'

'I suppose.' I took another chocolate.

'You can't miss what you've never had. Isn't that what they say?'

'Exactly. And then you see, Helen was born in . . .' I had to think for a moment. 'She was born in 1968. When Mum was very young. There was a big family fall-out, after that. Mum doesn't really talk to any of her brothers and sisters.'

Claire tutted. 'Cruel,' she said.

'It was cruel. They just shut her out. She's had to make her own way ever since,' I told Claire. 'She's actually a very strong person.'

'So Helen has a different father?'

'It sounds awful, I'm sure. She doesn't know him, either.'

'It doesn't sound awful at all. So, Helen must have been nearly an adult by the time you came along?'

I nodded. 'She started college around then.'

'So it was just you and Mum?'

'Helen would come home at weekends sometimes.'

'You loved that.'

'I did, actually.' Again, I was surprised – that she somehow saw that.

'She'd show up out of the blue, would she?'

'Yeah. You never knew when, but when she did she'd always bring a present for me,' I said. I remembered it. The doorbell ringing and knowing it was Helen. Sometimes, when I was very little, I'd be crying with excitement. 'Once she got me this toy rabbit. I had it for ages.'

'What would you do?'

'Anything. She'd bring me to the cinema. To McDonald's. Or if it was summer we'd go to a park. Or just play in the garden, when there was a garden. Just stuff.'

'And then she'd be off again.'

'That's it.'

'What's your mother like?'

At first, I didn't answer. 'Hmm,' I said eventually.

'Hmm.'

We laughed.

'Mum can be tricky, I suppose.'

'Yeah.'

I glanced at her. 'I don't think she was the most maternal type, if you know what I mean.'

'I do.'

'I remember this one time.' I hesitated. I had never told this story to anyone before. I wasn't even sure why it had occurred to me. Maybe it was because Claire had been so generous in telling her story that I felt I owed her a confidence in return. Or maybe it was because of the wine.

'Go on.'

'When I was small, she used to pick me up from crèche, if she had to work late, and take me to the solicitor's office where she worked as a secretary. It was a small, messy place. Her desk, by the front door, was always surrounded by boxes and piles of files. Then there was this narrow little hall leading to other rooms. The room I was left in was just off this hall. It had a desk and some chairs and a window that was always closed. She would give me crackers and a drink, colouring books, then tell me to be good and leave me there while she finished her work.'

'Her boss didn't mind?'

'I don't think so. He was this big, dishevelled-looking guy.' I shrugged.

'Go on.'

'Being good meant not coming out of that room to ask her anything. It meant staying there until it was time to leave. I could hear her speaking to people on the phone in there, or to other people in the office. Sometimes she would be talking to a client, sometimes to her boss. Then there would be these big gaps of silence. Once or twice, she would open the door and look in on me. When that happened, the right thing to do was to nod and say yes when she asked was I okay, was I having a nice time. One time, I really needed the bathroom, but she was on the phone. She'd been on it for a long time. I knew she was talking to a friend because she was speaking in a lower tone of voice than usual, almost whispering. It would only annoy her if I interrupted her. I must have been very young because I still needed her to help me in the bathroom.'

'Little mite.'

'There was a big plant in the room, in a large pot. At home, I'd seen the cat sometimes do her business in a plant pot.' I glanced at Claire again. All her attention was on me. 'So, after waiting as long as I could, I crouched down over it, and did my business. It didn't work, of course. Most of it ended up dribbling down my leg or going straight onto the floor. And then I stumbled and both I and the plant fell sideways.'

'Oh, no.'

'I'll never forget the expression on her face when she opened the door. I think that was worse than her shouting that I was a stupid girl, or even her hitting me.' I looked at Claire. 'It was the one and only time. It was the look she gave me. Like she hated me.'

'You poor thing.'

'She felt bad about it afterwards, though. On our way home she gave me money to buy sweets. I think she even let me eat them before my dinner.' I tried to laugh.

'It's a pity you and Helen didn't stay close.'

'She moved to LA the year I started secondary school. She was gone for four years.'

Claire nodded. 'Sad,' she said. 'You must have felt really let down, when she just left like that.'

I didn't know what to say. I wanted to make a joke, about feeling like I was on a therapist's couch. But I couldn't think of how to word it without it sounding like I was annoyed or something. So I started telling her about the place Mum and I lived, in the countryside, just before Helen moved away. Just to say something. It came to mind easily: being back in the countryside now had recalled it for me. We were living with my mother's boyfriend at the time. He had this big house, a few miles outside the nearest town. Across the road there was another house, and I befriended the little girl living there with her parents and her grandmother. Every day we used to play together in her garden, always climbing this big tree. When it rained, we used to go inside and read, in the kitchen, where her grandmother always was. There was a stove in there so it was always warm.

'Did you stay friends?'

'No.' I ran my finger along the rim of my glass but no sound came. 'I don't even remember saying goodbye to her. We had to move back to Dublin very suddenly. The man my mother was seeing had to sell his house and move away. There was some emergency – I didn't really understand it. We moved in with a friend of my mother's, back in Dublin. They ended up a couple after a while.'

'There's your emergency, I'd say.'

I didn't understand.

'The first fellow in the countryside probably found out she was cheating on him. Her new fellow was the man you moved in with.'

'No,' I said.

'No?'

I shook my head. 'She would have told me,' I said.

'My mistake. So. Back to Dublin and secondary school?'

'Yes.'

'That went okay?'

A blob of melted wax that had been just holding onto the side of a candle on the mantelpiece let go, splatted silently onto the marble below.

'It was a bit – cliquey. You know.'

'What was the new fella like?'

'Okay. He didn't really see me as his business.'

'That's bad.'

'It was actually fine. I didn't see him as my business.'

We both laughed.

'Then – I started college, in UCD. Mam gave me the money to rent a room in a house, instead of staying on with her. I made a good group of friends at college. We all moved in together for our last year. We were living in the same house for ages after we graduated.'

'Ah, good. You had fun.'

'I had fun. Up until recently, really.' I glanced at her. 'Three of the girls lost their jobs, with the recession.'

'Terrible. And you were okay?'

'Sort of. They kept me on freelance.'

'Who is they, now?'

'This massive global company I work for. Information development. I'm a technical writer for them. And a couple of other places.'

'That sounds very impressive.'

'It's not really. I mostly work on user guides for software, stuff like that.'

'Isn't that something?'

'It's pretty tedious, actually. But at least I got to keep doing it. The girls ended up doing stints in crappy casual work. Waitressing, stuff like that.'

'I know.' She smiled in a stiff sort of way.

'Oh, that's not what I meant to say. I'm sorry, I always stick my foot in it.'

'Don't be silly.'

'Two of them emigrated to Australia. And then the others had to move out.'

She was watching me keenly.

'I met Jason on their going-away night.'

'Aha.'

'We're only together a few months. But it's serious.'

'You know when it is.'

'Someone he's going to be working with put him in touch with Paul Gilroy. That's how we ended up here.'

She nodded.

'We liked this place, but Paul Gilroy said he needed someone to take it pretty much straight away. If I hadn't moved down early, we would have lost it. And I can live anywhere.' I waved my hand vaguely.

She nodded again. 'So, you're holding the fort until he arrives.'

'Exactly.'

She kept her gaze on me. 'I'd say he's given you the place for a song, has he?'

I found I couldn't lie. 'Yes.'

'Makes sense. Have a body in the place. Keep the mould out.'

'We pay the insurance.'

'You could save a lot of money, the pair of you, if you stay a while.'

'It's so unfair,' I said.

'Don't go around expecting life to be fair, Beth,' she said.

'I suppose not.'

'No, it's an opportunity for you both. Nothing wrong with taking an opportunity. If you stay long enough, you might save enough for a deposit. You'll get a house for nothing, these days. And then you'd be made up.'

'Maybe.'

She looked at me shrewdly. 'No, it's a good plan. As long as you're happy with this Jason fellow?'

'Of course.'

'Well, then. Now, are there any of these chocolates left?'

10

The next couple of weeks passed uneventfully enough. Work stayed busy and I got myself through week four, with Jason managing to get down that Saturday night, and then through week five. During that time, Claire and I met up twice. One evening, she came over to me for dinner. Another, we went to the local pub, where she chatted with the barman and some of the other people there, introducing me to everyone. People seemed to like her. She always managed to say something that made them smile. I liked her too. Of course I did. I mean, I was glad of her company. Why wouldn't I have been? She was so friendly to me. I think if I felt a little bit on edge around her, it must have been because of our different circumstances. I couldn't fully relax because that was always there. Her being kind and generous just made it worse. When I tried to bring it up, she would have none of it.

'Don't start feeling guilty, whatever you do. It's the biggest waste of an emotion there is. Especially in this country. Aren't I right? I'll get along fine. Now, same again?'

But I did feel guilty. Weren't Jason and I effectively exploiting a situation that was causing such misery for so many others? In that little estate alone, the Dorans and Claire were struggling to pay mortgages that were twice, maybe three times the value of their homes. And they were just a drop in the ocean. All over the country there were people in exactly the same situation. And there we were, waiting for the value of property to drop even further, to next to nothing, before snapping up something. What about the person we hoped would be selling such a place to us? What desperate situation would they be in? It hadn't really occurred to me before, that side of things. The more I thought of it, the worse it seemed, and the more uncomfortable I became with the situation. I began to see that there would be no shame in calling a halt to our plan. The opposite, in fact: there was shame in continuing with it.

By the time Jason made it down again, two weeks after his last visit, I decided I would say it to him. But in the end I didn't. He was in the worst form I'd ever seen him. His project had run into some problem. It took every trick in the book to soften his mood, to help relax him. And then he had to travel back early on the Sunday, sooner than I'd expected. I half considered just blurting it out before he got into his car, but in the end my nerve failed me. I suppose I felt sorry for him.

He seemed fragile. He'd been so annoyed, the last time he was down, when I was disappointed about him not coming the following weekend. Like he took it as a rejection of him, of our plan. Like the two were the same thing. It wouldn't be fair, I decided, to unburden myself just before he had to leave, go back to work, all alone.

In the end, I phoned him halfway through the following week, in the morning. I told myself I'd be better able to reassure him if I told him on the phone: it would be easier for me to stay composed and therefore to think straight.

I tried his work number first and, to my surprise, he answered almost straight away. I suppose he wouldn't have been expecting me to call him at work.

'I don't know if this was the brilliant idea we thought it was,' I said. I tried to make it sound as though I found it all a bit amusing. When he didn't say anything, I went on. I knew that if I didn't blurt it all out right away, I'd lose my nerve again.

'The thing is Jason, I've been thinking about this for a while. It just feels wrong. The other people living here are in such bad situations,' I said. 'Awful ones. Like Claire next door. She's so lovely. And you wouldn't believe what she's been through. It feels wrong to be trying to cash in on everyone else's bad luck. That's essentially what we're doing, isn't it?'

There was silence for a few moments. I could see him, sitting at his desk, blinking innocently at the shock.

'I'm sorry to land this on you first thing,' I said, 'but there was never going to be a good time to say it.'

Silence. 'I know you're under pressure,' I said. 'Please don't for a single second think this changes anything between us, because it absolutely doesn't. Jason? Are you still there?'

'Right,' he said, eventually. 'So, what? You're moving back to that house?'

'In Dublin? No! I didn't mean that.'

'You're moving in with your mother, or sister, or someone.'

'No! There's no one I want to move in with. I have no one. Except you. I'm not breaking up with you.'

'I don't understand.' He sounded tired. Like he didn't have the energy to try to understand me. 'What do you actually want, Beth?'

'I want us to be together,' I started. 'And I want us to have a future. But I want it to be like it was in the summer as well. And I don't know if I want to do the whole house thing any more. Not like this anyway,' I said.

It all sounded so vague. Weak, even. It sounded as though I *did* want to break up with him.

'I don't know how we'll make it work,' I said. 'But I know I want to make it work. Jason, please. Say something.'

Finally, he spoke. 'I'm guessing this has something to do with your friends going out to Sydney.'

'Sarah and Alice? How would it have anything to do with that?'

'No, the other two. It's on your Facebook wall. Went up yesterday. Have you not seen it? Hang on. I'll find it for you.' And then came the faint sound of his keyboard clacking.

I was a bit taken aback. In the summer, when he had made the case for us exchanging Facebook passwords, I had never imagined we were to go into each other's accounts on a regular basis, which, by the sound of it, was what he had been doing. The way he had put it made it sound like a symbolic gesture. Romantic. Everyone is doing it, he had said. It's the new exchanging of rings. And he had handed me a piece of paper with his password on it. It was a token of trust, he said. A new way of showing someone you really love them in our digital age. What could I have done but reciprocate? Not once had I gone into his account. It just felt wrong. Like trespassing. But here he was, acting as though this was completely normal. Like that had been the whole point.

Maybe it had been the whole point. Maybe this was just another case of me misunderstanding, like the time in the restaurant when I hadn't initially understood that the aim of the Plan was to get a mortgage together.

'Here it is,' he said. 'Jane writes, "Best impromptu trip to the other side of the planet." And there's a photo of the four of them. I presumed they'd asked you. Or at least said something to you about it.'

'This is the first I've heard of it.'

'So, you just want to move back to Dublin anyway.'

'I didn't say I wanted to move back to Dublin. It's nothing to do with the girls. We're not exactly friends any more. You know that.'

'Sorry, I don't understand. Where else would you go?'

'Well, I didn't think about that.'

'You didn't think about it.'

'I thought maybe we could figure out all that stuff together.'

'Did you? Look, if you're leaving, you're leaving. But I have to get some work done here.'

'But what about what I said?'

'Well, it's not like you're locked in a dungeon, is it? You can leave whenever you want. I'll see you, okay?'

He hung up.

I went online. There were loads of photos of the girls in Sydney, all from one night out. The four of them grinning, arms slung over shoulders, skin shiny with the heat. And loads of comments and likes from other people we'd known in college. I read all of them. One said, 'Where's Beth?' No one had replied.

I went and stood on the front porch. A sharp wind was tugging at a plastic sack on the green, held down by a concrete block. I stood there until it started to rain and then I went back inside.

Throughout the rest of that day I tried texting, then calling, Jason. I knew it would annoy him, but the longer his silence lasted, the worse it felt, until it seemed as though I could no longer restrain myself. In the messages I left, I told him to please ignore everything I had said that morning. That I had just woken in a bad mood. That talking to Claire, it had seemed so awful, what we were doing. That I just missed him. That I was his, and all that mattered to me was that we should stay together. That the Plan was all that mattered to me. That I would marry him in the morning, if he wanted me to.

11

The first attack happened that Sunday. At least, that was what I came to think of them as. Attacks. I was alone, as usual. I had spent the whole weekend alone. Originally, Jason had been supposed to come down but I hadn't heard from him since our phone conversation. He hadn't returned any of my texts and calls. So there I was, sitting on the sofa, just watching television, sipping sour-tasting wine left over from the previous night. On the television, a man was taking slates off a roof in the rain. I remember that because, at the moment a door shut upstairs, the man on the television lifted his head, as though he had heard it too.

I muted the television. It came again, loud and deliberate

– the click of the lock in the groove, a long silence, then the door opening and slamming shut.

Then it happened again. And again. As though whoever was doing it wanted me to hear them.

At first I just sat there. I must have left a window open, I thought. It must be the wind. But then the banging started again, over and over, in quick succession. Like they wanted the door to break in its frame. And then there was the clear, unmistakable sound of footsteps running down the landing.

Outside, I raced, through a freezing, rain-specked wind, straight to Claire's door. I rang her bell over and over. I shouted her name. I banged the knocker, my finger still on the bell. I banged the door with my fist. But she didn't answer. I ran across the green then, towards the Dorans'. Mud sucked my feet and I tripped on a concrete block, scraping my shin badly, and my hands.

Down there, in the mud, I could taste blood in my mouth. I had bitten my lip when I'd fallen. I looked back at the house and that was when I saw a light flashing on and off in my bedroom window.

All the lights were out in the Dorans' house, but when I approached, their dog started snarling behind the wooden fence. This time, his claws scratched the top of it, and he started barking loudly. I ran away, towards the entrance to the estate. I didn't know where I was going.

When a hand grabbed my wrist, I think I screamed. I think. I can't remember. But I do remember that first glimpse of Michael. He was standing right beside me. It was still raining but he wasn't wearing a coat, and his thin body was soaking wet. I think he was shouting at me. But if he was, I don't remember what he said. In my memory, it's like he's shouting at me through soundproof glass.

If Claire's porch-light had not beamed on at that moment, I don't know what I would have done next. Seeing it, though, and her standing there in her dressing gown, was enough. I shook myself loose of Michael's grip, and ran back across the green. This time, I managed not to fall.

'What in the name of God?' she said.

I found I couldn't speak. My teeth were chattering too hard.

'Come in, for God's sake,' she said.

She brought me to her sofa, and made me sit down. She put a blanket over my shoulders and gave me a cup of tea. 'Take your time,' she said. 'Get the cold out of you.'

As soon as my teeth had stopped chattering, I told her what had happened. The door slamming and the lights flashing. The young man who had grabbed my arm.

'Michael,' she said.

'You know him?'

'I do. He's been living in number one there since May.'

'Which one is that?'

'The one with the windows and doors in. By the driveway.'

Just where I'd seen him.

'A squatter,' I said.

'You could call him that.'

'I never saw him before.'

'Keeps to himself. I think he's harmless.'

'What's he doing there?'

'Ah, he's homeless. You know. I think he takes something. He was probably high off his head there now.'

'Could it have been him, do you think? In my house?'

'I'll tell you what I'm going to do,' she said. 'I'm going to call the garda station in Dunlone.'

'No. Yes. Do you think?'

'I do think. You hold tight.'

I watched as she padded over to the table, picked up her phone and made the call. She looked so much older, with no make-up on, her hair hanging down. In that moment, I felt grateful as she calmly spoke, describing how her neighbour had had a break-in. Gave the address. Then, when she had finished speaking to them, she handed the phone to me. 'They'll be here within the hour,' she said. 'You'll want to call your boyfriend.'

'He'll probably be asleep,' I said. 'It's almost midnight.'

'Give him a ring,' she said. 'Surely he'd want you to.'

I took the phone from her. I rang his number. He answered. Probably, it occurs to me now, because I wasn't calling from my phone. He didn't know who was calling him.

I told him what had happened. As I spoke, I started crying.

'I'll come down,' he said, when I'd finally managed to get the whole story out.

I didn't know what to say. I was glad, of course, that he didn't seem angry. Or at least that his anger had lessened enough for him to offer to come down. But, then, what if that meant he wouldn't come the following weekend? That was unthinkable. But if he didn't come, where would I sleep that night? I knew I wouldn't be able to go back to the house on my own.

'Would that not be an awful hassle?' I said to Jason, and I looked at Claire as I spoke, sitting there beside me, waiting patiently. I was half hoping she might offer me her spare room.

'Well, I'm awake now.'

'Are you sure?' My voice came out all high and reedy.

'If someone broke in, you shouldn't be there on your own. I should be down in an hour or so. The roads will be quiet.'

'Thanks,' I said.

While we waited for the guard and Jason, Claire told me a little about Michael. He had told her he was eighteen, she said, but she suspected he was younger. He was from Dublin and she had no idea how he had ended up on the estate. He had mental-health problems. Serious ones. That much was clear. He had told her he would be moving in with his aunt soon. That she had said he could, as soon as he was off the drugs. Once, Claire said, he'd banged on her door. That was the middle of the day, though. She occasionally gave him food. Maybe, she said, that was all he wanted from me.

'What did you do when he banged on your door?' I asked.

'I didn't open it to him,' she said. 'I told him to go home and sober up and I'd drop something in to him later.'

'Someone should call social services,' I said.

'Oh, I've done that. A couple of months ago. Out they came and asked me a few questions about him. Then they went across to his house. Dragged me with them. But he didn't answer the door. And off they went. I haven't seen them since.'

'It must have been him,' I said. 'In my house tonight.'

'It's likely,' she said. She looked tired. Exhausted, even. I knew I should tell her to go to bed, that I would be fine waiting for the guard on my own.

'I never saw him before,' I said again.

'No. Well, like I said, he keeps to himself. A man drops off coal for him every week or so. I don't know what he lives on.'

'Maybe he robs.'

'Maybe.'

'He wasn't wearing a coat. He was soaked through.'

'He'll die, I think, if he stays there through the winter.'

'He could be dangerous,' I said. 'If he has mental-health problems and he uses drugs. Even if he seems harmless. He could be dangerous, couldn't he?'

She shrugged. 'Of course. But he's not the only person living here.'

'You don't mean the Dorans? Why would they do something like that?'

She squinted into the empty fireplace. 'Oh, they wouldn't. It's just I don't trust him.'

'Mr Doran? Why not?'

She shrugged again. 'I don't know how he pays his way either.'

'But—'

'I don't know, Beth. I don't know what I'm saying. It was a long day.' She smiled. 'They would know a bit more about this place, though. They know the developer. Jim Doran used to work for him.'

'Building work?'

'Building work.'

The doorbell rang then. It was the guard. He was very tall – he seemed to stoop slightly coming through the sitting-room door. The kind of person who makes you feel safer just from looking at them. He politely declined an offer of tea. Then he sat on an armchair across from me, took a small notebook and pencil out of his pocket. 'Now,' he said. 'Start at the beginning and take your time.'

As I spoke, he took notes. When I had told him everything, he looked at what he had just written, sucked in his lower lip. 'And you saw no one?'

'No.'

'Any sign of damage to the front door?'

'None that I noticed.'

He nodded slowly. 'Would you be up for a return visit?'

Before I answered, the bell rang again. Claire went to answer it. I heard Jason's voice.

'You must have flown down,' I said, when he appeared in the doorway of the sitting room, his jaw rigid, his eyes big and lost-seeming.

He said hello to Claire and the guard. 'You've been very kind,' he said to Claire. 'We're very grateful.' Then he turned to me. 'Are you all right?' he said.

'I'm fine. I'm totally fine. Claire's been great.'

For a moment no one said anything. Then the guard spoke. 'We were just going back to the house. Will you come with us?'

At my front door, I realised I had locked myself out. Luckily, though, Jason had his set of keys, in the glove compartment of his car, so the three of us entered the house in silence. All the downstairs lights were still on. Straight away, I knew there was no one there. I think they did too. You could just tell, from the silence of the place. Still, the guard checked every window and the French doors at the back, and the locks. None showed any sign of damage. I led the way upstairs, where he checked all those windows, looked around for any sign of an intruder.

A small window in the bathroom turned out to be open. Just a couple of inches.

'Unlikely anyone got in through there,' said the guard.

'They must have had a key,' I said. 'That's the only explanation.'

'Did anyone live here before you?' asked the guard.

'No. No one.'

'Any neighbours have a copy of the key?'

'Not that I know of.'

'Go through it again,' said Jason, in a gentle voice. 'Are you absolutely sure the wind couldn't have knocked the door shut?'

'Yes. Definitely. It was way too – deliberate. And it opened and shut a few times. The wind couldn't do that, could it?' I looked at the guard. I looked at Jason.

'I wonder,' said the guard. 'If it didn't shut properly, I suppose that could happen.'

'But it did close properly.'

'And the light flashing,' said Jason. 'It was a pretty stormy night. Maybe the electrics went for a second, came back on.'

'No way. They were flashing on and off like crazy.'

'Yeah, but, love,' he said. He never usually called me 'love'. 'At that stage you were outside and you were scared out of your skin.'

'So?'

'So the mind can play tricks.'

I looked at the guard again. He pressed his lips together, put his notebook and pen back into the breast pocket of his uniform. 'I'll tell you what I think,' he said. 'I think anyone could get spooked living in a place like this. Myself included. It's nothing to be ashamed of, and you did the right thing in leaving and calling us. A good night's sleep will do you the world of good.'

'Someone was here.'

'No one's saying otherwise, honey,' said Jason. He squeezed my hand.

'Just with this weather,' said the guard, 'you wouldn't know what it could do. Playing tricks is what it does.' He put on his hat. 'I'll file the report. If anything similar happens, get in touch straight away, all right? And haven't you this fellow here now to keep you safe?'

We walked downstairs, said goodnight to the guard at the door. Then I followed Jason back into the living room.

He went to the coffee-table, lifted the bottle of wine that was still there, almost empty. He studied the label. He gave it a little shake. He lifted the glass, which still had some wine in it. He looked at me.

'I was just having one drink.'

'Were you?'

'To settle my nerves. Before I went to bed.'

'Fucking hell. Are you going to stand there all night?'

I walked to the dining table. He pulled out a chair. I sat down.

'Well, you may as well finish it,' he said.

I shook my head.

'What? You don't want any now?'

'No.'

'What's that?'

'No.'

'Don't start crying. Seriously. Don't even attempt that.' He filled the glass, and handed it to me. 'Here you go,' he said.

'I don't want any.'

'Sure you do.'

He was standing over me, holding the glass close to my face. 'Go on.'

I took a sip.

'You need to finish it.'

In the end, I just downed it.

'Did you enjoy that?'

'No.'

'Why are you trying to fuck with my mind, Beth?' he said quietly. 'I'm just trying to understand it. Are you trying to drive me crazy?'

I shook my head.

'Driving down here, on the motorway, I was worried about you. I was feeling guilty. Can you imagine? I was thinking, Maybe all that stuff she said on the phone, maybe she was picking up on some danger she couldn't put her finger on.

And now someone has broken in and she's been traumatised by it. I mean, okay, it was her idea to move down on her own, but I was the one who told her about the place. And then I find this.' He lifted up the wine bottle again, returned it to the table with a dull thump.

'This is nothing. I told you, it was just to help me sleep.'

'You know what else I find, Beth? I find bullshit.'

He stood.

'Where are you going?'

'I'm going to bed,' he said. 'I'll probably be gone by the time you wake.' He looked at his watch. 'In five hours' time, I've got to drive back down that motorway, and do a day's work. Not that that should bother you.'

'Jason,' I said. 'I'm sorry I dragged you down here. I really am. I'm so sorry. But there was someone upstairs.'

'Turning me into some kind of – monster.' He gestured towards the table, where he had made me drink the wine. He grimaced. 'That's not me.'

'I know it isn't, darling.'

'What are you trying to do to me?'

I put my hands to my face. I wanted to cry but no tears came.

'And what are you going to do instead?'

'Instead of what?'

'Instead of this.'

'I don't want to do anything else. I want to do this. Did you not get my messages?'

'I've changed my job on the basis of our plan. I did that on good faith.'

'I know, sweetheart.'

'This is about trust,' he said. 'Do you not see that?'

'Yes.'

'I need to trust that you will honour our plan. That you *can* honour our plan. Otherwise, what do we have? How can I trust you again? Do you not see it will only work if we actually stick to it?'

'I know.'

'Do you not see that what you have to do is very easy? I will be here, with you, in a few weeks.'

'I know that.'

'Do you not see the Plan is all you've got?' He looked like he was going to cry.

'I do see that now,' I said. I walked over to him. I put my arms around his neck. 'I didn't mean to hurt you,' I said. 'I'm so sorry.' I kissed him until he kissed me back. 'Let's go to bed,' I said. 'You need to rest.'

In bed, we had sex. I knew it would help things. And I knew that afterwards he would fall asleep, which he did, almost immediately. I lay there for a long time, wide awake, unable to sleep, the house around me silent. Finally I got up, found a pen and a notebook. I took them into the bathroom. I made a list.

1. The squatter

2. Mr Doran

3. Kids (but who?)

4. Someone from the village (who doesn't like the estate? Who doesn't like me?)

5. (Ghost???)

I looked at it for a while, then shut the notebook and put it in the sink cabinet. I sat there for a bit, listening to Jason's soft, regular snoring coming from the bedroom.

All I had to do was think of those hours of driving he did, all because he cared for me. His worried, lost look when he came into Claire's living room. The way he almost began to cry downstairs. In less than six weeks' time, I told myself, he would be living here with me, and with all this pressure gone, the two of us would go back to the way we had been in the summer.

All I had to do in the meantime was try to believe it was the weather that had had the doors opening and closing like that, the lights flicking on and off, like a message from somewhere terrible.

12

Torn-open rubbish bags covered the inside of the windows of number one. A cable stuck out of the wall where the doorbell should have been, its long black wires splayed and hanging. A sharp north wind was making them jerk back and forth.

Before I even had a chance to knock, the door opened. Standing there was the young man from the night before, his face pale and frightened. He looked even younger than I remembered.

I smiled. 'You beat me to it,' I said. I put out my hand. 'Beth, from across the way. We bumped into each other last night.'

His expression did not change.

'Is it okay if I come in? Just for a second.'

'What do ya want?'

His thin voice made him seem even younger. It made him seem a child. As he spoke, his gaze fixed on the shepherd's pie I had brought with me, still warm from the oven.

'Just to say hello. I brought you this.' I held up the pie.

He stepped back, held the door open.

Once inside, the smell hit me straight away – piss and shit, and something gone off, like sour milk. The hallway had the same layout as mine, but in every other way it was different – the walls unplastered, the floor concrete. An empty space where the staircase should have been.

An urgent scratching started up from the other side of the door to the living room. He went ahead of me, opened the door, and a small brown puppy ran out. It looked at me, and promptly pissed, there in the hallway.

'Oh, he's gorgeous,' I said, as he picked it up and scratched its head.

'It's a she,' he said. He was still looking at the shepherd's pie.

'You should eat this before it goes cold,' I said, handing it to him.

I followed him into the living room. There was not even a kitchen installed. The only piece of furniture was an armchair in front of the fireplace, in which a few small pieces of coal glowed. On the floor by the fireplace lay a cup, a kettle, a saucer filled with used teabags and a cardboard box containing some cutlery. Under the window there was a blue tent, a sleeping bag protruding from its entrance.

Michael put the dog on the floor and took a spoon from the

box by the fireplace. Then, standing in front of me, he began to eat. Occasionally, he threw a spoonful onto the floor, which the puppy licked up.

'Michael, isn't it?' I said.

He nodded.

'God, it's freezing in here.'

'The coal is nearly gone,' he said.

'Who gives it to you?'

He didn't answer.

'Claire said a man drops some around every week. Do you know Claire? Across the way?'

He ate the last mouthful of the shepherd's pie. Then he put the casserole dish on the floor for the dog to lick clean. 'He's awful hungry,' he said.

'That's grand.'

'Claire fills my water bottles,' he said.

'Oh, does she?'

He nodded. 'She gives me food sometimes.' Then his gaze fell on a book beside the armchair. On its cover was a red landscape, with jagged mountains in the distance.

'Any good?' I asked.

'Brilliant,' he said, and he picked it up, stared at the cover.

'What's it about?'

'Mars,' he said. 'Humans colonise it. It's in the future.' He looked at me. 'Do you read science fiction?'

'No. I'd like to. I always think there's so much of it. I wouldn't know where to start. I might never come back out.'

He looked at the cover again.

'So,' I said, 'last night was a bit like a scene from a science-fiction book, wasn't it?'

He stared at me. It was as though he was trying to remember something. As though last night was a long time ago.

I lifted the puppy. She was warm. I could feel her heart beating against my hand. She licked my face.

'I can get you one,' he said, his face lighting up. 'Do you want one? The man who gave her to me has more and he's going to drown them.'

'No, thanks. Do you remember seeing me last night, Michael?'

'I saw you,' he said eventually. 'Running across.'

'What were you doing outside?'

'I can't remember,' he said. 'Here, you don't have any fags?'

'No, sorry. I don't smoke.'

He was clearly disappointed. 'There's no teabags neither,' he said.

'Don't worry,' I said. 'I've had enough caffeine already to do me for the day.'

He looked at me forlornly.

'What age are you?'

'Eighteen.'

'Really?'

'Yeah.'

'You're very young to be living on your own.'

'I'm waiting till me aunt lets me move back in with her.'

'Is she in Dublin?'

He nodded.

'Why can't you live with her now?'

'The drugs,' he said. He suddenly looked like he might fall asleep, standing there. 'She has kids,' he said. He spoke more slowly. It was as though he was falling into a trance.

'I had a visitor last night,' I said. 'Banging doors, switching lights on and off. You didn't see anyone around the place?'

'I told you. I saw you.'

'But besides me.'

He shook his head. Then he scooped up the puppy – she had wriggled away from me – and sat into his armchair. She curled up on his lap and closed her eyes.

'I called the guards,' I said. 'They told me to ask everyone living here if they'd seen anything.'

He looked up at me. It seemed as though it took his last scrap of energy to do so. 'They didn't come round here,' he said.

'Did they not?'

'C'mere. What is it? I have a hole in my heart. Do you know anything about that?'

'A hole in your heart?'

'I had it since I was a baby.'

'Jesus. I'm sorry. I don't know anything about that.'

'And when I was in school I had to go to hospital with it, and there was this other boy there with it too, and he died. He died when I was there in hospital.'

'Why don't you call social services? I can call them now on my phone.' I took it out of my pocket.

'No point,' he said. 'I'm eighteen. I'm an adult.'

'But—'

'The last time they put me in foster care. There was lads

using in there. Anyway, I told you. I'm eighteen,' he said. 'I'll be going back to my aunt's in a few weeks' time, she said if I got to Christmas clean.'

He closed his eyes then. I stood there for a long while watching him. Both he and the dog seemed asleep. But when I went to pick up the casserole dish, he spoke. 'Here,' he said, his eyes opening. 'You don't have any more spare food?'

'I might do. I – I'll drop some over to you.'

'And coal or anything? Your man won't be here for another couple of days.'

'I have a few bales of briquettes. I can give you one of those, I suppose. Michael, did you break into my house last night? I'm not angry.'

'What would I do that for?'

'I don't mean to be rude.'

'Don't ya not? That's good anyways.' He smiled.

'It's just – it was scary. I'm there on my own. If we're neighbours, it would be nice to get along.'

He put a hand to his forehead. He started laughing quietly.

'Well – what else are we?' I tried to laugh too. 'And we're from the same place. Both blow-ins. We should maybe look out for each other.'

'Look out for each other.'

'Why not?'

'I wouldn't worry about them kids. That's all it is – kids messing.'

'Did you see them, then?'

'I'd say that's all it is. Or the wind.'

'It might have been the weather.'

'Or a ghost.'

'Why do you say that?'

'I think it was a ghost.'

'Very funny. Well, it was nice to meet you.'

He closed his eyes again.

'Goodbye then.' I walked to the door.

'Here. You won't forget about the food and the briquettes?'

'I won't forget.'

'Okay. Goodbye, neighbour.'

'See you, Michael.'

'At least you have electricity.'

'What?'

'And water.' He smiled thinly.

'Well, that's because I'm not squatting.'

He closed his eyes again. I stood there watching him for a while, his chest rising and falling, the puppy curled up on his lap.

'Michael?'

He didn't open his eyes. He really seemed to have fallen asleep, just like that.

Outside, I couldn't get enough of the cold, clean air. I sucked it in. It was still morning, but already it felt as though the day was preparing for darkness, the sun low in the sky. The rain had stopped but clouds to the south threatened more.

I kept my head down on my way around the green. I might not have heard Mr Doran coming out of his house just after I'd passed it if his door hadn't slammed shut.

'Hi there,' I said, turning to face him.

He looked at me, surprised.

He gave me a curt 'hello'. Then he turned and walked away, towards the entrance of the estate.

I went to meditation again last night. The same woman was facilitating it. Chenda. She spoke a little again at the start. She said it's normal for your mind to keep wandering when practising. That it's actually the act of drawing your mind back to your breathing that constitutes mindfulness. No one manages to stay with their breathing the whole time, she said, unless they've been practising for a very long time. She said if you just keep drawing your mind back to your breathing, it stays with it for longer periods. And that's how you slowly grow more and more mindful.

I put up my hand.

'Yes?'

'Is this the Eightfold Path? Is that what is meant by how to stop suffering?' I blurted.

'Well,' she said. She was frowning slightly, as though trying to figure out a way to reply. 'In a way, yes. It's part of it. It's a good start, shall we say.' She smiled. 'Don't get too hung up on the theory. The Buddha always taught that the Middle Way is experiential – we don't need a leap of faith to follow what he said. We just need to see for ourselves that it works. Does that make sense?' She smiled at me.

'Thanks,' I said. 'That's really helpful.'

I got on even worse with the meditation this time round. I'd say I did the observing-my-breathing thing for all of two minutes in total, before I was back thinking about everything and anything. And instead of feeling relaxed, I was almost panicky. Like I wanted to run out of the room. I almost did at one point. I even opened my eyes and looked around at everyone, silent and apparently observing their breathing with ease.

Afterwards, though, I hung around for the reading again. This one was easier to understand. It was called the Angulimala Sutta. Angulimala was this man who lived in a place called Savatthi, in India. He used to kill people all the time. Whole villages of them, it says. He killed people to make a garland of fingers to wear around his neck. People warn the Buddha from passing by this man's home when he's out collecting alms, but he ignores them. 'The Blessed One went on, silently,' it says. And when he does come upon Angulimala, he cannot reach the Buddha. This man used to be able to overtake an elephant, a chariot, and now he finds himself unable to overtake a simple monk. He asks the Buddha to explain. And the Buddha says, 'Angulimala, I have stopped for good, punishing living things. You are not restrained towards living things.' Angulimala throws away his weapons. He becomes a monk. But whenever he is out collecting alms, every time someone throws a clod of earth, or a stone or a stick at someone, *he* gets hit by it. He comes back to the Buddha all bloodied and sore and his bowl broken. The Buddha says, 'Endure it. Better to suffer the consequences of your past actions in the here and now than in Hell.' That's when Angulimala becomes enlightened. He does this speech where he says things like 'The negligent one became diligent and illuminated the world like the moon freed of clouds.'

13

Michael called on me the following evening. It was a Tuesday. I had been sitting on the sofa watching television when I caught sight of him through the window, walking towards my front door, holding two puppies tight to his chest, as though for warmth. One I recognised from the day before.

His smell hit me as soon as I opened the door.

'I got ya one,' he said, holding the other puppy out to me. 'He's drowning the rest of them, the farmer. I think he's already drowned them.'

The puppy tried to lurch forward, towards me. Then he did a tiny pee. It trickled off Michael's hands and onto the doorstep.

'For God's sake,' I said, 'I told you I didn't want one.' But I took the wriggling thing, by the scruff of its neck.

It whimpered.

'Don't hold it like that,' said Michael.

'This is how you're supposed to hold them.'

I looked at him, the puppy pee still dripping from his hand. 'Come in for a minute.'

In the living room, I put the puppy on the floor and Michael did the same with his. The one he had given me went straight to him and whined at him. The other stood beside him, looking happily from Michael to me, then at Michael again, as though daring us all to have a great game together.

'The sink is over there,' I said. 'If you want to wash your hands.'

He walked slowly to the kitchen area, the puppies following him.

'I couldn't have a shower, could I?' he said then. 'Just a quick one.'

'I don't think so.'

'I haven't had one in weeks. Months.'

By that stage, the smell had filled the room.

'There's a shower under the stairs,' I said finally. 'I'll get you a towel.'

I had to avert my eyes as I spoke. It was too pathetic – the way his face changed, his mouth hanging open in surprise. And then the way he moved so quickly towards the shower room, as though fearing I might change my mind.

'There's hardly any hot water,' I said, handing him a towel. 'It'll have to be quick. And this is just a one-off, okay?'

'Yeah. Put some newspaper on the floor. They'll piss on that.' And he was gone.

I looked at the puppies. I had no ham, or anything I thought they might like. In the end, I gave them buttered slices of bread, and a bowl of milk each. They swallowed the bread without chewing. They lapped up the milk so fast, some of it spilled onto the floor. Then they licked that up. When Michael came back into the room, I was buttering more bread.

'I don't have anything for them to eat.'

'You can feed them anything,' he said. 'They eat anything.' He looked even younger, with his hair made darker by the water, and back off his face. I was reminded of the first time I saw him, out in the rain.

'I suppose they do, if they're hungry enough.'

'He would be drowned now, if I hadn't taken him for you.'

'Well, I can't keep him.'

'Why not?'

'For a start,' I said, 'my boyfriend is allergic to them.'

'Your boyfriend?' he said. 'Where is he?'

'In Dublin.'

'He's hardly that allergic.' He took the piece of bread I had just buttered and stuffed it into his mouth.

'He comes down sometimes,' I said. 'That was for the dogs.' I took the towel he had left on the table and put it into the laundry basket in the utility room. When I came back he was already buttering another slice of the bread.

'I'm starved,' said Michael, but he threw a piece of bread on the floor. 'I haven't eaten anything since that dinner you made me.'

It landed close to the puppy intended for me. He lurched himself towards it, the same kind of movement he had made when he'd peed on Michael's hand, his body sort of leaping further than it could, so that he'd then land awkwardly. Like he hadn't learned how to walk properly.

'You know you're not my responsibility, Michael. And neither are these dogs.'

'Dogs,' he repeated.

It had already grown dark. Looking at the French doors, I could see a reflection of the kitchen, with Michael standing by the island, the puppies at his feet. A light steady rain had begun to drum against the panes. It was only seven o'clock.

'You can eat here tonight. But that doesn't mean you can do this again. Do you understand that?'

'Oh, I do. I do understand.'

'Okay? We're clear on that?'

'Clear, clear,' he said.

I put a frozen pizza into the oven and made a pot of tea. We ate our meal in front of the television, me on the sofa, Michael in the armchair, his puppy on his lap. Lurch – I started to think of him as Lurch as early as that evening – curled up beside me. Within minutes, both puppies were asleep.

After the pizza, Michael rolled a joint, his long, thin fingers steady and even graceful as he expertly crumbled the hash onto the tobacco and rolled the paper.

'What are you doing?'

'Do ya mind?'

'Well, yes, I do.'

'It's just the one.'

'We're not making a habit of this.'

'Ah, no.' He daintily licked the paper, sealed it. Then he lit the joint, inhaled. After a while, he passed it to me.

I had only ever smoked hash a couple of times when I was in college, usually at the end of a party. That time with Michael, it seemed very strong. I felt the effect almost immediately. It took a while before I could chance speaking again.

'So,' I said. 'What's your story?'

'How did I end up here, like?'

'Yeah.'

'I told you. Drugs.'

'Do you mean heroin?'

'No, I don't. I wouldn't go near that stuff. That's what killed my mother.'

'I'm sorry.' I passed back the joint.

'She got into the bed beside me before she died.'

'God.'

'My aunt found us.'

'What age were you?'

'Thirteen. I ended up on the streets, after.'

'What about your dad?'

He shrugged. 'I don't know who he is. Me brother's in jail.'

'Why didn't you go to your aunt? After your mother died?'

'She wouldn't have me. She says she will now if I stop taking drugs.'

'You should stop, then. What about your heart? It can't be good for that.'

'I have, except for this.' He took a deep drag. 'Once I stop taking this, I'm going to her.'

'What was it like, being on the streets?'

'Bad,' he said. 'I went around with some other lads. There are places you can go to get fed. I think it's better than jail.'

'Were you ever in jail?'

'Ah, no.' He passed me the joint. 'What about yourself?' he said.

'My boyfriend and I are saving for a deposit on a house. He's starting a new job in Dunlone in the new year.' I took a slow drag.

'So, how come he isn't down here with you now?'

'He has to finish his job in Dublin. If I hadn't moved in when I did, someone else would have got this place.'

'Ye got it cheap?'

I nodded. I was getting tired of telling that story. The story of the Plan.

'And then ye'll get married and have children.'

'That's none of your business.'

'The two of us are using this place to get somewhere better,' he said.

'I suppose that's right.' I stroked Lurch's head. 'I don't like it here,' I said.

'It's bad,' he agreed. 'It feels like the houses are watching you.'

'Yes! That's exactly it.'

'You have that fellow now anyway,' he said, nodding at Lurch.

'You came here with two dogs and you'll be leaving with two dogs,' I said.

'I won't,' he said.

'You will.'

At that moment, the Dorans' dog began barking loudly across the way.

'What's the story with them?' I asked.

'He's a cunt,' said Michael.

'Mr Doran? Is he?'

'Tried to get rid of me. Called the guards on me and everything.'

'He didn't exactly strike me as friendly. What about her?'

'You never see her,' he said.

'I wonder why they have that Alsatian.'

'For the debt collectors.'

'How do you know that?'

He shrugged.

A football match came on the television then and for a while we watched in silence. At one point, when the referee began to gesticulate with his arms, I began to laugh and couldn't stop. Michael was laughing too. The dogs woke and looked at us. That made us laugh harder. I worried I would never be able to stop laughing, until finally I did. Michael rolled a second joint then. As we smoked that, it became impossible to speak. It became impossible to move, even to pet Lurch, which occasionally I wanted to do.

I managed to get to the bathroom when I suddenly needed to throw up. That straightened me out a little. When I went back into the sitting room, instead of sitting on the sofa I stood behind it, my hands resting on its back. The air, I realised, was very smoky.

'All right?' he said.

I nodded.

He took a final drag, then dropped the stub into his cold tea, where it made a sad, short fizzing sound. Then he squished his hand into the pocket of his jeans and took out a small bag of white powder.

'No, Michael,' I said. 'You're not taking that here.'

He threw me a look and suddenly I was frightened.

'Just a line,' he said. He tipped some of the powder onto the table and inhaled it so quickly I didn't have time to object again.

'Come on, Michael,' I said then. I walked over to him.

'What are you doing standing there?'

'I should be getting to bed,' I said. 'I've a ton of work to get through tomorrow.'

'I'll stay here,' he said. 'You won't notice me.'

'That won't work,' I said. 'Come on. You'll be asleep before you know it, once you're in your sleeping bag.'

'I'll sleep on your sofa.'

'I don't think so.' I put my hand on his elbow.

'Don't fucking touch me.' He jerked my hand away.

'I—'

'I mean it. Don't fucking lay a finger on me.'

'Okay. But you need to leave now.'

'No.' He said it like a small child.

'Yes.'

'I'll kip here.' He sprang up, almost threw himself onto the sofa in one move, wrapping his feet around Lurch, who was still asleep there, managing to hold onto his own puppy as he did so. He pulled a blanket I had lying across the back of the sofa on top of himself.

'I said that's not going to work.' I opened the door to the hall. Then I opened the front door, let the frosty air steal through the smoke.

Michael didn't move. His eyes were shut.

'I don't want to have to call the police.'

'For fuck sake,' he said.

'It's not a big deal, Michael. Just go home and sleep there. I'll see you soon.'

'I'll fucking freeze.'

'You've slept there worse nights. Look, take that blanket if you want.'

'You were glad of the company while it suited you.'

'Come on.'

A sharp wind came through the door.

'I'm sleeping here,' he said quietly.

I googled Dunlone garda station. I put the phone on speaker and then I called the number. It rang a couple of times.

'Dunlone garda station.' It was a male voice.

'Fucking bitch,' said Michael. But he got to his feet. He walked past me, puppy and blanket in his arms, and out into the cold night. Slammed the front door behind him.

'Sorry,' I said. 'False alarm.' And I hung up.

Lurch whined at the door. He put his paws up and scratched it. He pissed right there on the floor. Then he turned to me.

14

The following evening I left Lurch in the house and walked around to the newsagent's to buy an apple tart. Then, back at the house, I sat for a while at the dining table, and tried to prepare. I told myself that, by its nature, visiting the Dorans was not going to be a pleasant experience. That way, if things went well, it would be a nice surprise. But if things didn't go well, I wouldn't feel too disappointed. I was on a kind of mission, I told myself, to find out whether or not they had something against me. And to let them know I was taking steps to protect myself. It was something I had to get through, if I was to last the next few weeks on the estate, just like calling on Michael had been something I'd had to get through.

I suppose what I really hoped was that those visits would dispel my worries. Look a source of fear in the eye and maybe it disappears. The fear, that is. If I learned that no one on the estate had anything against me, then maybe I'd be able to believe what Jason believed – that the events of that night were the result of bad weather and too much wine.

If it turned out that someone did have something against me, well, it was better to know.

I tried to remind myself of all this when Mr Doran opened his door and stared at me as I introduced myself. The bottom half of his face was dark with stubble, his eyes bloodshot.

I followed him into the sitting room, where Mrs Doran was sitting beside a coal fire, burning low. She wore a dressing gown, the baby again in her arms. On the other side of the fireplace, a television was flashing out some action film. She turned the volume off and looked at me.

'The young girl across the way,' said Mr Doran. 'Beth, isn't it?'

I smiled at Mrs Doran. I put the apple tart on the coffee-table. 'I hope you don't mind me just calling in like this,' I said. 'God knows what that's like.' I had decided to act naturally.

'Would you put the kettle on and bring out some plates?' she said to Mr Doran, without looking at him. I sensed they had just been arguing.

'Sit down,' she said to me, and she lifted some newspapers from the sofa and put them on the floor.

'Thanks,' I said, and sat on the sofa, close to her.

'You'll have to excuse the state of the place,' she said.

'It's grand. You should see my place,' I said. 'How's the little baby?'

'The little baby is fine,' she said. She stood and put him in a Moses basket on the other side of her armchair. 'You have to wait for him to be asleep a few minutes before you can put him down,' she said. 'Otherwise he just wakes up again. And cries his eyes out.'

Mr Doran came back in, with a tray carrying mugs of tea, plates and cutlery.

'How are you getting on across the way?' she said to me, as she cut three slices.

'Grand, thanks,' I said.

'I didn't know if you took sugar,' he said, handing me a mug of tea.

'No, thanks. This is perfect.' I took the mug. 'This is the same layout as my living room,' I said. 'Except you have a wall there, separating the sitting-room part from the kitchen. I don't have that.'

She looked at the wall.

'How old is he, did you say?' I asked, glancing at the baby again.

'Nearly three months now,' she said.

'What's his name?'

'James.'

'That's a lovely name. James.'

'After his daddy.'

For a minute or two, we sat there, watching the muted television, no one saying anything.

'You're paying eight hundred a month for the place,' said Mr Doran then, turning to me.

'That's right.' My face grew hot.

'We looked into renting out this place. We weren't going to be getting close to that.'

'And your boyfriend is coming down in the new year, is that it?' said Mrs Doran.

'That's it, yeah. Well, Christmas. He starts the new job in Dunlone in January.'

'That'll be nice for you,' she said. 'I wouldn't fancy being here on my own.'

'Where's the job?' said Mr Doran.

The name of the company escaped me. 'It's this huge pharmaceutical company in a business park in Dunlone. This side of the town.'

'I know it,' he said.

'Do you?'

'I worked on the new buildings they have there. A couple of years ago.'

'Oh, the new labs. Wow. That's such a coincidence. That's where Jason will be based.'

He nodded, looked back at the television screen.

'Claire mentioned you worked for Paul Gilroy,' I said.

'Used to,' he said.

'Actually,' I said, 'I wouldn't say it's going great, to be honest. In the house, I mean.' I took a sip of my tea.

'What do you mean?' said Mrs Doran.

I put my mug on the coffee-table. 'Just . . . weird stuff has been happening.' I cleared my throat.

'Weird stuff,' she said. 'Like what?'

Mr Doran was watching me.

'Well, like someone turning the lights on and off. Upstairs. And banging the doors.'

'God,' she said. 'A break-in?'

'Yes. I mean I don't know.'

'Did you call the guards?' he said.

'One came out,' I said. 'Very nice. He could find no sign of a break-in. But he said I'm to call straight away if anything else happens.'

'You must have been scared out of your wits,' said Mrs Doran.

'He said to ask around as well,' I lied. 'Check in with the neighbours.'

'We haven't seen anything,' said Mr Doran. 'Have we, Fran?'

'Us? No. No.'

'Could be kids messing, I suppose,' he said.

'Yeah, that's what the guard said. He asked me if anyone else had keys to the place, but I didn't think so. I mean, they couldn't have, except Paul Gilroy. It's not as though anyone else has ever lived there.'

Neither of them spoke.

'It's a bit of a mystery, I suppose. But he said to call straight away if anything else happens. He said it's on the books now, and they'll send someone out quickly. So at least that's something.' I forced myself to look at them, each in turn. 'It's weird,' I said.

'Maybe it's a ghost,' he said.

'Jim.'

I smiled at him. 'I actually wondered that. But if no one lived there before . . .'

They exchanged glances.

'Unless this place is built on an old graveyard or something,' I said.

'You can feel the winter coming in, can't you?' said Mrs Doran.

'This place is not built on a graveyard. I can tell you that for a fact.'

'Jim,' said Mrs Doran, again. She shook her head.

'Who told you no one lived there before?' he said.

I looked at him.

'In the house you're in now,' he added.

'Paul Gilroy,' I said.

'No wonder.'

'Jim, just let it alone.'

'What is it?' I said. '*Did* someone live there before me?'

'Well, they did,' he said. 'For close on a year. Would that be right, Fran?'

She didn't answer.

'What happened?' I said.

'He hanged himself,' he said. 'In the living room.'

Mrs Doran put her cup down. 'For God's sake,' she said. 'You'll only be frightening her.' She peered into the fire, which had grown even lower.

'I don't think so,' I said. 'I would have heard.'

'From who? He didn't want to put you off, did he? He

needed someone to keep the place from going damp. He needed someone to stop it becoming the haunted house, that's what he needed.'

I looked at Mrs Doran. 'Is it true?' I said.

'It was very sad,' she said. 'But it was a while ago now.'

'Not that long,' said Mr Doran. 'It only happened about this time last year.'

'Why? I mean, why did he do it?'

'Money problems,' said Mrs Doran.

'Didn't he lose his job a month after signing the mortgage? When everything started going belly-up?'

'He was prone to depression, they said.'

I sipped my tea. It had gone cold. I thought of my living room. I tried to think how he would have done it. But it was as though my mind had stopped working. I couldn't think, even though I wanted to.

'A young couple,' he said.

'Will you stop it.'

'I'm telling her for her own sake.'

'But I'm sure Paul Gilroy said—'

'You believe that little prick?' He took a pouch of tobacco and papers out of his pocket and started rolling a cigarette.

'You can't smoke that in here,' she said flatly.

'I know that, don't I? No one told you that.' He shook his head.

'No one told me that.'

The baby began to cry. Mrs Doran looked in at him. When he kept crying, she lifted him out of the basket. She stood and swayed. 'Sssh-sssh-sssh,' she went. 'Sssh-sssh-sssh.' But the baby only cried harder. It arched its back and wailed.

'I'd better go,' I said, standing. 'Thanks for the tea.'

'Not at all,' said Mrs Doran, glancing at me, then away. 'Walk her out, Jim.'

As soon as we got to the door, he lit his cigarette. 'The best thing for you would be to get back in your car and head back to your boyfriend in Dublin.'

'Would that be the best thing?'

He looked at me when I said that. Like he was seeing something in me he only realised then, or like he was trying to figure something out. 'I don't care what you do,' he said. 'It doesn't make any difference to me.'

'Okay. Goodnight.'

'I'll see you across,' he said.

'No, you're fine. Thank you.' I started to walk away. Then I turned back. 'You said it happened in the living room,' I said. 'Where exactly?'

'Forget about it.'

'I need to know.'

'I think they said it was off one of the beams.'

'Of course. You don't know which one?'

He shook his head. Then he dropped his rollie to the ground, extinguished it with his heel, then put it into his pocket. 'Goodnight,' he said, and went back inside.

*

The sky was clear that night, but there was no moon. I walked very slowly back to the house, so as not to fall or walk into something. Even at that, I managed to bump into the Portakabin, the side of my face pressing for an instant against the burning cold of the steel wall. I had forgotten to use my phone as a torch, as I had done on the way over.

15

The following week came the letterbox banging. It was a Wednesday, and I was upstairs in bed. I had spent the whole evening there, as I had done every day that week. Once it got dark, I could no longer bear being in the living room on my own. Not after what Mr Doran had told me about what had happened there. If I hadn't had Lurch with me that week, I don't know if I would have been able to stay there. He slept on my bed every night, and when I tried to work, he was there under the table. I think, too, that he was the only reason I still bothered going for a walk every day.

I still hadn't told Jason what Mr Doran had told me. I couldn't find a way to do it that would *not* make him think I was trying to mess up the Plan again. I could never be sure

I wouldn't start crying or something stupid like that, once I started telling him. So when we spoke on the phone, I just acted like everything was fine. He was so absorbed in his work, he didn't notice anything different about me, if there was anything to notice.

Each day, I would work until it was time to close the curtains, and then I would bring Lurch and a bottle of wine with me up to bed. I would just drink a couple of glasses while browsing Facebook, even though I hardly ever commented on anything any more. Or I would watch old TV episodes on YouTube, with Lurch curled up at the foot of the bed. Something like that, until I knew I was going to fall asleep.

That Wednesday night I was about to drift off when it started up, sudden and urgent. Clack, clack, clack, clack. Silence. And then off again. Clack, clack, clack, clack, clack.

I knew I wasn't imagining it because Lurch sat up. He growled.

'Sssh,' I said.

I got to the window, but I couldn't see anything except raindrops hitting the glass hard. When the banging stopped, I looked at my closed bedroom door, then back at the window. I tried to imagine climbing down the drainpipe, but I couldn't work out how I would do it without risking the pipe coming away from the wall.

When the banging started up again, I pulled on a pair of jeans, a sweater, boots. I stuffed my keys and phone into my back pocket, lifted Lurch and held him tight against my chest.

I was going to make a run for it, but not, obviously, through the front door. I had to go out by the French doors. From there,

I could cross into Claire's garden, and bang on her back door until she woke. If she wasn't in, I would run up the driveway to the pub. Or I would cut through the golf course to the club. I'd decide which once I was outside.

I think I shouted out as I made a run for it, down the stairs, through the living room and into the darkness. I don't think the letterbox clattered at all as I did that. At least, I don't remember it. I do remember the intense feeling of someone observing me, though, as I tried to turn the key in the French doors – my hands were shaking so much it took a few attempts. But then I was outside. I was dropping Lurch onto the lawn on the other side of the fence. I was banging on Claire's French doors, calling her name as loudly as I could.

I had already knocked on her door twice that week, but neither time had she been in. So, when her hallway light finally came on, I could have cried with relief. It seemed to take her for ever to reach the door. I almost shouted to her to hurry, but then she was there, in her dressing gown and woollen socks, her eyes heavy with sleep.

'What's happened?' she said.

'Someone,' I said. 'Something was trying to scare me.'

'Come on,' she said wearily, holding the door open.

Neither of us spoke again until I was sitting on her sofa, a blanket over my shoulders. Just like the last time.

'Now,' she said. 'What's happened this time?'

'I can't believe this is happening again,' I said.

'*What*'s happening again?'

I told her what I had heard. 'I don't want to call the guards,'

I said. 'They'll think I'm mad. Or they'll just say it was kids. Or the wind.'

'It doesn't sound like it was the wind.'

'No, it doesn't.'

'Someone is trying to frighten you.' The calm, matter-of-fact way she said it made it seem even more frightening.

'I called in on the Dorans last week.'

'What did you do that for?'

'I don't know. See if I could find out anything. You said he used to work for Paul Gilroy.'

'Did I? I shouldn't have opened my mouth.'

'You knew, didn't you? About the couple who lived in my house.'

She looked at me again, almost sharply this time. 'I didn't want to frighten you, telling you about that. What good does it do?'

'I'm being haunted.'

'You're not being haunted. Ghosts aren't real. Or if they are, they don't go around banging people's letterboxes.'

'Well, then, who is it? Who's trying to scare me?'

She said nothing.

'Why would someone kill themselves like that?' I said. 'Why would they do that?'

'People have a breaking point, I suppose.'

'You're tired. I'm sorry. I should just go home.'

She didn't say anything.

'Do you think it was Mr Doran?' I asked.

'No. Why would he want to scare you?'

'I don't know. It doesn't make sense. Do you think it was Michael, then?'

'Not impossible, I suppose.'

'Kids?'

'You're going round in circles. You're no wiser now than you were the last time.'

I started to cry. But they were tearless sobs.

'Are you still determined to stay on the estate?' Claire asked.

'I have to.'

'The Plan,' she said.

'The Plan.'

'Well, then, we have to call the police. In case something happens again.' She stood, walked over to the kitchen island and picked up her phone.

'No,' I said. 'Please don't.'

'Why not?'

'I don't want you to think badly of him. He's under a tremendous amount of pressure right now.'

'Your boyfriend.'

I nodded. 'It's just . . . it's taken a lot for us to get here, and it means so much to our future. Like – everything. If he has to come down again, and sees me like this . . . again. Especially when nothing really happened.'

'Except that something did happen.'

'It just wouldn't be fair to him. It might be too much.'

'What if we call the police and you don't tell Jason?'

That hadn't occurred to me.

16

Jason phoned the following evening, just as I was about to retreat to my bedroom. I had spent the day sitting at the dining table, as usual, trying to work, Lurch at my feet. I had a deadline that Friday, which was lucky because it kept me focused for some of the time. And bringing Lurch for a walk gave me a reason to take a break, get out of that room for a while. I brought him for three walks that day. But I was falling far behind on work. I kept thinking about the guard the night before, looking at me as though I was crazy – just like the last time he came out, there had been no sign of a break-in. I kept going on these websites about exorcisms, and searching weird forums for discussion threads about how to get an angry spirit to leave a house. I tried to imagine a conversation with Claire, in which I would ask if I could stay with her for a couple of nights, but it never worked. I knew somehow she didn't want me to ask. I figured she would already have offered, if she'd thought it was a good idea.

'Hey-ho,' said Jason.

'You sound happy,' I said.

'Slight overstatement,' he said drily.

'Sorry!'

'We met a deadline today.'

'Pressure off?'

'Hardly.'

'No,' I said.

'Lessened, maybe.'

'A reprieve,' I tried.

'Sort of. So. How is week nine going?'

'Well, interesting.'

'Oh. Here we go.'

'Don't worry. I'm handling it.'

Taking care to speak calmly, I told him about my visit to the Dorans and what Mr Doran had told me about the couple who had lived in the house. The man who had killed himself. I only lied about the reason for my visit, making it sound as though they had invited me over. Then I told him about the letterbox banging. I made sure to stay calm so he wouldn't assume I'd been drunk and imagined it. I told him how I had gone to Claire's, and how she had insisted I call the police. I made it sound like I'd taken it all in my stride. Like I didn't think any of it to be such a big deal.

'Probably just kids messing,' I said. 'That's what the guard thought.'

He said nothing.

'Ghosts don't bang at letterboxes, do they?' I laughed.

'No,' he said. 'They don't.'

Another pause. For once, I managed not to fill it by babbling on.

'Could Doran have been bullshitting you?'

'No, Claire knew about it too. She hadn't said anything because she didn't want to freak me out.'

'Not like that dickhead.'

'Hm.'

'You sound very calm.'

'There's not much point in overreacting.'

'That's right.' There was a pause. 'I'll get down tomorrow. For the weekend.'

'Don't put yourself under pressure. I know how busy things are for you.' It felt like a gamble, saying that.

'No, no.' Another pause. 'I might even be able to leave work a bit earlier than usual. Might. We'll see.'

'That would be great. Wow, it'll be so good to see you!'

By the end of the day, I knew I didn't have a hope of finishing the report I was working on in time. Usually when that happened, I would work through the weekend, submitting it first thing Monday morning instead. That was almost always okay for a Friday deadline. But this time I emailed my old boss, saying I'd come down with something and would check back in after the weekend. Then, instead of working, I spent all of Friday cleaning the house, taking particular care to hide every last trace of Lurch, like all the hairs that had accumulated on the sofa. Once that was done, I drove to a supermarket outside Dunlone and bought groceries. Back in the house, I made a huge pot of chilli. I did everything as quickly as I could, but by the time the dinner was cooked, it was almost seven. Jason could arrive at any moment. I poured some of the chilli into a bowl, threw all of Lurch's stuff into a bag – bowls, food, lead – and went round to Michael's house.

Each time I saw him, he seemed to look younger than the time before. It took me a moment to realise his pupils were dilated.

He was holding onto the door with one hand, leaning into it and staring at me, as though not quite sure who I was, or where I came from.

I held out the chilli. 'It's still warm,' I said.

Slowly, he pulled down the sleeves of his hoodie to cover his hands and took it. 'Are ya comin' in?'

'Can't. I've a favour to ask you. Could you mind this fellow for the weekend? My boyfriend's coming down. He's allergic.'

He looked down at Lurch. He managed to smile. 'I'll look after ya. Won't I, buddy?'

'Great.' I handed him the bag. 'I'll be over Sunday evening at the latest.' He took the lead but stayed there, leaning against the doorway. I glanced at the driveway: still no sign of Jason.

'Here, you don't know anything about the people who used to live in the house I'm in, do you?'

'I don't know anything about anyone around here.'

'No.'

'I'm not *from* around here. I told ya that.'

I was just back inside when Jason's car pulled up. If I had delayed another few seconds at Michael's, he would have seen me standing at his door. He might even have spotted Lurch. I would never have managed to make up a good excuse for that. Not that quickly, anyway. It had been too close – way too close. As it was, I barely had time to pull my coat off and fix my hair in the mirror before the bell rang. As I opened the door, I noticed that my hands were shaking.

Jason didn't notice anything, though. And soon we were eating our dinner on the sofa, a romantic comedy on the TV. During the ad breaks, he muted the TV and spoke. At least, that's how I remember it – him speaking to me. I don't remember me saying much at all. I don't think anything occurred to me to say, even though he said a lot. And all of it seemed to make sense. How it was awful – terrible – what had happened in that room, but how it didn't actually change our situation. How it had nothing to do with us. It was something that had happened in the past and which belonged in the past. How it might seem as though things were connected – what I had learned about the previous owners and then some kid banging at the letterbox like that. But obviously, in the clear light of day, they had nothing to do with each other at all.

I'd said it myself, the guard had agreed. Kids messing. That's all it had been. If it had even been that. Now it was already the end of November. There were only three and a half weeks to Christmas. To him moving down. That was a lot less than the time I'd already been there. We were going to spend Christmas together. And that would be a celebration.

The beginning of a new, positive chapter in the life of the house. And then, every day, he would come home to me in the evening. And every night we would go to bed together. And every morning we would wake up together. And when we had children, they would have a better life because of the decisions we were making now.

The next day, we drove into Dunlone and went to the cinema. And on the Sunday morning we went back to Dunlone for breakfast, to a nice place overlooking the river. We bought the papers and, after eating, ordered more coffee, then just sat there, reading. Just like we used to do in the summer.

At one point, he looked at me. I had stopped reading and was gazing out the window.

'You've been very quiet this weekend,' he said.

'Have I?'

'Are you sure you're okay?'

'Yes. It's like you said. It's in the past, what happened. It doesn't matter.'

On the other side of the river, a woman was pushing a buggy. She was grinning down at her baby as she walked.

'So you're still on board? With our plan?'

'Of course.'

'No smiles for me?'

I smiled. He came round to my side of the table, put his arm around me again. 'Isn't this nice? This is what it will be like. Soon.'

'What about our budget?' I said.

'Maybe,' he said, 'just maybe, there will be room for a small bit of manoeuvre. Occasionally.'

'Really?'

'A little might go a long way. That cheered you up, didn't it?'

On the way back to the house, we stopped off at a hardware shop and Jason bought a motion-sensor porch-light, which he installed over the front door as soon as we got back. Just for peace of mind, he said. I almost certainly wouldn't need it.

After that, he had to leave pretty much straight away – he had to go straight to his lab and make up for the time he had missed on Friday. Work was about to get incredibly busy, he told me. The next few weeks were so important.

'You'll be down next weekend, though?'

'We'll see,' he said. 'I'll try my best.'

That meant no. It always did.

We were standing outside the house, by the car, his bag already in the boot. He smiled at me, pressed me to him. I put my arms around his neck. 'Don't go yet,' I said, into his shoulder. I barely said it.

'We're nearly there,' he said. 'I'm really proud of you, okay?'

He loosened his grip. I tightened mine. I hadn't planned on doing that. But it was as though my body had different ideas from my mind.

'Beth. Come on now.' Awkwardly, he unlocked my hands, managed to get them back by my sides. 'You'll be grand. Remember what we said? Keep busy. Why don't you call Paul Gilroy? I'd be interested to hear his side of things.'

I waited until his car was back on the road and out of sight and then I went to Michael's house to collect Lurch. It took him a long time to answer my knocks; my knuckles were stinging when the door eventually swung open. He stared at me suspiciously, and I could see straight away he was in a bad state. With one hand, he held onto the door, while with the other he pulled at the zipper on his hoodie. Up and down, up and down. His jaws were moving mechanically.

'Just wanted to pick Lurch up,' I said, as cheerily as I could manage.

An urgent scratching started up then, from the other side of the living-room door.

'Speak of the devil,' I said. 'I'll just grab him.'

I sort of squeezed past Michael and opened the living-room door. There was Lurch, whining. I picked him up, got back outside.

Michael was still standing in his doorway. I smiled at him. He stared hostilely back.

'Thanks a million,' I said.

It felt like he wanted to say something then, or maybe ask something, but he didn't and, anyway, I didn't wait around. I just walked back across to my own house, as quickly as I could, Lurch still in my arms. I only looked back when I reached my doorway. He was still standing there, still watching me.

After feeding Lurch, I did what Jason had told me to do: I stayed all evening in the living room. I poured myself a glass of wine from my stash, which I had hidden under the bed in the spare room before Jason came down. While drinking it, I tried to write an email to Helen, apologising for my behaviour. But I couldn't get the words right. Then I called my mother. When it went to voicemail, I left a message, asking her to please phone me back. I rang three more times after that – sometimes if she was busy she didn't always answer the phone. But still there was no reply. So I returned to my laptop, tried to do some work. I wasn't able to concentrate, though. I went onto Facebook instead, and looked at pictures of the girls in Sydney, and then of my mother's fancy-dress party. I didn't write a comment anywhere. I couldn't think of anything to say.

I logged out and starting googling words like 'exorcism' and 'haunting' again. I searched 'get rid of spirit in house' and passed the evening reading more articles and forum threads about how to do your own exorcism. Then I made a shopping list. Crucifixes. Holy water. That kind of thing.

17

The next morning, I phoned the developer, Paul Gilroy. It rang a few times and then it went to his voicemail.

I left a message, asking him to call me back. 'I need to speak to you,' I said, trying to sound assertive. 'It's important.'

After that, I managed to work for a couple of hours. But I was so far behind that I kept scrolling through the outline document, to see how much was left, and would get disheartened. When that happened, I would just stare out the window at the golfers. At lunchtime, I emailed my old boss, said I was still not well but hoped to get back to work in the next day or two. I fed Lurch. And then I drove into Dunlone. I hardly ever did that except to go to the supermarket. It was almost like breaking a rule to drive past the supermarket and keep going, right into the town centre.

I parked near the castle, by the river that flows through the town. First, I went into a religious shop, which I had noticed when Jason and I had gone for breakfast at the weekend. I bought five small crucifixes, a set of plastic rosary beads and a large bottle of holy water. Then I spent a few minutes looking at the menus outside a couple of cafés close by, including the one Jason and I had been to. The religious items had used up every last penny in my personal account. All I had left was a five-euro note in my wallet. In the end, I picked up a cheap sandwich from a shop down the road and ate it in my car. It had rained heavily the night before, and the river was high and choppy. Tacked to a railing in front of where I had parked was a Samaritans poster. 'Talk to us if things are getting to you,' it said. And then there was a freephone number.

I tried to imagine the courage it would take to climb the railing and step off the pier into the dark, pain-cold water. And then not to fight. Not to reach for a rock or the wall, but to allow yourself to be pulled down by the water.

Back in the house, I poured the holy water into saucers, which I then placed at various points throughout the house, just as I had read online. I put one on the windowsill in the hallway, one midway on the stairs, one on the kitchen island, one on the coffee-table and one on the sill of the sitting-room window that overlooked the estate. I did the same thing with the crucifixes. The rosary beads I put on the locker beside my bed. It's not that I'm religious or anything. Mum never brought us to Mass when we were little or anything like that. It was just another thing I'd read online.

After that, I went back to the email I had been trying to compose to Helen. But again I couldn't finish it. I walked to the window and looked out at the grey Portakabin and the Dorans' house across the way. Already, the sun had sunk behind the trees on the golf course. The nervous feeling was growing in my stomach.

When Claire's car pulled up next door, I waited a few minutes and then I went around.

'Beth,' she said, when she answered the door. She was pale, despite the make-up. She gazed at me warily.

'Hey,' I said. 'I was hoping you'd be in this evening.'

'Were you?'

'What's that?' I asked. Behind her, in the hallway, was a folded-up camp bed. She glanced at it, then back at me. She didn't say anything. She just shook her head, like it wasn't even worth explaining.

'Have I called at a bad time?'

'No. No, not at all.' She held the door open. 'Come on in.'

Over tea, I talked about anything I could think of. I told her every detail of the weekend with Jason – the film we saw, the café we went to, even what we ate for dinner. I told her about Michael's visit to me, a few weeks back. I hadn't told her that, even though she knew about Lurch. I told her about my work project that I was not getting done. I even started telling her the plot of a television programme I was watching.

'Why are you staying here, Beth?'

At first, I thought she meant her house. Then I realised. 'What?' I said. I tried to laugh.

'You're befriending Michael. Do you not see how strange it is? The person most likely to have broken into your home is the person you invite over for tea.'

Normally, she would have smiled at least, after saying something like that. But she didn't smile. She seemed almost angry.

'You're friends with him too,' I said.

'Don't be silly,' she said. 'I occasionally give him something to eat. There's a big difference between doing that and having him round.'

'Well, anyway, I'm not befriending him,' I said. 'And we don't know for sure if it was him.'

'A man committed suicide in your living room. And the people across the way hate you.'

'I wouldn't say hate.'

'Well, someone's been trying to frighten you. You're not safe here. Jason cannot understand this, not properly. Or he wouldn't make you stay.'

'He's not making me.'

'Christ, this is not a place for tourists.'

'Claire,' I said, and I put my hand on hers.

'Why don't you leave? I don't understand.' She pulled her hand away.

'It's our plan.'

'This plan. I can't hear about this plan again.' She stood, took our half-full cups of tea to the sink and clattered them down. She stayed there for a while, her hands rigid as they held the sides of the sink, her eyes closed.

'Lurch helps,' I said, just to break the silence. 'To be honest, if I didn't have him, I probably would have left by now.'

It was true. I hadn't realised that before. But Claire didn't say anything in reply, not straight away at least.

'Sorry, Beth,' she said. 'It's not your fault.' But she kept staring out the window, even though it was too dark to see anything, and she still looked angry.

'What isn't my fault?'

'I may as well tell you. The bank is repossessing my house. I'll be leaving here soon.'

'No.'

'Yes, Beth. You'll be on your own then.'

'I meant how awful for you. Where will you go?'

'I haven't figured that out yet. A flat in Dunlone, probably. I don't know. A bedsit, maybe.'

'When?'

She turned around to face me. 'A couple of weeks. Three at the most. I'll be out before Christmas.'

'I'm sorry,' I said. It seemed unimaginable to think of Claire reduced to such depressing living circumstances. I remembered the camp bed in the hall. Was that to be her new bed?

'Thank you, Beth. I'm sorry myself. I'm very tired this evening. Work was crazy.' She attempted a smile.

'I'll let myself out,' I said. 'Thanks for the tea.'

She didn't say anything.

'Maybe you could come round for dinner one evening.'

'Maybe.'

She didn't walk me to the door or anything. She just sat there and, after a moment or two, I let myself out, went back to my house.

In my living room, I turned on the television and for a while I managed to do a little housework – tidying away some things strewn around, loading the dishwasher – before opening a bottle of wine, my last, and putting a frozen lasagne in the oven. I poured a glass and then I went back to the email I'd been trying to compose to Helen. But reading over what I'd written earlier, I began to feel angry. Why should I apologise? Why was I always cast as the injuring party instead of the injured? All those little comments and silences from her when she was over, each one designed to belittle my life. Who asked her? A white rage hummed through me. I deleted everything I'd written and wrote a new email. In it, I told her I could see through her supposed concern for my welfare. That, really, she didn't care for me and never had. That she had nothing to do with me. That I had found someone who did actually care for me, and that I was truly happy for the first time in my life. That I was absolutely fine. That the biggest favour she could do me, if she had any feelings for me at all, was to leave me alone.

After I had pressed send, I went onto Facebook and blocked all the girls from my account.

When the wine was gone, I emptied the little jar I kept loose change in. I went through my bags and the pockets of my clothes until I had enough. Then I walked all the way out of the estate and down to the village pub.

'Hi,' I said to the barman. 'Can I buy a bottle of wine off you? To take home.'

He looked at a shelf, chose three bottles and put them on the bar. I pointed at the cheapest one. I was picking through my change when I realised that Mr Doran was standing beside me.

'Hello,' I said.

'There she is,' he said. Though his voice was quiet, it was obvious that he was very drunk.

'Neighbour,' he said. He sat down heavily on a stool and put his drink on the bar. He smiled at me. 'Howdy, neighbour.'

The barman was watching him.

'Fair dues to you anyway,' he said. 'Nothing upsets my wife nowadays.' He raised his glass at me. 'Makes her cry, you know.'

'I can't see how I could have done that,' I said.

There were two other people in the bar, and they had stopped talking.

'She comes in,' he said, addressing the entire pub, 'with an apple tart, would you believe, and tells us that as far as she's concerned, we strike her as the kind of people who would break into her house.' He took a drink, returned the now almost empty glass to the bar.

'I didn't mean—'

'All right, Jim,' said the barman.

'All right?' said Mr Doran. 'What's all right about it?' He was staring at me, but I kept my gaze on the bar. 'You'd think butter wouldn't melt,' he said. Then he got off his stool and walked out the door.

'Are you all right?' said the barman.

'Yes.'

'He's had a few too many. I wouldn't worry about him.'

Behind me, the voices started up again. A low pretend conversation. I wanted to shout something angry at them. But I just paid for the wine. Then when the barman gave me my change, I dropped it all on the floor. No one helped me to scoop it up so I hunched down and picked it up myself.

I got really drunk that night. When I'd finished that second bottle, I went and stood outside the front door. It had been unseasonably warm that week during the day, but once the sun went down and the sky filled with stars it got very cold. I could feel it through the drunkenness. But I stayed there, hugging myself and looking around. All I could see was the living-room light on in the Dorans', as usual, and, to my left, the Portakabin, squat and incongruous as always. I picked up some stones and started to throw them as far as I could. One hit the Portakabin, making a startlingly loud rattling sound. Others landed further out, in the dark. I began to laugh, as loudly as I could. I started flicking my porch-light on and off. Not a single curtain moved, at least not one that I could see. I smashed the empty wine bottle on the driveway.

18

When the doorbell rang the next afternoon, my first guess was that it was Claire, wanting to apologise for how angry she had been the day before. Then I wondered if maybe it was Michael. Or Jason. Could it be Jason? Could it even be Mr Doran? The living room was a mess again – empty wine bottles still on the table, leftover food on the kitchen counter, clothes lying everywhere, dirty dishes on the table and the counter. It smelt from the bin, which had not been emptied in days.

Though it was almost four, I had only just got up, and was still wearing a dressing gown. I waited until the bell rang again, this time for longer, and then I opened the door to find

Paul Gilroy standing there, all clean looking in his suit and expensive-looking coat, shiny car behind him in my driveway.

Looking at him, it felt as though something had been punctured. I blinked.

'Hi, hi,' he said.

'Hello.'

'Sorry to call around unannounced like this.'

'Come in,' I said. 'It's a bit of a mess.'

He stepped inside, glanced around him.

'It's not usually like this,' I said. 'I usually keep it clean.'

He shook his head, eyes closed, as though it wasn't even worth mentioning.

'I'll just be a second,' I said, and ran upstairs to throw on some clothes.

When I came back down, he was standing in the exact same place, just by the door, his coat folded neatly across his arm. Lurch was at his feet, gazing up at him.

'I'm minding him for a friend,' I said. 'It's just for a couple of days.'

He scratched Lurch's head. 'Late night?' he said.

'Sort of. Would you like some tea?'

'I'll have a quick cup.'

I let Lurch outside, through the French doors. Then I cleared the dining table and opened the curtains. I made the tea, which we drank black because there was no milk.

'You were a bit shook by what you heard,' he said.

'You could say that.'

He nodded. 'I probably should have said something. In fairness.'

'You should have. I have to work in this room every day.'

'You've had a rough time of it.'

There was something in the way he looked at me that made me feel grateful. At last, somebody understood what I was going through. Initially, I had told myself I was going to be okay with what Mr Doran had told me, about what had happened in that room. Whenever I thought about it, I felt strangely numb – like it had been muffled, like it wasn't real. And all those things Jason had said, about us creating a new, happy chapter in the house, they made sense to me. I clung to all that. But something was changing. Ever since my visit to the Dorans, being in that room made me feel like I was carrying a weight, one that was getting heavier and heavier with each passing day. It made it hard to work or tidy. It made it hard to do anything.

'Did you find him?' I asked Paul Gilroy. 'The man.'

'Oh, God, no.'

'His wife, probably.'

'Probably. Awful business.'

I looked at him. 'What do you think I should do?'

'I think you should leave. That's what I'd say. It's no good here. Now.'

'That's not what you said when you showed us the place.'

'I suppose not.'

I stared at my black tea, now gone cold, a thin broken film of limescale on the surface. For a while, neither of us said anything. Then he awkwardly covered my hand with his own, just for a second. On his ring finger there was a fat gold wedding band. It pressed against my hand. He smelt nice, I remember.

'Why don't you call the boyfriend, get him to come down sooner?'

I shook my head. 'He can't. He's very busy finishing up his work.'

'Is he?'

'It's not his fault.'

'No, no.'

'He'll be down by Christmas for good.'

'Not too long.'

'No.'

He cleared his throat. 'I had a phone call this morning,' he said, 'from one of your neighbours. I was going to call out anyway but—'

'My neighbours?' Then I remembered – how I had stood in the doorway, throwing stones out into the night, laughing like a madwoman. Smashing the wine bottle onto the ground. 'Oh, God.' I put my head in my hands.

'It's coming back, is it?' He smiled.

'Who called you?'

'I can't be telling you that. No, it's nothing to be worried about as long as it's a one-off.'

'It is. Was.'

'Well. I suppose I'd better be getting back,' he said. He didn't say where.

'Do you mind about the dog?' I said.

'Doesn't matter a damn,' he said flatly.

'That's kind of you.'

He stood. Put his coat back on. He took his time, buttoning it up.

'Your wife will probably be expecting you. Not going out to comfort silly girls,' I said.

For a moment, I couldn't quite believe what I'd said. It was like listening to someone else speak the words.

He kept his gaze on his task. Said nothing.

'Thanks again,' I said at the door.

Outside, there was already a handful of stars in the sky. It was time to close the curtains. It wasn't even five o'clock.

'Goodnight now,' he said.

'If you ever feel like calling again,' I said, 'the dog and I would be glad to see you.'

Not long after he had gone, Jason phoned. When I asked if he would be down the coming weekend, he said he would do his best but it would be difficult. He said he could definitely come the weekend after that. And then it would be less than two weeks to Christmas. Imagine that.

'Imagine,' I said.

The following afternoon, when I got a text message from the developer, saying, *How about this evening? Paul*, I told myself I would delete it. But I didn't. And when it grew close to the time when I had to draw the curtains, I replied: *Around eight works.*

I told myself it didn't have to mean anything I didn't want it to. That, as far as I was concerned, it was just a friendly visit.

By the time he showed up, a bottle of wine in his hand, I had tidied the place a bit. I'd even blow-dried my hair for the first time in ages. Put on some make-up. I told myself I did it all just to show I was fine and normal and there was no reason to worry about me as a tenant.

He looked even more polished than the day before. Wearing a suit again, the same cologne, only more of it.

I opened the wine and poured two generous glasses. He sat beside me at the island.

'Cheers,' he said.

'Cheers.' I drank. It hit my empty stomach. I hadn't eaten anything since lunch time. 'Wow,' I said. 'That's nice.'

He nodded.

I put on the radio, to Lyric FM. It was an opera, a man singing angrily. For a while, we sat there listening, sipping our wine, without talking.

'You're very quiet,' I said.

He refilled our glasses.

'My wife hates me,' he said brightly. 'How's that for conversation?'

'Ah,' I said. I didn't know what to say. Already I was feeling a bit drunk.

'I couldn't get you out of my head, you know,' he said, 'that first time I showed you around this place.'

'Really?'

'You haunted me. A pretty young girl, brave or stupid, I couldn't tell which. Setting up shop in this place, all on her own.' He shook his head. Then he looked down at Lurch, who was lying on the floor. 'And you, sir,' he said. 'According to the terms of the contract, you should not be here, should you? No pets allowed.'

By the time he put his hand on my thigh, I was very drunk.

'Poor girl,' he said. Then he kissed me, pushing his tongue inside my mouth, far back so that I felt like I might gag. As he kissed, he pushed his head towards mine so that the back of my neck ached. It was difficult to break away from him.

I don't remember going upstairs with him. But we did, because the next thing I do remember is being with him in the spare room, and he was taking off my clothes. Then he spent what felt like a long time running his hands up and down my body. Then he opened his trousers and then he was inside me, hard and foreign.

I let him do what he wanted. I let him lie down on me, enter me, and when it hurt I said nothing. I let him finish, the old stranger. I told myself it made no difference, that once it was over, it would be over.

It did not take long. But instead of leaving straight away, as I thought he would, he just lay on the bed, long after his breathing had returned to normal. I lay beside him, staring at the ceiling, which was just about visible from the light that crept in through the edges of the doorway.

Then he was pulling my arm.

I shook my head. 'I'm tired,' I whispered.

'Go on,' he whispered back. He kept pulling my arm.

And so I did. It felt easier than ignoring him, or saying no again. This time, he came in my mouth, groaning awfully as he did so.

We must have slept for a couple of hours. When I woke, he was standing at the bottom of the bed, getting dressed.

'This has been fun,' he said, from the doorway.

I didn't say anything and eventually he left. I lay on the

bed, listening to his footsteps down the stairs, the front door click behind him, the engine start up, the sound of the car reversing, then driving away. I was reminded of times, when I was young, when I would lie in bed listening to a man my mother had been with leaving in the same way. Clip-clopping down the stairs, the delicate way they would always click the front door shut.

While brushing my teeth, I threw up into the sink. In the shower, I thought I would never get the smell of him off me. I stayed in there until the water ran cold. Then I went downstairs and drank what was left of the wine he had brought. I drank it standing there at the kitchen island.

And that was when I heard a noise, coming from outside the front of the house.

It was a sharp squeal, but too mechanical a sound to have been an animal. Like a gate that needed to be oiled. I went and stood by the front door. Through the frosted glass, I could see that my porch-light had come on. Then, suddenly, came the sound of footsteps and the blur of someone running past the door. I opened it, but all I could see was the outline of the houses, the clear sky.

After that, I sat up for what felt like a long time, Lurch beside me on the sofa, the television turned down low, the curtains still drawn. Finally, I fell asleep, still on the sofa.

It must have been a couple of hours later when it happened. I woke knowing someone was in the room with me. So did Lurch, whose hair was stiff: he was growling quietly. Maybe that was what had first alerted me to the presence. Or maybe the sound of soft footsteps, coming from the hallway.

19

What I remember next is this: hugging my knees to my chest, my nails digging so hard into my skin that one bent and splintered, then closing my eyes and letting a scream out of me. As though that was the best way of protecting myself from what was about to happen – by being as small and as loud as possible.

Because I knew something bad was going to happen to me.

Then it happened. First, a dull cracking sound. Lurch yelped once. Then, pain, at the back of my head, sharp and sudden.

I must have passed out, because the next thing I remember is looking at the curtains, and there being light along their edges. That meant it was morning. Well into the morning too

– it was the beginning of December by then, when daylight starts late. Maybe that was why, but I knew straight away that Lurch and I were alone. That whoever the intruder had been was long gone.

On the floor by my feet lay Lurch, his eyes closed. He was sleeping. I watched him breathing for a while, his chest filling and emptying steadily. After a while, I leaned forward to pat him, and that was when I got sick. I remember the vomit was a lurid red, and then yellow. It splattered onto the floor, my legs. Lurch slept on.

I waited a while and then I got to my feet, very slowly. I had a terrible headache. If I moved my head even a tiny bit, it got worse and I felt like I was going to get sick again. Only by moving very slowly did I manage to walk to the kitchen, find some tissue paper, clean up. Then I went to the sitting-room window, looked through the curtains. It was a sunny day, a clear blue sky. For a second I wondered if it had really happened. I went to the French doors, looked out: there was no one on the golf course. I remember it seeming that the trees knew something, that they were swaying fat with some secret they were not going to share. I stood there and waited until a golfer appeared. I watched as they stilled themselves, bent over a ball, took a shot, gazed ahead, then walked down the hill until they had disappeared.

Lurch was still asleep. I went back to the sofa and fell back to sleep myself. When I woke again, it was mid-afternoon. Lurch was by the French doors. He looked tired but he wanted to go out so I let him. Then I put the heating on. I managed a shower, got dressed. I made myself a cup of tea, took paracetamol. I waited until Lurch scratched to come back in. Then after feeding him, I lay down on the sofa again. I pulled a blanket over me and went straight back to sleep, Lurch at my feet.

When I woke a third time, my head still ached, but not as badly as before. Gingerly, I traced my fingers over the back of my head: there was a sharp bump. At least, I thought, no one could tell me I was imagining that. I realised I was starving, so I boiled some pasta, ate it with olive oil and cheese, which was all there was. I decided to call on Claire, but when I went outside, her car was not in the driveway. I rang the doorbell anyway, even though I knew she could not be at home. I listened to it ringing inside, looked across at the light on as usual in the Dorans' sitting room.

Back in my house, I pulled up the number of Dunlone garda station again. But in the end, I didn't call them. I think I knew I was never going to. Like the other times, there were no signs of anyone breaking and entering. And it wasn't as though either of the other call-outs had made any difference. I knew what Claire would say. She would say I had to call them, that this time was different. But it was easier when she did it. When she was with me when they showed up. If I called, it seemed to me that they would assume I'd just been drinking too much again. They might not even call out at all. And I would have to tell them about Paul Gilroy visiting. Or lie about that. What was the point of asking them to come if I was just going to lie to them?

There were seven missed calls on my phone, all from work. A conference call had been scheduled that morning with my old boss and another technical writer, so she could clarify a few aspects of the last report I'd been working on, which had since been passed on to her. I was pretty sure that I wouldn't be able to clarify anything for her. I was pretty sure that, after the phone call, I wasn't going to be working for them again. So I told myself it didn't matter, that there was no point in calling them.

In the end, I just turned on the television. Flicked through the channels until I found a gardening programme. My plan was to check at every ad break to see if Claire was back. If she wasn't home by eight o'clock, I would call the guards. At least, I told myself this was what I would do.

I had managed to pass a couple of hours like that when Michael appeared at the sitting-room window. By then, it was almost dark. He pressed his face up against the pane. Then he knocked on it. He was staring at me.

'Go to the door,' I said, 'and I'll let you in.' Then I ran to it and pulled across the Chubb lock.

The doorbell rang, long and loud.

'Go home, Michael,' I said.

He rapped on the door with the knocker. He rattled the letterbox.

'I'm half froze,' he said.

'Go back to your own house, then.'

'Let me in, would you?'

'If you don't go away now,' I said, 'I'll call the police.'

'You won't.'

'What do you want off me?' I said. 'What do I owe you?' My teeth had started chattering. It was hard to get the words out.

There was no answer. I waited a couple of minutes and then I opened the door a crack, the chain on. There was no sign of him.

Then banging started up, on the French doors. It was Michael again. When I came into the kitchen, he was pulling at the handle.

'Come on,' he kept saying. 'Come on.' His voice was thin and distant through the glass. He kept looking at me, as though expecting me to realise my mistake. Then he was shouting. 'For fuck sake.'

He put his hands on his head. He started kicking the door.

'Go away,' I shouted. I slammed my palms down on the dining table. 'Go away.'

He kept kicking the door. It would have broken, if he had kept kicking it like that.

I took out a long knife for cutting meat. I held it upright in front of me. I walked right up to the door. 'Get away from here,' I shouted. 'The police are on their way.'

He stopped kicking the door. For a moment, he kept looking at me, like he was waiting for me to realise my mistake. I stood there, my grip tight on the knife, until finally he walked away, out of sight. I was about to put the knife on the table when he suddenly reappeared, gave the doors one final kick.

'Get out of here,' I screamed.

He gave me a final hard stare, and then he was gone.

I must have stood there for a long time after, straining to hear anything above the TV. When I made out the sound of a car, I thought at first it must be Claire. But then it pulled up outside my house. The headlights swooped through the sitting-room window, the engine stopped. I knew it wasn't Jason – his car sounded different. At least I have this knife, I remember thinking.

The doorbell rang long and loud. There was only a short pause before it rang a second time, this time for even longer.

When the letterbox started to clatter, I went to the French doors, tried to unlock them. I had a vague plan of running down my garden and through the golf course to the clubhouse over the hill. But my hands were shaking so much I couldn't open them. And all the time, the doorbell was ringing on and off, on and off, the knocker banging.

I just had the doors open when a woman's voice called out, through the letterbox.

'Beth? This fecking thing. Beth! Are you home or what?'

Helen.

It was Helen.

20

The lighting in the restaurant was soft and low and the place was full of people. Lots of couples, and then a big group of women who took up a long table by the window, all dressed up for the night. By their table a fat, brightly lit Christmas tree. I kept blinking, not quite able to take it in – that all this was happening just around the corner from where I had been living. By luck, the waitress had said, they'd just had a cancellation, and she'd led us to a table by the fireplace, where a turf fire burned.

'So many people,' I said again. It was all I'd said since we'd sat down. But it was true, and the fact that this was taking place just a five-minute drive from where I lived astonished me.

'It's lovely here,' I said. 'Isn't it?'

Helen had said nothing since we arrived, except to murmur agreement. She had said nothing on the short drive there either or back in the house, after I had opened the door, still holding the knife.

The first thing she had done was gently take the knife out of my hand and place it in the sink. Then she had got me to sit down, sat beside me. 'What's going on, Beth?' she said. 'You have to tell me.'

But I couldn't say anything.

'You're coming with me,' she said.

I shook my head. 'I'm hardly moving to London, am I?'

'You can't stay here.'

I knew she was right, but I also knew I couldn't leave.

'I have to,' I said. 'Stay here.'

'Why?'

'I just have to.'

'Let's go to dinner,' she said then. 'Let's get some food into you. You're so thin. When did you get so thin?'

I didn't know. I didn't answer.

'Isn't there a restaurant attached to that pub across the way?'

'I think so,' I said. 'I don't know.'

She drove us the short distance. I suppose she was hoping that once I got out of that place and ate something she'd be able to talk sense into me. And I suppose, in a way, that was what happened. We each ordered the Christmas special – roast turkey and ham, vegetables and mashed potatoes, gravy – and just a glass of wine each. Actually, she did the ordering.

I just sat there, staring at the turf fire burning beside us.

And when the food came, we ate without talking, though she kept sneaking these quick stares at me.

'I still can't believe you flew home just to see me,' I said, after we'd finished eating. 'I mean, why did you do that?'

She thought about it for a second. 'It was your email,' she said.

'The one where I told you to leave me alone?'

'I decided it was a cry for help.'

'That was imaginative,' I said, remembering all the awful things I'd said in it.

'I think it was the "absolutely".'

'The "absolutely"?'

'"I am doing *absolutely* fine." I wasn't buying that.'

We lapsed back into silence.

'I'm sorry,' I said after a bit, 'about that email. I was drunk when I sent it.'

'I'm glad you did,' she said. 'Now. Are you going to tell me why you were holding that knife?'

'Michael,' I said.

'Who the hell is Michael?'

'This guy. He's squatting in one of the houses. He's actually probably harmless. He wanted me to let him in. He freaked me out for a second.'

'Had you already met him?'

'Oh, yes. He gave me Lurch. The dog.'

'So, what happened?'

I ended up telling her everything. About that night back in November, when the doors had slammed shut and the lights had flashed upstairs, and I had run out into the estate. About Claire, and her helping me, and the guards coming, and what Mr Doran had told me when I visited them. About Michael. About the time with the letterbox banging, and how the guard hadn't seemed to think it was anything. About the intruder from the night before. Her eyes widened as she felt the bump at the back of my head.

'It was probably Michael,' I said, 'who did it. Don't you think?'

'I don't know,' she said. 'It might have been.'

'Do you think I should call the guards again?'

'Probably. No. I don't know. Beth, you need to leave this place. You know that, don't you?'

'I think I would agree with you,' I said, 'if there weren't only two weeks to go.'

She straightened her cutlery. 'Before Jason moves down.'

'Yes. He'll be here in time for Christmas.'

'For Christmas. Does he know what's been going on?' She asked it lightly.

'Sort of.' Then I told her about how he had been so busy at work he had only been down four times since I had moved in. How obsessed with work he always was. I told her about our budget, and how all my earnings went into an account that I still didn't have access to, that I was living on a measly sum he paid into my personal account every month. I felt guilty telling her all that, even though there were many things I didn't tell her, like how angry he'd got when he came down that time, after the first attack.

'He's abusive,' she said, when I stopped talking. She tried

to say it in a matter-of-fact, neutral way, but she could not keep the shimmer of anger out of her voice.

'I don't know,' I said. 'His work is very stressful right now.'

'Fuck his work. What do you mean? How can you mean that? How, Beth?'

I took a sip from my wine. 'Well, no one's perfect. I haven't exactly been perfect.' Then I told her about Paul Gilroy. Not every detail. Just the bare outline.

'Oh, Jesus Christ. The disgusting creep. Beth, you're vulnerable. You're being taken advantage of.'

To my shock, she started crying.

'It hasn't been that bad,' I said, ready to tell her about Claire again.

'Don't,' she said. 'Stop.'

We sat in silence.

'Are you going to tell Jason? About what happened tonight?'

I shook my head. 'I don't know,' I said.

'No. Well, maybe I'm being too hard on him,' she said. You could tell she found that difficult to say, that she didn't really mean it. 'Maybe he has been so absorbed in work he hasn't been able to see what it's been like for you.' She sounded as though she was trying out the idea, saying it out loud to see if it rang true after all.

'Yes,' I said. 'Exactly.'

'Right. So, imagine this. We go back to the house just to pick up some of your stuff. We get a taxi to drop us at that Travelodge outside Dunlone. We spend the night there, and in the morning we get another taxi back to my car and we go to my flat. You can stay there.'

'Just leave?'

'Imagine. You'd never have to spend another night in that house again.'

'But. Is your flat empty? It's still yours, I mean?'

She nodded. 'I'll be moving back into it in the new year,' she said. 'When I come back from London.'

'Unless,' I said. I'd had an idea. 'If I was to stay in your flat up to Christmas. Just for the next two weeks.' It occurred to me that I might get away with doing that without Jason even knowing.

'Yes.'

'Then I could move back down with Jason.'

'We'll figure all that stuff out. That stuff is figure-out-able. That's the thing, Beth. You've no perspective. All that's happened is you've made a mistake.'

'Maybe.'

'There's no maybe about it.'

'So I just leave tonight.'

'You leave tonight.'

She went to the bathroom then. When she was gone, I looked around the room. It was even busier than it had been when we arrived. All the tables were taken. More people had joined the big group by the window. They were all laughing at something the waiter had said. One caught my eye, and she smiled at me. I smiled back. Then I put my hand on the back of my head. The bump was still there – and the sharp pain when I touched it. I took my phone out of my bag and looked at the screen. As usual, there was no message, no missed phone call. I wrote a text to Jason. *I'm okay now*, I wrote. *Helen has come down. You don't need to worry about me.* I pressed send.

When Helen came back, we ordered dessert. Then she told me about the television series she'd just got a part in. A Gothic drama set in Dublin. It was not a major part, but it was not a small one either. For a while, as I listened to her, I forgot all about the estate and Jason. I was so engrossed in this news, this idea of Helen's big break finally coming. At one point, when she was talking about how she was planning on finding a bigger place in Dublin, maybe even buy somewhere, something she said – I can't remember what exactly – seemed to imply that I might move in with her then. Of course I knew that couldn't happen. By then, Jason would be down in the estate, and we would be living there together. Anyway, what a bizarre idea, Helen and I being flatmates. I said nothing directly in reply. In any case, the way she'd put it, it seemed more a throwing of the idea out there, even to try it out for herself, rather than in a way that demanded any kind of response.

Back in Dublin, though. Getting a new job. Meeting new people. In this imagined future, of course, there would be no Jason. Why did that not feel like a problem? I didn't want to analyse it too much.

'Right. Time to grab your stuff, I think,' said Helen, as though she'd read my thoughts.

'And just leave,' I said again.

'And just leave!'

The relief felt physical. I thought of that cliché – a weight lifted from my shoulders.

'You okay?'

'Yes.'

'Come on, then.'

Outside, it had grown dark. Helen drove carefully the short distance back to the estate, down the driveway. When she slowed down to a halt, just outside Claire's, I assumed at first that she had mixed the houses up.

'Whose car is that?' she said, nodding ahead. 'Is it Jason's?'

Sure enough, parked in the driveway of my house, there it was. I could see his outline, in the driver's seat.

21

Yesterday, after the *sutta* reading, I'd hung around while Chenda spoke to some other people from the class and then, when they finally left, I asked her if she had time for a quick chat.

'It won't take a second,' I said.

'Beth, isn't it?' she said.

'That's right.'

She was looking at me, waiting, her gaze so clear and focused on me. As though our conversation was the only thing that was happening at that moment, as far as she was concerned. Which it was, of course. But most people are thinking about something else, or trying to do something else even as they're talking to you, especially if they don't know you. With her it felt like everything else evaporated as soon as I had her attention. It was unnerving, in a way. It made me wish I had prepared better what I wanted to ask her.

'What would you like to ask me about?' she said.

'I'm interested in becoming a Buddhist nun,' I blurted. 'Like you.'

'Oh.'

I laughed. 'That probably seems ridiculous.'

'No,' she said. 'It doesn't.'

'Oh. Well, good. I suppose I wanted to know how to go about it.'

'You do. Well, you know, it's a very slow process,' she said.

'Do you live in a monastery?' I asked.

'No.' she said. 'I live in a small flat in Rathmines.'

I nodded. 'But is there a monastery in Ireland?'

'Not that I'm aware of.'

'Oh.'

'There's a community,' she explained. 'Here in Dublin, there are thousands of us. But it's not something you can become overnight,' she said. 'It took years from my first meditation class to becoming a nun,' she said.

'Years?'

'Years. And lots of people – in this class, for instance – don't become monks or nuns. They just integrate meditation into their lives.'

'Right.'

'How are you finding the practice?'

'Great,' I said.

'Wow,' she said. She has a huge smile. Serious to delighted in a moment.

'Well, you know, it's hard,' I said. 'Of course. But I want to keep at it.'

'That's good. Are you practising at home?'

'Yes,' I lied.

'Good,' she said again.

'I do find it hard. But I think I just need more time at it. I'm getting used to it. I'm getting used to all the sitting still.'

'The body adjusts.'

'That's right.'

In the silence that followed, it felt as though the room was ringing with the sound of my voice. As though, if I uttered one more word, the air would break.

Then she spoke. 'You're on the right track. There's no need to make any big decisions. Slow and steady. Does that make sense?'

'Yes.'

'See where that leads you.'

'Right.'

'You know, sometimes people come here to get away from problems. But meditation does not get you away from problems.' She smiled when she said that but she kept looking at me, waiting for an answer.

'I know.'

'You understand that.'

'I do.'

'Good. Well, just keep doing what you're doing now. Okay?' Another clear-as-day smile.

22

'I'm literally just after getting your text,' said Jason. 'Hello there.' He smiled at Helen, extended a hand to her.

Helen seemed to hesitate. Then she took his hand briefly.

'This is Helen,' I said. 'My sister.'

We were all standing in the hallway.

'It's so nice to meet you,' he said to her. 'I've heard a lot about you.'

'Have you?'

'Yeah. Don't worry, all good.' He turned to me. 'You never said anything about Helen coming down.' He turned back to her. 'I literally got Beth's text two minutes ago,' he said again, 'just after pulling up.' He looked back at me. 'I'd thought you were all on your own.' Then he pinched my nose, the way you would a child. He was wearing aftershave and his hair shone with gel. He was smiling at me, like he was very amused by the situation and expected me to be too. I wondered if maybe I should be.

'I didn't know,' I said.

'It was an impromptu visit,' said Helen, in a flat voice.

'Snap,' he said. 'Surprise. Don't I feel like a right twat now?'

'I don't understand,' I said. 'What day is today?'

'What day is today? Jesus!'

'Thursday,' said Helen.

'Can we go inside and I'll explain it to you?'

In the living room, he stared around him in open amazement at the mess – dirty plates, mugs and glasses cluttering up the coffee table and kitchen worktop, then all the saucers of holy water and crucifixes.

Right then, Lurch started scratching at the utility-room door.

'What the hell is that?' said Jason.

There was nothing to do but open the door. Out ran Lurch straight away. He tried to jump into my arms. He whined.

'What the fuck?' said Jason. Then he looked at Helen. 'Sorry. Is it yours?'

'That's Beth's dog,' said Helen. 'Did you not know she has one? She's scared out of her wits here.'

'Helen,' I said. I turned to Jason. 'This kid gave him to me.'

'A kid.'

'Michael, he's called. He's squatting in one of the other houses. Did I not tell you about him?'

I knew I had but Jason just stared at me.

'He said the dog was going to be put down, if I didn't take him. I was just hanging on to him until I found him a new home. I put an ad up in the window of the newsagent's across the way,' I lied. 'I can show you if you like.'

Lurch jumped up on me. I held him for a second. Then I carried him back into the utility room, where I dropped him onto the floor. I emptied some dog food from the packet into his bowl. My hands shook so much some of it spilled on the floor. I closed the door, Lurch staring up at me. I prayed he wouldn't start scratching it again.

'Claire next door said she might take him,' I said, turning back to Jason and Helen. 'Now, we need tea. Why don't you two sit down? Put the telly on or something.'

Jason walked to the sofa. But instead of sitting down, he lifted the blanket lying on it. It was covered, I knew, with Lurch's hairs. As was the sofa. But Jason just looked at the blanket, folded it neatly and placed it on the floor. Then he glanced around, taking in fully the mess of stuff on the coffee-table – bowl with leftover spaghetti and oil congealed, bottle of wine and glass, roll of kitchen paper, mugs with black tea at their base.

Finally, he sat.

Helen tried to catch my eye as I cleared the table, put the heat on, filled the kettle. I just pretended not to notice.

'What text?' she whispered, coming up to me. 'What did you tell him?'

'Nothing much,' I said, in a normal voice. 'Jason, what did I say to you in the text again?'

'Just that Helen had come down. You were fine. Something like that.' He turned the television on. 'I'd say I was on the road ten minutes when you sent it.' Then he turned off the television. He stood. 'Look, I'm sorry. It was a stupid idea, coming down as a surprise. I'll head back. Don't want to ruin your girlie night.'

'Don't be ridiculous,' I said. 'Where are those biscuits? There were definitely biscuits here earlier.'

'Beth,' said Helen. 'We were going to leave this place, remember? You were going to move out.' She turned to Jason. 'Someone hit her. Someone broke in here and attacked her. There's a bump on the back of her head.'

'A bump?' Jason looked at me. There was a smile twitching about his face.

'You find that amusing?' said Helen.

'He's not laughing at that,' I said.

'Then what the hell is he laughing at?'

Jason walked over to me. He ran his hand along the back of my head.

'Ouch,' I said.

'Someone broke in here and attacked you. When did this happen?'

'Yesterday. Last night, I mean.'

'What happened? Did you see them?'

'No.' I quickly described what had happened.

'What did the guards say?'

'I didn't call them.'

'No? You hadn't been drinking when this happened by any chance? Beth?' He cupped my chin, tilted my head until I looked at him. He smiled.

'You think she imagined it?' said Helen. 'Is that what you're saying? You think she dreamed up that bump on her head?'

'Any sign of a break-in?' he said.

'No.'

'No. Why doesn't that surprise me?'

'This is a big joke to you,' said Helen.

'It's not a joke, I promise you,' he said, all traces of amusement gone from his face. 'I hope you believe me, Helen. If I really thought Beth was in any kind of danger here, I would not be laughing.' He kept his gaze on her. Like he wanted her to see how sincere he was being. 'It's just – we've been here before, more than once. Haven't we?' He looked at me and I nodded. 'This is your first time down, isn't it?' he said to Helen.

'Second.'

'Second. That's no problem. I'm not having a go at you. It's just – a lot has happened in the last few weeks. I agree it hasn't been easy on Beth. But all that's happening is that she's been badly spooked. That's pretty much what the guard said last time. Isn't it?'

I nodded again.

The smile returned to his face. 'You realise you two stink of booze. How much did you put away tonight?'

'We hardly had anything to drink,' said Helen. 'I found her holding a knife, you know. Frightened for her life.'

'It was just Michael,' I said to Jason. 'He came around,

banged on the door.' I looked at Helen. 'He's probably harmless.'

'Harmless. What about whoever hit you?'

'I don't know,' I said. 'I actually was a bit drunk when it happened. I'd made this big deadline.'

'The drinking does need to be sorted,' said Jason. 'That is of concern.'

'I need to eat something,' I said.

'You just ate,' said Helen. 'We drank hardly anything,' she said again.

'Have some tea,' said Jason, and he went back to the sofa. 'It'll sort you out.'

'Beth,' said Helen, loud enough for Jason to hear. 'What the hell?'

I made a pot of tea, which I put on the coffee-table, along with three mugs. Then I sat beside Jason. He put his arm around me.

'Come on, Helen, sit down and drink your tea. You'll feel better for it,' I said. I kept my gaze ahead of me as I spoke. I didn't dare to look at her, though I could feel her stare on me, on the two of us, as she tried to figure out what to do.

Jason turned to face her again.

'Look, I know Beth's situation down here isn't ideal,' he said, his face all serious now. 'I've been trying to get down as often as I can. But it's nearly over. I'll be here with her very soon.'

'I was really upset when Helen turned up today,' I said to Jason.

'Oh, yeah?'

'She was brilliant.'

'Well, she's a good sister. She just proved that.'

'Come on, Helen,' I said. 'Have tea with us. Please.'

'It's not like you can go anywhere until the morning anyway,' said Jason. 'Jesus. How much did you ladies put away?'

'Shut up,' I said. I gently whacked his stomach and he doubled over, pretending to be in pain. 'Idiot.'

Finally, without saying anything, Helen sat down. She stared at the television screen. Handing her a cup of tea, I caught her eye, mouthed, 'Thank you.' But she just looked at me as though she didn't know me.

23

I woke in the morning with a dry mouth and a headache.
Beside me, Jason was snoring lightly. Though it was still
dark and quiet in the house, just like the last time I knew
Helen had already left. I peered out the window and, sure
enough, her car was gone.

I got dressed and went downstairs. I let Lurch out and put
all the saucers and the crucifixes and the bottle of holy water
in a drawer. I loaded the dishwasher, cleared the surfaces,
swept the floor. Then I called Lurch back inside and fed him.
When he had finished eating, I took him to Michael's house.

I knocked until he answered.

'I need you to mind Lurch,' I said, and I held out the lead.
When he didn't take it, I dropped it on the ground.

'You wouldn't let me in last night,' he said.

'You scared the life out of me. Look, I'll bring you over some food later, okay?'

'You had a knife.'

'That's because you scared the shit out of me. You were trying to break into my house.'

'I wasn't.'

I put my hand on the bump at the back of my head. It still hurt. But, looking at him standing there, I couldn't believe it had been him. 'Were you in my house, the night before last?' I said.

'No.' His skin had a grey hue. He looked miserable.

I glanced back at my house. There was no sign of Jason. 'Well, I have to go. I'll bring you something to eat later, okay?'

He nodded. When I handed him the lead again, he took it.

I walked to the shop for milk, bread and the paper. I wanted to have breakfast made by the time Jason came down. I didn't take the car in case it woke him. But I might as well have, because when I came back, he was standing at the French doors, looking out at the golf course. On the table lay all the crucifixes and the bowls, in a neat row.

'Good morning,' I said.

He didn't answer.

I put on the kettle, put two slices of bread into the toaster. I put teabags into the teapot. Still, he didn't move or say anything. I made the tea, I buttered the toast. I put it all on the table. And then I sat down and waited.

He sat beside me. He stared at me until I could no longer bear it.

'What?' I said.

'What? What's all this shit, for a start?'

'Just – stupid stuff. I got spooked. Like you said.'

'Spooked.' With one swipe of his arm, all of it was on the floor.

'The dog,' he said.

'The dog is gone. You don't need to worry about that. I've given him back to Michael.'

'Just like that.'

'Just like that.'

'Why did you take him in the first place? Why should I believe a single word you say?' His voice rose with the second question and he swiped his hand across the table a second time, this time sending his cup and the plates to the floor. The cup handle snapped off as it hit the tiles.

I waited a few seconds and then I started picking things up.

'Stop that,' he said. He took hold of my arm. He held it so tight, it hurt. 'Sit back down,' he said. I did as he told me. He was still staring at me. It felt like a physical pressure, that stare, as if it alone could hurt me, if he wanted it to.

'*You don't need to worry about me any more.* That's what your text said. How do you think that made me feel? And then I learn you're planning to leave. Who clearly thinks I'm some sort of monster. God knows what you said to her about me.'

'We were drunk. It was a stupid, drunken plan. I was going to go straight to you anyway. She was going to drive me. This morning. That was the plan.'

'Shut up, Beth. Can you do that? Just shut up.'

'Sorry.'

'I come down, find you living like a fucking tramp.'

'I'm sorry.'

'You lie to me.' He was looking out the French doors at the golf course again. His voice sounded incredulous and sad. I thought he might start crying.

'I've been selfish,' I said. 'But I just hate it here.'

'You hate it here. Of course.' He rubbed his face with his hands. 'I tell you what, Beth. I'm going for a drive. And when I come back, you will have this place the way it should be. Then we'll see.'

'See what?'

But he was already putting his coat on.

I woke to him kissing me. I was lying on the sofa, where I had gone after I'd finished the cleaning. I must have been exhausted, to fall asleep like that. I suppose as well I was so relieved I'd had a chance to change the sheets in the spare room, which I'd only thought of after he left.

'That's an improvement,' he said. 'Now you need to clean yourself.'

I showered and dressed, and then we drove to a supermarket to buy some food – for dinner that evening, and then for me for the week ahead. It was already growing dark by the time we got back to the house. I started to prepare a meal. As I chopped vegetables, he set out what was going to happen between then and Christmas. I was going to stay on in the house. He would get down for each of the two Saturday nights left before Christmas, even though that would be very difficult for him. I was going to stop drinking. It was no wonder I hadn't had enough money for food, he said, when I was spending it all on cheap bottles of wine. I was going to walk every day, for an hour, after lunch. I was going to get healthy again. I was going to stop entertaining stupid ideas of ghosts and I was going to pull myself together.

I didn't dare tell him that I had almost certainly lost my main client, and that work from my other clients had slowly reduced to almost nothing. I didn't know how I was ever going to tell him that. Listening to him, it seemed that somehow I was going to have to fix that problem myself. The old Plan was flickering back into focus.

'You don't have to tell me what you and Helen were planning,' he said. 'I can't force that out of you.'

He looked so hurt when he said that that I told him.

'But I was wrong,' I said. 'I see that now.'

He shook his head.

'I'm not her,' I said. Because I knew he was thinking about his ex. 'You *can* trust me.'

'If you want out, you just have to say so.' He sat back in his chair and gazed at me.

I wasn't sure what he meant – if I wanted out of the Plan, or out of the relationship. At that moment, the way he said it, it seemed as if the two were one and the same.

'I don't want out,' I said.

'I really thought this would work,' he said.

'It's going to work. It's working. I've just had a couple of wobbles. It's nearly Christmas, you said it yourself.' I put my arms around him and kept them there until he put his around me.

'I thought we were okay,' he said.

'We're more than okay,' I said. 'We're great.'

Then I turned on the news, and we sat there together, listening to its usual inventory of doom and gloom. Unemployment rates had grown worse. A housing development in Dublin, built only a couple of years previously, was revealed to be structurally unsound and all the residents were being evacuated. A child somewhere had been reported missing. Emigration rates had not been so high since the 1980s. A man had been shot dead on the streets of Dublin. In the history of the state, the country had never seen such high numbers of homeless families.

24

There was no answer when I knocked on Michael's door the following morning, after Jason had left. Banging on the windows didn't work either. The black rubbish bags that covered them, from the inside, were stuck on with tape, no gap to see through. When I went round the back, I found all the windows and the French doors there were also blacked out. I managed to find a small gap, though. I could just about make out the blue tent, the armchair.

No Michael. No dogs.

'Hello,' I called. 'Michael?'

I waited awhile, until I was too cold to be standing around, and then I walked out of the estate, up the driveway and onto the road. There, I turned left, on a whim, I suppose, away from the village. I had never taken that route before. It wound a lot: once I'd turned a corner, another appeared ahead. It was a bright, clear morning, the low sun shining right into my eyes.

I was about to turn back and try Michael again when I stopped to look at a farmhouse. I don't really know why. I suppose it reminded me of the house of the girl I'd befriended during that brief period when I was young and living in the countryside. The girl I'd told Claire about. I remembered how we would pretend we were fairies who lived in one of the trees in a field beside their house. She was good at climbing it, always going further than me. Her grandmother used to make these thin biscuits, which we would take with us and pretend were fairy biscuits. Or sometimes, if it was raining, she and I would play inside, in their kitchen, while her grandmother baked or washed up. We would sit by the range and the grandmother would let us read her missionary magazines and *Reader's Digest*s. If one of us had finished a page before the other, she would wait until the other had caught up, then turn it. The grandmother used to call us the twins, even though we didn't look alike.

Then I remembered what Claire had said – that my mother must have been having an affair, and that was why we moved back to Dublin so suddenly, before I'd even had a chance to say goodbye to that girl. At the time, I'd dismissed the idea but standing there on the road I realised she must have been right. We hadn't even brought all our stuff with us – Mum had just loaded the car with what she could find and told me to get in.

I don't know how long I'd been standing there when an old woman came around the side of the house and started walking slowly towards the gate. She raised her arm in a wave, making it clear I was the reason she was coming down. I waited for her. It seemed too rude to walk away, even though that was what I wanted to do.

'A fine day,' she said, once she was within hearing distance.

'It is.'

'Aren't we due one?' She reached the gate, leaned her arms on it. 'You'd still feel the cold, mind.'

I nodded.

'I've seen you in Martin's,' she said.

'Martin's?'

'The shop there. The newsagent.'

'Oh. Yes.'

'Are you living in the estate?'

'That's right.'

'All on your own?'

'My boyfriend will be joining me at Christmas. His job starts in January.'

'How are you finding it?'

'Grand.' I touched the back of my head, where the bump was.

'Did you hurt yourself?'

'Oh. No. I mean. I just— I was in a pub. In Dunlone. I went there with my friend and there was this low door. I just banged into it. I took a step back to make way for someone.'

She winced, frowning slightly. 'Did you put ice on it?'

'I must do that, actually.'

'Where's the pup?' she said. I must have looked surprised then because she added, 'We don't miss much around here.'

'A friend is minding him,' I said. 'My other friend, who was down last night, is allergic.'

'That sounds very complicated.'

'Claire. Claire is minding him.'

'Claire Walsh.'

'Do you know her?'

'I do indeed. Claire Walsh. She'd be your neighbour.'

'There was no answer when I called over to her. She might be out with him herself.'

'Is that it? Well, I saw you standing there and I said I'd come down to say hello.'

'I probably looked a bit odd, standing here. I was admiring the view.' I gestured vaguely at the fields to the left of her house.

'Not at all. You're welcome now to come in for a quick cup of tea. You look half froze.'

'You're very good. But I should be getting back.'

'Are you sure?'

'Honestly. I've a ton of stuff to do before tomorrow. My boyfriend is coming down for a few days.'

'Oh, is he? That's good.'

'See you now.'

'Goodbye, love.'

I set off towards the estate. I couldn't hear her walking up to her house, but I didn't look back. It seemed to have grown even colder, the sun giving out no warmth. Even the trees in the field appeared to be feeling it, but were choosing to endure it, each on its own, rather than huddle together for warmth. There was a crow on a branch, staring out towards the road. He flew off silently, overhead, without looking at me. Birds, it occurred to me, never seem to look at you, but they always see you.

Back at Michael's house, I banged my fists on the door as hard as I could; it was less painful that way to my numbed fingers. Then I banged on the window. I shouted his name. Again, there was nothing. I listened for a whine or a bark but there was only the sound of the wind against the side of the house.

I walked across to Claire's, but even though her car was in the driveway, no one came to the door. I called her name, but again all I heard was the wind, moaning around her house. Beside it stood mine, its shadow so long that it reached the Portakabin.

I was waiting, I suppose, for Claire to come home, or for her to open the door. But in the end, it was Michael's front door I heard slam shut. And when I turned, it was Michael I saw, standing in his doorway, looking across at me.

25

My first instinct was to run to my house, and then to lock the doors, call the police. But I was too scared. As long as he didn't move, I didn't move. It felt like, if I ran, it might startle him into running after me. So we just stood there, me on Claire's porch, he on his own, staring across at each other.

He looked cold, in his fleece, and thin. He looked so angry. Or desperate.

'Your dog is gone,' he shouted across at me, after a while.

'Where?'

'He ran off.'

He seemed to be hesitating. Still neither of us moved. I couldn't take my eyes off him, even as I wanted to cast my gaze around for Lurch. When he finally took a step forward, I did the same. I felt in my pocket for my keys, fisted the jagged metal. I took another couple of small steps, alongside Claire's car. He did the same, so that only the road separated us.

'Don't worry about Lurch,' I said. 'I'll look for him. My boyfriend is back down later and he can help me.'

'It wasn't my fault,' he said.

'It's okay,' I said, as lightly as I could.

'What?'

'I have to go,' I said.

'You should go,' he said.

'See you,' I said, raising my hand. Then I started to walk towards my house, slowly at first, then faster.

There was a faint bang before I reached my door. A door slamming. I looked around and, sure enough, he was gone. At Claire's house, there was still no sign of her. All her lights were still out.

I didn't find Lurch's body until the next morning. After that encounter with Michael, I'd been too scared to do anything all day other than call him from the front door. I did get into my car one time, after it grew dark, and drove slowly up and down the village main street, but by then I'd already been drinking, and when a passing car blared at me, I went back to the house. After checking that every window and door was locked, I spent the evening watching TV and finishing that last bottle of wine, every now and then getting up to open the front door and call for Lurch again, until finally I fell asleep on the sofa, not waking until sunlight was shining through a crack in the curtains, right onto my face.

The first thing I did was go to the French doors to look for an early golfer, which I'd got into the habit of doing first thing in the morning. I don't think I'd even thought of Lurch until I saw him lying in the middle of the back garden, as though he was asleep.

I pulled a blanket around me and went outside. I knelt beside him. There was no sign of injury on his body. No blood. But he was hard and cold, and his eyes were open and staring ahead. I had to lie down on the grass, which was stiff with frost, for us to be looking into each other's eyes, and even then he seemed to be gazing past or through me.

'I'm sorry, Lurch,' I said. 'I'm sorry.'

Back inside, I called the guards and told them I had reason to believe my dog had been poisoned. I was almost shouting at them, I think. Then I went around to Claire, and this time she answered the door. I was so glad, I started to cry. Real crying, with real tears. When she put her arms around me, I only cried more. I thought I wouldn't be able to stop.

She brought me inside, sat me down at her table and gave me a glass of water. When I managed to get out what had happened, she insisted I stay with her until the guard came. We could bring our chairs around to the front window, she said, and that way we would see the car when it pulled up. It was the old Claire, the one I knew. Concerned and caring and making things better. She said she was sorry for being in such bad form the last time I'd called: she'd felt really bad about that. She said she'd been meaning to come around but she'd been so busy these past few days, looking for a place to rent in Dunlone. I ended up telling her about the break-in, even though I'd told myself I wouldn't. I put her hand on my bump. She looked grave, as she felt it. She said we must tell the guard about that too. Yes, I said. I know.

The guard who came was the same one from the night of the first attack, with the lights flashing upstairs and the door banging. I told him about the attack, two nights earlier. He and Claire followed me into my house, where I showed them where Lurch and I had been struck. He took out the same type of notebook as the time before and, as I spoke, he made a couple of short notes in it.

'And there was definitely no sign of a break-in that night?'

'None.'

'And you had no visitors? Besides the intruder. Your boyfriend wasn't down?'

'No. No visitors,' I said.

'Why did you not report this sooner?' You should have called us as soon as you woke.'

'I think I had a concussion,' I said. 'I wasn't thinking straight.'

He didn't say anything for a while, frowning at the sofa. You could see that it didn't make sense to him.

'Right. And then you say yesterday you gave the dog to this lad to look after?'

'Michael, yes. My boyfriend was down. He's allergic to dogs.'

He was waiting for more. 'So you had some sort of friendship with this Michael?' he prompted.

'With Michael? I wouldn't say friendship.' I looked at Claire.

'He's a vulnerable young man,' she said. 'He doesn't always seem dangerous, does he? He probably isn't always dangerous.'

'He has mental-health problems,' I said. 'He shouldn't be there on his own.'

'You say social services came out here?' he said to Claire.

'About three months ago.'

'I might follow up on that,' he said. He turned to me. 'Do you want to show me where the dog's body is?'

They followed me into the back garden. I had not moved Lurch's body but I had put the blanket over it, which I removed for them to see. I watched the guard's face.

'He couldn't have just frozen,' I said. 'He would have scratched on the door, or barked. I would have heard him.'

He didn't say anything.

'If he had frozen, he wouldn't just be lying there in the middle of the lawn. He definitely wasn't there yesterday night. I must have gone out looking for him ten times. Twenty times.'

He nodded.

'Can you find out?' I asked. 'If he's been poisoned?'

'You have a licence and all that.'

'A licence. No.'

'The thing is, it'd be hard to imagine someone doing this on purpose if he wasn't making a nuisance of himself. It's been known to happen if a dog is a danger to someone's livestock, but that wasn't an issue?'

'He's just a puppy,' I said.

Claire put her hand on my shoulder, squeezed it. 'He can't have suffered much,' she said. 'Not for long anyway.'

'You'll have to come in and make a statement about Wednesday night,' said the guard. 'Okay?'

'Thank you, Guard,' said Claire.

'He thinks I let Lurch freeze,' I said, after he had left. 'That I forgot about him.'

'Never mind,' she said.

'He thinks I'm just a drunk. A drunk who can't take care of their own dog.'

'No.'

'Is that what you think?'

'No. Or, at least, if that was the case, it's only a reflection of how badly you've been affected by everything. How badly you're feeling.'

'I would have heard him scratching,' I said. 'I always heard him scratching.'

'I know, love. But do you really think you should keep living here? This kind of thing would unhinge anyone.'

Unhinge. Like a gate suddenly swinging loose.

'Now,' she said.

'Jason.'

'He's just made a mistake. You both have.'

I thought of Helen saying the same thing. 'I'm not calling him.'

'No. Well, why not go to him?'

'What?'

'Pack up and hit the motorway.' She said it almost cheerfully.

'I don't know.'

'Ring Paul Gilroy. Hand back the keys. He can't object if you've already moved out. Or you could just give them to me. I'll make sure he gets them.'

I knew I wasn't going to give back the keys, or any of that. But something had occurred to me. What if I did turn up at Jason's place, like Claire had suggested, because I had already made it to the end? Who would care either way, if I was in the estate for those last two weeks or not? Who would even know? I could stay in Helen's empty flat. And I could tell Jason that my old boss wanted to see me in the office a lot between then and Christmas. I could tell him I had cleared it with Paul Gilroy and, just for that time, it made more sense for me to stay with him during the week.

Claire was right – if I went to him, instead of the other way around, it would no longer be a simple matter of him getting into his car and driving away.

By then my mother was about to leave for Spain. And Helen would be back in London. Otherwise I might have gone to one of them.

It didn't take too long to pack – just my clothes and toiletries, my laptop, a few books. It didn't even take that long to clean, despite how bad it had got with Lurch's hairs everywhere and nothing having been cleaned properly in ages. Claire helped me – that was what made it so easy. In a couple of hours, the place was close enough to the way it had been the day I moved in, and all my belongings were in the boot of my car. By then, it was already almost dark.

'I wish I could return the favour when you're moving,' I said to her, after she had helped me load my stuff and we were standing beside my car in the semi-dark. 'Do you know when that will be yet?'

'A few days, I'd say. A few days. Now. No last-minute doubts?'

I shook my head.

'Didn't think so. Well, it's been lovely knowing you. You're a lovely person,' she said.

'No.' I wanted to say that it was she who was the lovely person, but I couldn't get the words out.

'You are now. That's it. The wrong rabbit hole. That's what the past few weeks have been. Nothing more.' She spoke brightly, the way you would to an upset child.

'Will you be okay?' I managed.

'Oh, I'll be fine.'

And then I was on the motorway, amid all the other cars zooming along, lighting their way through the dark and the rain. It would have felt heartening, I think, I might even have started feeling optimistic, if all the time the image of Lurch lying dead on the cold ground wasn't stuck in my mind, like a kind of shadow. Still, I told myself, every second took me further away from that wrong rabbit hole, as Claire had called it, and closer to – what? Over and over, I tried to imagine the conversation with Jason, where I'm standing at his door, telling him that it was over, that I'd made it, that I'd be spending the next two weeks with him. That I hadn't called in advance because – why? I didn't know how I'd explain that in a way that would satisfy him. And the further away from the estate I got, the harder it became to imagine his reaction when I showed up.

By the time I'd reached the edge of the city, I just could not see it happening.

26

Rush hour had passed so it didn't take long to reach the area where Jason lived. It's a nice part of the city, and it was particularly pretty that night, with all the Christmas lights on and the big Christmas tree in the middle of its small square. The streets were full of people, going in and out of restaurants, or smoking outside them, or queuing for takeaway, or going into the supermarket, or just walking home. Festive. That was it. I remember feeling reassured. As if nothing very bad could happen.

Before I reached his place, I took a free parking space, at the top of a narrow cul-de-sac off the road his house was on. Then I walked back to the main street, and went into a small, brightly lit café just on the corner. I had some change in my pocket and I told myself I just needed to eat something and have a chance to think about exactly what I was going to say to Jason before I knocked on his door.

The café was all window, countertops and high stools. I bought a latte and a croissant and took a seat looking out onto the street. It was warm in there and the croissant tasted good dipped into the milky coffee. Beside me sat a young man wearing earphones. He was staring at the screen of his laptop, occasionally tapping out a few words. He reminded me of myself before I moved to the estate, how I used to go to a café occasionally to finish something I was working on, or to break through a difficult bit.

By now, though, I no longer had any work. An email from my old boss the previous week had confirmed what I already knew – that they no longer required my services. And I hadn't heard from any of my other clients in ages. I hadn't figured out how I was going to explain that to Jason. He would have been expecting a payment to come through around then. He was sure to ask me about it. Maybe, I thought, I could tell him it had been delayed. Then wait until the new year. Perhaps by then I would have a new client, or have persuaded my old boss to give me a second chance. Maybe, now I was back in Dublin, I could call in to the office and explain things.

But that was not the problem before me. I could figure that out later. It was figure-out-able, I thought, remembering the phrase Helen had used about me living on the estate. The problem before me was convincing Jason that it really was going to be fine for me to live with him over the next couple of weeks. That it would make no material difference to the Plan.

I tried again to imagine him answering the door to me. The mute surprise on his face when he saw me standing there. I couldn't decide if it would be better for me to seem upset at that point, or cheerful. I would blurt it all out, I thought, whichever way I managed it. Cheerful might be better. I would know when I saw him.

All the while I'd been thinking this through, I'd been staring into the distance, without really registering anything before me. It was only when the man in the earphones glanced my way that I realised. There, right outside the window, a man was staring in at me.

It was Jason.

I tried to smile as I put my coat back on and went outside. 'Surprise,' I said.

'What's going on?'

'Don't look so shocked,' I said. 'It's not like I was on another planet.'

He just stared at me, his eyes all glassy. He smelt of drink and had in his hand a bag with a bottle of something in it. Either he had stopped at a pub on the way home from work, and bought something to have at home – it was a Sunday but by then he was working weekends – or he had been drinking at home, and just nipped out for more. Sometimes in the summer, he would drink at home like that after a long day at work. He needed to, he said, to unwind. We used to do it together.

I was glad, when I saw he'd been drinking. I thought that maybe I could drink with him, and it would be like old times. And we would wake up in bed together in the morning and he would have to accept it then. And maybe that way he'd see it really wasn't such a big deal.

'What's going on?' he said again.

'Let's walk,' I said. 'It's freezing.' I linked his arm with mine and after a moment we started walking towards his house.

As we walked, I told him I had meetings coming up in Dublin, all of a sudden. That Paul Gilroy had called in on me, unexpectedly, just the day before. That, believe it or not, he had suggested I base myself in the city for the last two weeks before Christmas.

'The hard bit is over,' I said. 'We did it. Ta-da.'

When I said 'ta-da' like that, he stopped walking.

'You didn't think of running any of this past me first?' he said. He was slurring very slightly.

'Well, I did,' I said. 'But there didn't seem any need, when I thought about it.'

'No need to tell me?'

'I thought it would be nice to just – surprise you with the news.'

'You think I'd swallow that? Paul Gilroy suggesting it?'

'What? He did.'

'You've fucked it up,' he said. 'You've always wanted to fuck it up.'

'Honestly, Jason, I haven't.'

'The whole point,' he said, 'was for us to stay there. You think you can just walk out on that, come up here and stay with me?' he said. 'Without even asking?'

'Just for two weeks,' I said.

'There are other people living with me.'

'They didn't mind me being there in the summer.'

He started walking again, this time gripping my arm. He gripped it so tightly it hurt. All the time, his whole body was hardening beside me.

The silence was unbearable. I started talking again. I told him about finding Lurch dead in my garden. I lied and said the guard had said it definitely seemed someone was trying to intimidate me. Then I told him there really had been an intruder who had hit me, the night before he and Helen were down, that I had glossed over it so as not to worry him. Because I knew how much it meant to him, me staying on in the estate. I told him about Michael, and how threatening he had seemed the last time I saw him. I told him that Michael kept trying to get into the house. That I thought he wanted to hurt me, and Claire thought so too. That even the guard seemed to think that. I told him it was probably only temporary but that at that particular point I had no work on. That I had missed some important deadlines. I told him I was afraid I really was developing a drinking problem. He stopped walking then and, for a moment, I thought he was finally going to say something, but then he was walking again, this time faster than before. I talked on. The more I spoke, the more fantastical it all sounded, yet I was unable to stop myself. I told him I was afraid I was having a nervous breakdown. I told him I was frightening myself – that I had started doing things I would never normally do. I told him that Helen said I was vulnerable. That Paul Gilroy had taken advantage of my vulnerability. I told him something had happened with him.

Something I had never wanted. Something I couldn't bear to think about. I started crying then.

By that point, we had reached his front door. He put his key into the lock, pushed the door open. We went inside. It was cold in there, almost as cold as it was outside.

'Hello?' he shouted. 'Anyone home?' He turned on the light. 'Hello?' he roared, louder this time. Again, no one answered.

'No one home,' I said.

He turned to me then, and in that short moment before he punched me, it all tumbled forward in my mind – the summer we'd spent together in Dublin, his weekend visits to the estate, right up to that moment. And I swear I saw in his face what I think now I must have known deep down all along. Not only did Jason not love me, he hated me.

I might have cried out when he punched me, at the shock of the pain. I definitely tried to get back outside. But before I could open the door he had flipped the lock. And then he punched me in the stomach, and I fell to the floor. I remember trying to recover my breath, then trying to pull my knees to my chest, my eyes clenched shut, as the kicks to my back came hard and fast.

And then he stopped. It had all taken place in a matter of seconds.

But I could still feel him looming over me. And there was a high-pitched wailing sound. It took me a moment to realise that it was coming from me.

'Christ,' he shouted then, suddenly. And he kicked the door, before going quiet again.

I stayed as still as I could, too scared to try to open the

door again, because that would mean standing up. All the while, I was waiting for him to start kicking me again.

'Come on,' he said, after a while. I felt him leaning down over me. He was gripping my arm then, trying to pull me to my feet.

I let out a scream.

'Oh, Jesus,' he said then. 'It's too much. It's too much.' He kicked the door. After a short silence, he stepped over me and walked down the hall. I heard a door open, a tap come on, go off. Then he was back, kneeling beside me, slowly prising my hands away from my face, then wiping my face and hands with a tea towel. Then he started rubbing the floor with the tea towel, which was already red from the blood that was coming from my nose.

'Let me go,' I managed to say. It was more like a whisper, really.

'You can't go anywhere like this,' he said. 'We'll have to fix it, okay? We're going to fix it.' It was as though he was talking to himself, rather than to me.

'No,' I said, and started to cry.

At that moment, there was the sound of a key turning in the front door. Jason sort of wrenched me from the floor so that I was sitting up, and put his arm around me, just as a man and woman came in. At first they didn't register us. They were taking off their coats and laughing about something when the woman glanced down.

'Jesus,' she said, staring at me. The man turned, stared too.

'She's just been mugged,' said Jason.

'Oh, Christ,' said the guy.

Jason squeezed my shoulder.

'Have you called the cops?' she said. She was staring at me.

'Not yet. It literally just happened.'

'Jesus,' he said again. 'Would you like a cup of tea or something?'

'Actually, would you guys mind giving us a bit of space? I think she's in shock.'

'Of course, of course. Sorry.' But still they stood there, staring at me.

I knew that was my chance. My only chance.

'I need to go,' I said. I kept my gaze on her. On the woman.

'Beth,' said Jason, and his grip tightened on my shoulder.

'Can you open the door?' I said, my voice breaking. 'He did this. Jason did this. I need to get away from him, okay?'

The girl's eyes seemed to grow bigger.

'Are you mad?' said Jason. 'She's confused. Jesus, I hope she's not concussed.' But there was nervousness in his voice.

'I'll call the guards right now,' I said, 'if you don't let me walk out that door.'

'She's confused,' he said again.

But the woman took a step towards the door. All the while, I kept my gaze locked on her, and she gazed back at me. It was like a lifeline. I know it sounds silly but, right then, I knew that if that gaze between us broke, I would not escape. And it was like she knew that too, because she kept that sort of frightened, determined stare on me, even as she unlocked the door and pushed it open.

'You need to let her go now,' she said then, in a low, clear voice.

'Do you need any help?' said the guy to me.

'No. Just. Make sure he doesn't follow me. Okay?'

'Do you have someone to go to?' said the woman.

I nodded. 'Let go of me or I swear I'll go straight to a garda station,' I said again to Jason, without turning to him. And, to my immense relief, his grip on my shoulder finally relaxed. I took a painful step forward, ducked under the woman's arm, which still held the door open. I stepped outside, back into the night.

Out in the cold, I cautiously touched my lip. It was already swollen. Around it, my skin was wet with blood that Jason had missed. Or maybe it was new blood. The pain was extraordinary. Every breath intensified it.

All I knew was I had to get to the car. But I had only managed a couple of steps when the woman came out after me. 'You can't be on your own. Let me come with you.'

I shook my head. 'My car is just up here,' I said.

'You're not going to be able to drive.'

'Thank you,' I said, 'but I'm well able to drive. My mother isn't far, okay? I'm going to her.' I glanced at the house. I kept expecting Jason to come running towards me.

'Don't worry,' she said. 'He's not going anywhere. We said we'd call the guards ourselves, if he went near the door. Fucking bastard.'

I said nothing.

'I can bring you to the garda station,' she said. 'There's one really close to here. You could make a statement.'

'I'm not doing that,' I said flatly.

'Why not? Look what he did to you. You can't let him get away with it.'

She was standing beside me now, a hand tentatively touching my elbow, her face all worry.

Looking back now, I wonder why I didn't go with her to the garda station, make a statement. But then all I had was this pressing urge to get as far away as I could. I was ashamed, I suppose, of the state I was in, in front of that pretty young woman. It was so deeply humiliating.

'I will,' I said. 'I'll do all that. I just want to go to my mother first. Okay?'

'Okay,' she said reluctantly.

All the while I was walking, slowly and painfully, back to my car, I could feel her gaze on me, though I didn't look back until I had reached the side street where I had parked. She was still standing there, arms folded, that worried expression on her face. I managed a stiff wave and then, once I was around the corner and out of sight, I vomited, there on the street. It was dark and quiet; I don't think anyone saw me.

Back inside my car, the first thing I did was take some painkillers, which by luck I had in my bag. Then I drove away, and I did not stop until I was outside my mother's house, even though I knew she was on her holiday by then. I was hoping, I suppose, Helen might be there. Sometimes she would stay there if she was back in Dublin for a couple of days. But the house was all shut up. And when I rang her phone, I got that long dial tone you get when someone is abroad. I checked under the mat, in the unlikely event that she had left a spare set of keys for someone to water her plants or something but there was nothing. If only she hadn't moved house after I had started college. Then I would have had a key. But she had moved house. She was always moving house. That last time, she never offered to give me a key to her place. The thought would never have occurred to her.

There was nothing for it but for me to get back into my car.

At that point, I considered spending the night in the car. I even managed, slowly and painfully, to take some clothes out of my bag, and put them on over what I was wearing. But after putting on tracksuit bottoms over my leggings, a fleece between my jumper and coat, a wool hat, I was still very cold. And I was still in awful pain, with every breath still delivering another sharp shock of it.

It only occurs to me now that I could have gone to a garda station on my own. Or even phoned a women's refuge. But it never entered my mind, or at least it never made its way to my conscious mind as an option. The shame of it all was too much. I couldn't bear to admit to the world how low I had fallen.

It was shame, then, that had me driving all the way back to the estate that night. I would clean up in my house first, I had decided, and then I would go to Claire. She was the only person I could imagine actually telling what had happened. Right then, she seemed like my only friend in the world.

27

By the time I was back on the motorway, it was snowing. The further I got from the city, the thicker it fell, until the windscreen was completely covered for a split second, before being wiped clean again. The pain in my chest was awful. The painkillers didn't seem to have touched it. I sat hunched over the wheel, pressing my hands into it as I drove. It wasn't safe, driving like that on the motorway, and anyway I had no money for the tolls, so I got off at the first exit and made the rest of the journey home on the old roads. They were so quiet, as were the small towns I passed through, each one lit with a string of lights. As I drove, the pain got worse, but when I pulled over, thinking I couldn't keep going, I found that being still was no less painful. So I drove on. I was sort of moaning. It helped a little to do that.

When I reached the estate, it was almost midnight and the snow was falling hard. All was in darkness, except for the Dorans' downstairs front window. Claire's downstairs light was not on, but to my great relief, her car was in her driveway. I remember noticing that her boot was open, which seemed odd. But I didn't give that too much notice. I would shower and change, I decided. Fix my face as best I could. And then I would go straight to her.

I was just about to put the key in the lock when the Portakabin door creaked open and slammed shut behind me. When I turned around, all I could see was snow swirling and, across the way, the dim square light from the Dorans' house. Only then did it occur to me that my porch-light had not come on, as it should have done. I turned on the flashlight on my phone, shone it upwards. The glass pane over the bulb was broken, the light-bulb inside shattered.

The door of the Portakabin creaked and slammed shut, then creaked open again. I shone the flashlight in its direction. It was just about visible in the snow – the doorway gaping open, then the door slamming shut.

It made no sense, of course. That door had always been locked shut. The whole time I had been down there, no one had ever used the Portakabin.

I suppose I was tired of not understanding. I got to the door before it swung open again, managed to grab it.

I held it open. Shone the flashlight ahead of me.

The first things I saw: a desk, a chair, windows painted black.

Then the bed. Just a small camp bed, by the wall. And in it a girl under a grey blanket. About eight, maybe nine years old. She looked like she was sleeping.

28

The girl was very still. But when I put my hand on her forehead, it felt warm. And after a few moments of staring at her, I saw that her chest was rising and falling, rising and falling.

'Hello,' I said absurdly, first in an almost-whisper, then again, more loudly. 'Hello.'

Nothing.

'Wake up,' I shouted.

Still nothing.

I shook her shoulders, lightly at first, then harder. It made no difference.

I hesitated to lift her – the pain in my chest was still so sharp and constant; I didn't think I'd be able to bear it getting any worse. But as I was standing there, wondering what to do, the door slammed shut behind me, before almost immediately creaking open again. I strained to hear anything that might suggest someone was out there, but the only sound was the wind.

I managed to lift her then, one arm under her back, the other under her knees. I even managed to get her outside. But before I had reached my car, I stumbled and we were both lying on the snow-covered ground. Still she slept, the snow falling on her clothes, her face, her hair.

I was trying to lift her again when I heard Michael's voice call, 'Beth?'

I could just about make out his shape, standing outside my front door. He was looking towards me, but I couldn't tell if he could actually see me. He was hugging himself against the cold.

I dragged her to the car, managed to open the back door, get her inside, shut it.

'Hey, Beth?'

'Go away,' I shouted, or tried to shout. Then I sat into the driver's seat. I got the keys out of my pocket and into the ignition. I was about to turn on the engine when he took a step towards me. I turned the key anyway. I switched on the headlights. He shut his eyes against the sudden glare. He squinted towards me. In that moment, as I remember it now, he looked confused. But he might not have looked confused. He might have looked angry, or hostile.

Him looking confused right then fits with the truth. Which I know now. I didn't then.

Maybe I'm remembering things differently from how they actually happened.

'Don't move,' I shouted, but of course he couldn't hear me, inside the car, the engine running. I glanced back at the girl – she was still asleep.

'Don't move,' I shouted again.

But he took another step towards me. I revved the engine again, louder this time.

There was a moment, then, after I had revved the engine that second time, and he still hadn't moved and . . . I don't know. He couldn't have seen me, with the headlights on like that. I knew he couldn't have seen me. But he still seemed to be staring at me.

Why didn't he just walk away? That's what I don't understand. Why did he just have to keep standing there, in front of a car with the engine revving? Any normal person would have moved and moved quickly. Surely that's what I assumed he would do, when I put my foot on the accelerator and the car moved forward? Faster than I'd intended and I braked almost immediately. I'm sure I did. The car didn't even touch him. But he fell to the ground all the same. His hand clutching his chest. He fell and then he just lay there, staring up at the snow falling.

Afterwards, as soon as I had been discharged from the hospital and was back here living with Mum, I looked it up on the internet. It wasn't a normal heart attack. It was a specific type, caused by the hole in his heart. It can happen if the hole lets new oxygen blood get mixed up with old oxygen blood. When that happens, the blood circulating in the body can have less oxygen in it, which makes the heart work harder. And sometimes, especially if someone isn't getting proper treatment, or I suppose if they're very weak, their heart can just give up. What happens is, the heart gets tired and one day it just stops. It's rare among children apparently, which technically Michael was: he turned out to be only sixteen. But I suppose he wasn't in the best of health, with the drugs he was taking and where he was living and everything.

I don't think he had been lying there very long when Mr Doran ran past my car, up to Michael, knelt down beside him and started doing mouth-to-mouth resuscitation, alternated with chest compresses.

He had to shout at me a couple of times before I understood.

'Call an ambulance,' he was saying. 'Call an ambulance.'

29

When I think of what happened next, it's like recalling the memory of a film. Calling 911. Giving the address, telling them about Michael, and about the girl who slept on in the back of my car. Getting out of my car, and walking up to where Mr Doran was still giving CPR to Michael. The way Michael still seemed to be staring at the sky, his body jerking with every thump to his chest. Mr Doran shouting at me to get a blanket and how I found myself, at the doorstep of my house, incapable of going inside. Like there was an invisible wall between me and the door. Taking off my coat and putting it over Michael's body – I don't remember feeling the cold. Then Mrs Doran beside me.

'Oh, my God.' Her hands to her face.

'Go back inside,' said Mr Doran to her.

'What happened to him?'

'Go back inside.'

'There was a child,' I said to her. 'I put her in my car.'

'What's she talking about? What's happened to you?' She was staring at my face.

I walked back to my car and she followed me. I peered through the window at the girl. She was still unconscious.

'I couldn't wake her,' I said to Mrs Doran.

She opened the door. She looked inside.

'Oh, my God, Jim. It's a child. In the back of her car.' She bent over the girl, trying, I suppose, to hear her breathing. She put a hand on her chest until, I suppose, she felt that steady rise and fall. Then she stood. Closed the door. Looked at me.

'What happened?' she said again.

I touched my swollen lip. 'I found her in there,' I said, pointing to the Portakabin.

As she looked at it, the door swung open in the wind, slammed shut.

'What was she doing in there? Was she on her own?'

I nodded.

'You've called an ambulance?'

I nodded again. She was staring at me intensely, with fear or concern or both.

'Hang on,' she said. She ran to her house, came back with a duvet and a blanket. She opened the car door, gently laid the duvet on the girl. She shut the door quietly, as though afraid of waking her. Then she put the blanket over my shoulders.

'What were you at?' Mr Doran shouted at me. He had

stopped doing CPR on Michael's body. 'Revving the engine at him like that. What were you at?'

At first, I didn't say anything. I didn't know what to say.

'I thought he was going to hurt me,' I said eventually.

'This lad?' said Mr Doran. 'This child? Did you think he was going to hurt you?'

'I thought he had something to do with her,' I said, looking at my car, where the girl slept on. 'I don't know.'

'Jim,' said Mrs Doran. 'She's hurt.'

He went back to doing the compressions. For a while, that was the only sound – that and the occasional squeak and slam of the Portakabin door. Until the screaming sirens came, lights flashing, people suddenly everywhere. I heard someone declare Michael dead, watched as they zipped a body-bag over him, loaded it onto a stretcher and into an ambulance, which immediately drove away. While this was going on, others were moving the little girl from the back of my car onto another stretcher, which was put into a second ambulance. Someone asked me if she had been responsive at any point. No, I told him. No. Did I have any idea what might have happened to her? No. I just found her, in there. He went into the Portakabin with a flashlight, emerged with what looked like a syringe and a small container. He said something to another medic. I didn't hear all of what he said but I thought I caught the word 'insulin'.

A third ambulance arrived. One of the medics pushed a wheelchair towards me, asked me to sit in it. He put one of those foil blanket things over my shoulder and told me they were taking me to hospital.

My last image from that night is of the Dorans standing close together in their doorway, staring through the still-swirling snow as one of the medics wheeled me backwards up the ramp and into the ambulance. He was holding her hand against his chest tightly.

Once out of the estate and on the road, the ambulance picked up speed. We seemed to be moving really, really fast, but there weren't any windows so I couldn't get a sense of our speed. The other thing was how bright it was in there. Everything was visible. I kept blinking in the brightness of it. I felt like I couldn't adjust to it.

In the hospital, they took an X-ray of my ribs and found two of them cracked. Just hairline fractures, they said. They would heal in a couple of weeks. Then they took my blood pressure again, checked my temperature, waved fingers in front of my face, asked me to turn my head and a hundred other things. They told me I was fine, but that they would like to keep me in for the night. To give me a chance to rest. I was dehydrated. I had had a shock. Yes, I could talk to the guards now, but only if I was sure I was up to it. Did I have family or friends I would like to call? A boyfriend? No? Well, we would see in the morning. Everything would seem easier, after a few hours' sleep.

All they could tell me about the girl was that she was in intensive care. That her parents were with her. That there was no need to worry myself.

I made my statement to a guard that night, in a room there in the hospital. I had been expecting the male guard who had come out to the house, but it was actually a youngish woman I hadn't met before. She was a good listener, hardly ever interrupting. I talked up to the point where I got back to Dublin. I sort of stopped there. I didn't want to tell her what Jason had done to me. I wasn't ready to talk about that yet.

She frowned a little then, in the way people do when they're trying to figure something out. 'So what happened,' she asked, 'when you got to your boyfriend's house? Jason, isn't it?'

I nodded.

'Can you tell me what happened then?'

'Well. I called in.' I looked at her. 'I just decided to come back to the estate.'

'Did you argue?'

'Sort of.'

'So you drove to Dublin to see him and not long after you arrived you came back down to the estate.'

'Yes.' We looked at each other across the table. I didn't cry. I didn't feel like crying.

'Okay,' she said, after a while. 'What happened next?'

I told her about what had happened when I got back to the estate. When it came to the part about Michael, I told her it had seemed as though I was in danger. Which was true. I told her I'd revved my engine, just to scare him away. That was when he fell over, I told her.

She just listened. Didn't ask me to repeat what had happened or anything.

'And that was when Mr Doran would have arrived, isn't that right?' she said.

I nodded.

'And you called for an ambulance.'

'Yes.'

Only then did she ask me about my injuries. But I just shook my head.

'Have they anything to do with what happened on the estate? Anything at all? Michael didn't go for you, did he?'

'No.'

'I'm sorry, Beth. I know this is hard. But I need to ask you. How did you sustain your injuries?'

I shook my head.

She waited.

I looked around the room. It was like a room where you came to see a consultant. The desk I was sitting at across from the guard. The bed behind us. There was a poster behind her, showing the human body, all its organs. Writing on it in a font too small for me to make out. The top right corner was hanging down. I wanted to stick it back onto the wall. For a second, that was all I could think of.

'Beth,' said the guard.

'Yes.'

'What happened to you?'

I looked at her. Then I looked back at the poster.

'I'm not pressing charges,' I said. 'I don't want that.'

'Okay.'

I looked at her again. 'He did it.'

'Your boyfriend.'

I nodded.

'Right.'

For a moment, neither of us spoke.

'This happened in Dublin?' she said.

'I got back into my car. My mum wasn't home. She's on holidays in Spain. So I came back.'

'To the estate?'

'To the estate.'

'Okay.'

'I just wanted to get away,' I said. 'When I revved the engine like that. That's all I wanted. I was trying to get away.'

'It's all right,' she said. 'It's all right now.'

'It's my fault he died,' I said. 'Is it?'

'We don't know why Michael died yet,' she said. 'The post-mortem will shed some light on that. But, from what you've said, it doesn't sound like it was your fault. If anything, it sounds to me like you're a victim.'

It was two days later that I found out about Claire. They had kept me on in the hospital until my mother got back from Spain, and I had found myself drifting in and out of sleep all that time, not eating much, until the second morning when I woke in my small ward to daylight and a ravenous hunger. There were two other patients in that room, both women. They were sitting up in their beds, eating breakfast. At the end of my bed, there was a tray with a boiled egg, toast and a little pot of tea on it.

First I went to the nurses' station. I asked if they knew how the girl was.

'We can only talk to family about a patient,' said the nurse. 'As far as I know she's stable. Now eat your breakfast. The social worker will be in to you soon.'

As I ate, the two other patients kept glancing my way.

'Can we have the news, Nurse?' one called out.

The nurse turned to me. 'Are you okay with that?' she asked.

'Of course.'

There was a small wall-mounted television in the corner of the room. She turned on the news channel and there, on the screen, was a photograph of Claire, smiling her big smile. The guards were appealing to one of the residents of the estate to come forward, the newsreader said, to help them with their investigation. She lived on the estate where Grace Kennedy, the nine-year-old victim of a recent kidnapping, had been found in the early hours of Saturday morning.

'I hope she gets what's coming to her,' said the woman in the bed opposite mine.

'She had nothing to do with it,' I said. But that was when I remembered. The insulin the medic had found in the Portakabin. Claire was a type-one diabetic. She had told me herself, that night I had gone round to hers for dinner.

'Are you joking?' said the other woman.

'Did you know her?' said the one opposite. She was staring at me, as though she didn't want to miss even the tiniest gesture.

'She was my neighbour.'

'You found the child.'

I nodded.

'She had that child in the Portakabin for three nights. You never heard anything?'

'It's a mistake,' I said.

'She'd have come forward by now if it was a mistake. You never heard anything?'

I said nothing.

'The guards probably took a statement off you.'

'Do you think she killed the young fellow too?'

'Maybe he saw something.'

'They should string her up. When they find her.'

They looked at me again. 'You never saw nothing?'

I shook my head.

'The poor little mite.'

The social worker turned up then. She came straight over to me, drew the curtains around my bed.

30

It's been over a week since I wrote in here. Now, I just spend the mornings in bed. I've stopped going for my midday walk. I don't watch films on my laptop any more in the evenings. I don't really do anything. I haven't even gone to meditation. I don't imagine I'll ever go back there. It's too hard. Anyway, it just makes everything worse.

I can pass whole days sitting on my bed, or lying in it, watching the shadow of the house slowly swallow the daylight on the laurel and the chestnut tree, then the darkness descending. At this time of year, it still gets dark very early.

I suppose I'm just tired from the effort of writing it all down. I suppose I just need to wait this out.

I was sitting here earlier today, pretty much as I am now, when the buzzing of the phone gave me a shock: it hardly ever rings these days.

I answered it. 'Hello?'

'Hello, Beth? Beth Sheehan is it?'

I recognised her voice straight away. It was the nice guard, the one who had taken my statement in the hospital. The results of Michael's post-mortem were through, she said. Death by natural causes. So there was to be no inquest. She wanted to tell me as soon as she heard.

'Didn't I tell you?' she said. 'You can relax now.'

'That's great. Thanks.'

'Take care of yourself, Beth,' she said, and hung up.

I imagined Mr Doran hearing the news. I imagined him turning to his wife, or whoever was sitting beside him in the pub. Whoever would listen. Scared him to death, he would say. She would have run him over, if he hadn't fallen to the ground first. I was just sitting there, thinking of Mr Doran and staring in that vacant kind of way at the chest of drawers, when my mother knocked on the door. She has a distinctive way of knocking – light and fast, like she's hoping I won't hear.

'I'm here,' I said.

The door opened. As usual, she stayed on the other side of the doorway, and spoke without looking at me. 'You'd better come down and watch this.'

'Was it on the news? About the post-mortem? The guard just rang me.'

She looked at me blankly.

'Natural causes,' I said. 'There'll be no inquest.'

Her eyes widened. 'Oh,' she said. 'It wasn't that, no. I came up to tell you they're doing that woman on the television.'

That was how she always referred to Claire. That woman.

I followed her down to the living room. On the television, a man was looking directly into the camera as he spoke, and I felt for a moment as though he was addressing me specifically. He was wearing a coat, the lapels turned up. The wind was whipping his hair to one side. I recognised where he was: it was the estate. Behind him stood Claire's house.

He was from a current-affairs programme that I had occasionally watched in the past. I'd never seen him presenting from anywhere except the studio before, though. They must have decided that this event was special. Even though by then two weeks had passed since Claire had confessed to the police.

'We decided to take a closer look at the thirty-nine-year-old woman behind these shocking events,' the man on the television was saying. 'The perpetrator of the crime, who hid for two whole days in a neighbour's hayshed before going to the nearest garda station and making a full confession.'

The camera turned onto the Portakabin, briefly capturing the house beside Claire's. The one where I used to live. Curtains all drawn. Door shut.

My mother flashed a glance at me. 'Was that your place?'

'Yes.'

The Portakabin had that yellow crime-scene tape around it. But besides that, and a new lock holding its door shut, it was just the same. The windows were still blacked out.

'For three nights,' continued the presenter, 'Grace Kennedy

was kept here, in this Portakabin. Walsh, a type-one diabetic, used insulin to sedate her. She would have made regular visits to the Portakabin in the dark to administer it.'

He went on to talk about the advantages of hiding the child in the Portakabin, rather than in Claire's house. Distance from the crime, should the police be somehow led to the estate in searching for the girl. A reduced likelihood of her ever recollecting where she had been held. And, of course, the fact that she would never be discovered in Claire's home by a visitor: according to neighbours Claire, he noted, was very popular. People often dropped in for a cup of tea or just a chat. Listening, I was reminded how cars used to pull up outside her house and later drive away.

As he spoke, a photograph of Claire filled the screen. She looked like the Claire I knew. Smiling, hair perfectly straightened. Beautiful, friendly Claire. I wondered who had given it to them. Her husband, maybe. Then it disappeared, to be followed by a series of short interviews with people who knew her, most of whom I knew, too. Mr and Mrs Doran. Paul Gilroy. The man in the newsagent. The woman in the farmhouse, whom I had spoken to that one time. Claire's boss in the café in Dunlone. I waited for someone to mention me but none of them did. All of them spoke of how nice Claire had always seemed. How shocked they were when they learned what had happened.

It was so strange to see them all speaking one by one on the television like that. The sight of Paul Gilroy especially made me flinch. My mother glanced my way, but said nothing.

'There was another resident of the estate,' said the

presenter then. 'Walsh's neighbour, who was renting the house beside her.'

The camera returned to rest on the house where I had lived. There was nothing to indicate what had happened that night. No yellow tape or anything like that. The ground where Michael had lain was just as it always had been – concrete paving slabs, the front doorstep. It might never have happened at all. It might have been a dream.

'In fact, it is understood that it was this resident who discovered Grace Kennedy in the Portakabin and alerted the authorities. She has refused all requests for interview.'

'You should have talked to them,' said my mother. 'It looks funny that you didn't.'

'What has been confirmed,' continued the presenter, 'is that ten years ago Claire Walsh worked for a year as nanny to the Kennedys. At that time, Grace would have been just a baby.'

A large red-brick house, thick woods behind it, appeared on the screen. The presenter described how the two youngest children – Grace and her brother – used to play in those woods behind the house, every day after school, before they were called in to dinner. How their older siblings, now all in university, used to play there too. Claire, he said, would have remembered that. And it would have been easy for her to spy on the younger children, to learn that they, too, played in those woods, and when they did so. The week the kidnapping happened, he said, the weather was unseasonably warm. Claire must have been watching and waiting for an opportunity, waiting until Grace was playing there alone.

When that opportunity came, he said, she took it. If she had not kidnapped Grace that day in mid-December, she might never have gone through with her plan. Two days later, that unseasonably warm weather was to be replaced by freezing temperatures and snow.

I remembered what Claire had said to me, of the family she had nannied for all those years ago. All the cash dealings. The new baby Claire had cared for. It would have been Grace.

The kidnapping, he said, probably took place within a matter of minutes, on an otherwise normal Wednesday evening in December. And it seemed that Claire had delivered the ransom note on her way home, demanding eighty thousand euro in cash and warning the parents not to go to the police, the girl, presumably unconscious, in the boot of her car. It specified that the parents should meet her at midnight on Friday – two days away – at a layby on the M6.

Then the programme switched back to the studio, where a second presenter sat with a panel of experts, waiting to discuss the case. A crime journalist, an economist, a psychologist.

'So it is highly likely,' said the presenter, 'that had Grace not been discovered in the Portakabin that night, she might have been returned to her parents. Walsh's plan might have succeeded. We might never have heard of this case. After all, the night the victim was found in the Portakabin was the very night she was to be returned to her parents, had all gone to plan.' She went on to describe how Claire had successfully applied for a second passport, only two months previously, the second under her Irish name: Clár Breathnach. Both passports had been found in a car in a Tesco car park very close to the motorway layby where she had arranged to meet the Kennedys. Along with the passports, there was a single plane ticket to Costa Rica. Where Claire had gone on her honeymoon, I remembered. Where she said she had been so happy. They showed fuzzy black-and-white CCTV footage then of a large, deserted car park at night. After a few moments, a hooded person got out of a car at the furthest edge of the car park and walked quickly out of view. The presenter explained that that had been Claire in the footage, a week before the kidnapping had taken place. The car had been bought for cash that very day, for a very small sum. It seems Claire planned to abandon her own car somewhere close by, straight after the exchange on the motorway, before walking to the Tesco car park and making her way from there to the airport.

The presenter turned to the crime journalist.

'What would have been the reasoning behind the two passports?'

'Two passports,' he said, 'would have given Walsh a distinct advantage. She could have flown to Costa Rica on her original passport, then used the one with her Irish name when checking into hotels and such. Having two passport numbers would certainly complicate any efforts to track her down, had police identified her as a suspect. Which might never have happened, of course.'

They began discussing Claire's plan. It was clearly a horrific act, they agreed. To put a child in danger like that. She was still in hospital. It was not yet clear that she would make a full recovery. It was unimaginable that someone could not only conceive of but actually execute such a plot. Besides which, it was fraught with risk, involving a strong element of wing and prayer. What if the note had not reached the parents the next day? This, said the presenter, can only be seen as an astonishing game of bluff, one whose success depended on the child's parents believing their daughter was in the hands of someone who would harm her if they did not do as they were ordered.

But, they acknowledged, it was also clever in its simplicity. It might have worked. They seemed to find that fascinating. If it had, eighty thousand euro would have been enough to set Claire up for a few years in relative comfort somewhere in the developing world, someone said. Maybe in the meantime she might have succeeded in getting a false identity for herself.

The reporter went on. What was clear was that these were the actions of someone who was not only desperate for a new chance at life but also of someone with very little to lose. Someone for whom the prospect of a long-term prison sentence was not much worse than how her actual future was looking. Significantly, Claire Walsh's house was about to be repossessed by the bank. The previous year, her husband had left her, stranding her with a sizeable mortgage, possibly three times the current value of her house. This was a woman who had celebrated her wedding in one of the most exclusive venues in the country, who, at the age of thirty-nine, was about to start renting a flat or bedsit in the nearby town of Dunlone, while every month a substantial proportion of her income as a waitress would go towards the colossal debt left from that repossessed property, a debt she could probably expect not to pay off for decades, if at all.

'And what of the vulnerable young man,' she asked, 'Michael Doyle, who was squatting in one of the unfinished houses on the estate, and who tragically died from sudden cardiac arrest that same night?'

I'd been hoping they wouldn't bring him up.

'According to the coroner's report, released only today, his death was due to natural causes. But was his death that same night just a coincidence, or is there more beneath the surface here?' She went on to say the story presented more questions than it did answers. She asked what its message was. Was it a story of the Great Recession? Of what people might feel impelled to do in desperate circumstances? Or was it a cautionary tale, a warning of the limits of endurance among the increasing number of people in Ireland who had been financially ruined by the current crisis?

A panel discussion began then, about the property bubble and the impact of its collapse. I turned the television off.

'Well,' said my mother.

'Well.'

'I suppose you're pleased there's to be no inquest.'

I didn't say anything.

'That child still hasn't recovered,' said my mother, her voice all indignation. 'That was in the papers as well.'

'I wouldn't believe everything you read in the papers.'

'Brain injury, they're saying,' she added, ignoring my comment. 'She might never recover fully. Well, if that woman ever sees the light of day again it'll be too soon.'

She gave me another one of those keen, nervous looks she's been giving me ever since I moved in.

'I've booked another holiday,' she said suddenly.

'Oh,' I said.

'Well, the last one was cut short.'

'Sorry about that,' I said.

'There's no need to be smart.'

'Is that what you've been wanting to have a go at me about?'

She looked at me.

'You've obviously been pissed off with me for ruining your Christmas holiday. But you haven't been able to have a proper go at me because you can't actually blame me for what happened. As much as you'd like to.'

'Don't be ridiculous.'

I thought she was going to say something else then. But she just looked down at the coffee-table, pretending to be annoyed by an invisible mark on it.

I made myself some toast and went back to my room.

31

To visit someone in prison, you can't just show up. First, you have to get on their list of approved visitors. Then you have to make an appointment. That was what I was told when I phoned the women's prison yesterday, the morning after that television programme.

'If the prisoner has not already nominated you,' said the man on the phone, 'one of the officers here could ask her for you. Or you could write to her yourself.'

My first instinct was that I would write to her. But how do you compose a letter with nothing but questions?

'If someone could ask her,' I said.

When I called again the following day, I was expecting to

be told that she had said no. So I was surprised to hear that my name was there.

'Beth Sheehan,' I repeated. 'You're sure?'

'You're here all right. Do you want to book a visit?'

I booked in for tomorrow morning, which is a Saturday, even though it was only Tuesday when I called them and it's not as though I'm busy. I regret that now, as the impending visit has hung over every waking minute of this week, making the days seem interminable. Every time I've tried to imagine how it would go, to think of what I might say to her, my mind goes blank. I keep thinking of that photo of her that was on TV. Claire, with her perfectly straightened hair and perfectly applied make-up. And then of what the reporter had said – about how she had hidden in a hayshed for two days, after that last night.

But she's added my name to her list. I can't cancel or just not show up. It wouldn't be fair. And then there are all the questions I still have. Everything that I still don't understand.

32

The women's prison isn't far from the city centre, but in an area I don't know very well. I had to use the map on my phone to get there, walking slowly from where the bus left me, on a clear-sky day, the wind cutting through my coat. As I walked, I stared at my phone, like a tourist, until it told me I was there and I saw, across a busy road, the prison – a high and imposing red-brick wall that gave the entire street a desolate feel. Even though it's a modern building, there's something medieval about it – the fundamental hostility of the height and thickness of those walls, the small square windows.

No one else was walking on that side of the road, but when I reached the entrance – a high metal door set into the wall

– a man and three young children were standing there. The children regarded me silently as I joined the queue behind them.

Presently, there was the sound of locks turning, and the heavy door was opened by a prison officer, who asked for ID before ushering everyone ahead of him, down a corridor lit entirely by electric lights, towards another locked door. We waited as he unlocked that door, then had us again walk ahead of him, this time towards a security gate with a conveyor-belt. Just like in an airport, we were instructed to put our bags and coats onto the belt, and then we continued down another long corridor, through another locked door, which opened onto a courtyard, surrounded by the red-brick complex you see from the street. There were trees and lamps in the courtyard, a small lawn. All the small windows looking down onto it had curtains. It felt more like a dreary apartment complex than a prison.

We followed the officer across the courtyard to a small one-storey building. The room he led us into was full of people – adults and children – all sitting at round tables and talking. There was a Christmas tree and decorations hanging from the ceiling, even though it's already February. Some of the children were chasing each other around the room.

I suppose I'd expected something much quieter. More restricted, even. Maybe even a glass screen between each prisoner and visitor, like you see in films.

'Just up here,' said the prison officer to me.

I think I registered Claire before I actually saw her, if that makes sense. Alone, hunched over her table at the other side of the room. Something, at least, made me stop in my tracks.

The officer stopped walking too. He looked at me blankly.

'Okay,' I said. And I nodded to let him know I was ready to continue walking towards her.

I followed him through the crowded room to where she was sitting, as far as possible, it seemed to me, from everyone else. She was staring intently at the table in front of her, as though there was something written on it. She kept staring, even though she must have sensed us approach and stand beside her.

'Claire,' said the prison officer. 'I have your visitor here. Beth Sheehan. All right?'

She raised her head. It seemed as though she had to force herself to look, first at him, then at me.

'Visiting is until twelve,' he said to me. 'You've the guts of an hour.'

I wanted to tell him I wouldn't need near that long.

'Okay,' I said. 'Thank you.'

Then he left, and it was just me and Claire.

She looked pretty much as she always had. On one level, at least. For example, she was wearing make-up, as well as her own clothes. And her hair had been washed and blow-dried.

I suppose I had expected her to look more like a prisoner. To be wearing some kind of uniform, at least. And upset. I had expected her to be upset. Or, at least, to seem remorseful.

On another level, she looked like a different person. Like a mask had fallen.

She didn't smile and you could tell straight away that

being in my company was the last thing she wanted. She had a small pencil in her hand that she was turning over and over.

'You should sit,' she said, and gestured at a chair on the other side of the table.

I sat. Only then did she regard me properly.

'What happened to you?' she said.

'What do you mean?' I asked, my voice coming out all icy. She couldn't have been referring to my face, which had long since healed. And I had made some effort with my appearance. At least, more than is usual, these days. Just like she had, I suppose.

'You look like a train wreck,' she said.

I stared at her, shocked at her insolence. 'I don't think so,' I said.

'Fair enough,' she said. 'How's Jason?'

'We broke up.'

'That's terrible,' she said. I could swear she almost smiled. 'The Plan came to nothing in the end, then?'

'I suppose you could say that.'

'You're better off without him,' she said, her voice now flat. 'You know that yourself.'

'How are *you* doing, Claire?' I said.

'Fine,' she said. 'I'm fine.'

'I was surprised you added me to your list of visitors,' I said.

'Were you?'

'I was.'

She flicked a keen glance at me. 'So, why did you come, then?' she said.

'Sorry?'

She coughed. Said it again. 'Why did you come?'

'Well,' I said, 'I'm not sure.'

When she didn't say anything, I continued, 'I suppose, for one thing, I was wondering if maybe you wanted to apologise to me.' I hadn't known I was going to say that. It just came out.

'No,' she said. 'I don't.'

She didn't say it angrily or anything. She sounded tired. Almost bored.

'Why not?'

'Excuse me.' She stood, walked over to a water cooler. I watched her fill two plastic beakers. She was wearing a top I'd seen her in before – a dark pink hoodie. I'd recognised it when I first saw her, and looking at her at the water cooler, I remembered. She had worn it that night she had cooked dinner for me. I had a flash then of her standing at her kitchen island, emptying ladles of fish stew onto our plates, smiling as she spoke. How I had admired her.

Now it looked as though her hands might be shaking a little. As though it was taking all her energy not to return the glances of the other people in the room. To pretend she didn't notice she was drawing so much attention.

'You must hate me,' I tried, when she was sitting opposite me again.

She frowned, as though trying to understand the question. She looked exhausted by the effort. 'I don't think I hate you.'

For a while, we sat there, neither of us saying anything.

'I need to ask you a favour,' she said then.

'A favour?'

'My mother's in a nursing home in Dunlone,' she said. 'I think I might have mentioned this to you before.'

I nodded.

'I need you to visit her. Just once, to check if they've changed her room. They were supposed to move her after another resident died. I wrote to them about it a couple of weeks ago, and they said they were considering it. But I think they're bullshitting me.'

I looked at her blankly.

'Her room has a terrible view,' she continued. 'Just the car park and the road. They were supposed to move her to a room that looks out at the fields. I've been on at them for ages about this.'

'Right.'

'She lived her whole life on a farm.' She gazed at me expectantly. 'She would be used to seeing trees. And the other thing is, I need you to tell her I love her. And that I'm fine.'

Then she took a small photograph out of her pocket, slid it across to me. It showed Claire and an older woman standing in front of a grand staircase. Claire is in a wedding dress, her arm around her mother. Both of them are smiling into the camera.

'I don't get it,' I said. I didn't pick up the photo.

'What don't you get?'

'If your plan had worked, you would never have found out about her room. Whether she'd been moved or not. Isn't that right?'

'That's true,' she said. 'But it didn't work. Look, I'm not

expecting you to understand. You don't need to understand, okay?'

'Oh, right.'

'Just hear me out. You can tell them you're her niece. I'll write to them, tell them to expect you. There won't be an issue. Just phone them in a couple of days to let them know when you'll be coming.'

'She'll know I'm not her niece.'

'She won't. She recognises hardly anyone. Besides me. She knows me.' She drank from her cup again. 'You don't have to stay long or anything.'

'Do I not?'

'They probably haven't moved her,' she said. 'She's probably still in her old room. Number three, on the ground floor. If that's the case, tell them I'm getting my solicitor on to them. Tell them I'm really concerned about it. That it's all I think about.'

'Why do you think I'd want to help you?'

She looked annoyed. Impatient, even. 'I'll get to that,' she said. 'But there's something else. I want you to find out how Grace Kennedy is doing.' She was speaking quickly now, the words tumbling out over each other, as though she was scared I would suddenly get up and leave.

'But . . . you can get the papers in here, can't you?'

'They're no good. I need you to see her. Actually see her. Speak to her. And then come back and tell me.'

'How would I even do that? It's not like I could call on them.'

'Why not? They'd probably want to meet you. Say thanks.'

The fact was, they had already written me a letter, in which they said they would like to meet me. I hadn't replied.

'I'm not going back,' I said. 'I'm not doing any of that.'

'It's not like you'd have to go back to the estate,' she said. 'It would be one trip. You could call into the nursing home, that will only take five minutes, then visit the Kennedys on your way back to Dublin.'

I said nothing.

'If you do that for me,' she said, 'and come back to tell me, then I'll answer any question you have. I'll answer *all* the questions you have.'

'How will I know you're telling the truth?'

'You'll know. Why wouldn't I tell the truth? Now, I mean.' She gestured vaguely around her.

'Was it you,' I asked, 'who hit me that time? On the back of my head?' Instinctively, I felt where the bump had been.

'I'll tell you everything you want to know,' she said, 'if you promise to do those two things for me.'

'That's why you're asking me,' I said. 'No one else would have questions for you. Not that you could answer, anyway.'

'You're the only person who's visited me. That's why you.'

33

Yesterday I went to Dunlone.

First, I went to the home of Grace Kennedy. The girl who had been kidnapped. Their house was just outside a village a couple of miles east of Dunlone, on a road skirting a huge lake. All the houses around there seemed to be big and impressive, and every road looked the same as the previous one, all of them winding along a wood, every now and then a gap in the trees giving a glimpse of the lake and its small islands. Even with my phone and the precise directions Mrs Kennedy had given me when I'd called, I struggled to find it. But when I eventually came to it, I recognised it immediately from the television – a squat red-brick split-level house in the middle of a large landscaped garden, with woods behind it that were dark even in the daytime. The only thing different was the 'for sale' sign by the gate.

I didn't even turn onto the drive. The realisation had been unfolding inside me slowly, all the way down, but it was only when I saw the house that I understood I couldn't go in. Instead, I pulled in at a gate to a field from where I could still see the house. I sat there for a while, trying to imagine them inside – the parents and the girl – sitting together on a sofa, biscuits and tea ready. Waiting for me. The mother had been wary on the phone at first, but when she was assured I really was who I said I was, she had been very eager for me to visit. She said Grace had been asking about me, and that they would all like so much to meet me. They had asked the police, she said, about meeting me before, but they had told them what I had said – that I didn't want to talk to anyone.

As I sat there watching, the front door opened, and Grace and her mother walked out into the garden. At first, I thought they had seen my car, and knew somehow it was me, but I soon stopped worrying about that. There was something about them – the pace they moved at maybe – that told me they hadn't seen me, that they didn't know they were being watched. Hand in hand, they slowly made their way down the driveway towards the gate. At the gate, they stood for a while, still holding hands, looking out at the road, before walking back up the driveway and into the house.

It didn't necessarily mean that they were looking out for me. Maybe they did that walk every day, down to the gate and back. It might have been part of Grace's rehabilitation or something. Or maybe they had forgotten I was coming. Or maybe the mother had detected hesitation in my voice, on the phone, and had not even told the girl, in case she would be disappointed. That was what I told myself, as I drove away.

At least I went into the nursing home, where Claire's mother lives. It's on the very edge of the west side of Dunlone, between a housing estate and open countryside, abruptly reached by taking the last motorway exit for the town. It had grown dark by the time I got there; the cumulus cloud in the sky felt full of rain.

It was a modern structure, with a large, bright lobby, leather armchairs and big windows that looked out onto fields. Still, you could tell straight away it hadn't been renovated in a long time, perhaps not since it was first built. The colour scheme was dated – the salmon paint on the walls, the grey-green linoleum of the floor – and in places the paint had peeled. There was a smell too – of disinfectant and something more stifling, something warmer, as though the windows had never been opened.

I went to the small desk by the door and told the woman sitting behind it who I was.

'Oh, yes,' she said. 'I was speaking to you on the phone.'

'That's it.' I had called ahead, as Claire had suggested, half hoping, of course, to be told I couldn't visit. But there was no problem, the woman had said, as long as I arrived during visiting hours.

There, in the nursing home, her eyes narrowed briefly as she took me in. 'I don't think we've met before now.'

'No. I haven't been able to get down.'

She regarded me almost brazenly. 'You're a cousin of Claire's, isn't that it?'

'Yes.'

'Terrible business.'

'I know. Terrible.'

'And nobody saw it coming. You'll probably say yourself, no one could have seemed nicer.'

'That's true.'

She kept looking at me.

'Is now a good time for a visit?' I asked.

'I'd say it is. Hang on and I might call one of the carers. No. Do you know what? I'll take you down to her myself.'

We walked along the dingy corridor together. Besides one older man sitting in one of the armchairs, the place seemed empty.

'Most of them go back to their bedroom after breakfast,' she said. She had stopped outside a door with the number three on it. 'I think I said to you on the phone,' she continued, 'Phyllis hasn't seen any of it on the news. No one has said anything to her about it.'

Phyllis was Claire's mother. 'I won't mention it,' I said.

'No. Maybe don't say anything about Claire at all. Just in case.'

'Okay.'

'It's very advanced now. The dementia. I'm sure Claire's told you. The past year, she wouldn't always have known who Claire was even. We find at this stage it's often better to go along with what the person is saying. Even if it isn't our version of reality. You know?' She was looking sharply at me, as though it had just occurred to her there might be something else to it.

'Don't worry, I won't stay long.'

'Probably best if you don't.'

'Five minutes,' I said.

'Fine. That'll be fine.' She rapped the door sharply. 'Phyllis?' she called. 'I have a visitor here for you.'

There was no sound. She knocked again. Still, nothing. 'Phyllis?' She opened the door.

It was a small room. On the edge of a single bed a woman sat, dressed neatly in a grey skirt, a white blouse and navy cardigan. Her white hair looked freshly curled. Her hands resting on her lap, she was gazing at me expectantly. It was as though she had been waiting for me. On a small dresser there was a hairbrush, with short white hairs in the bristles. On the locker by her bed lay a set of rosary beads.

From the window you could see the car park, the road with its sad string of shops on the other side, and houses beyond. Claire had been right. Her mother clearly had not been moved to the room with the better view.

'Now, Phyllis,' said the woman, 'you have a visitor.'

'Hello,' I said. 'It's Beth, your niece. I hope it's okay to call on you like this?' I smiled at her.

'Isn't that nice,' she said. She had a high voice that wobbled as she spoke, but she smiled back, tentatively, at me.

'Okay, Phyllis,' said the woman. 'We'll need you to help us lay the tables for lunch soon.' She winked at me. 'I'll leave you to it,' she said.

She left before I had a chance to bring up the issue of the room. I told myself I'd do it on my way out instead.

'Is it okay if I sit down?' I said to Claire's mother, who was still sitting on her bed, still regarding me silently.

Her eyes widened as I sat in the chair but she didn't say anything.

'How are you?' I said.

'I'm all right,' she said, in a frail voice. 'Thank you.'

'That's good.'

'What will I do now?' she asked. She spoke the words politely.

'Oh. It's a funny time of year, isn't it?' I said. 'It'll be nicer when the summer comes.'

'Yes.'

'You can go for walks in the summer.'

'That's right.'

'I saw some snowdrops,' I told her, 'on my way here.'

'Yes,' she said. 'Did you bring me some?'

'No. I never thought of it. I should have.'

There was another long pause. I was hoping she would ask about Claire, but she just kept looking at me, as though she was waiting for me to say something.

'Do you like your view?' I asked, gesturing to the window.

She glanced outside. 'Oh, yes,' she said.

'That's good.'

'I was expecting my sister,' she said.

'Your sister?'

'My sister Margaret. Have you seen her?'

'I haven't. Sorry.'

'She's forgotten me.'

'She might have been delayed. The traffic is bad in town.'

'That's probably it.'

My palms had started to feel clammy.

'It isn't your daughter you're thinking of?' I said. 'Claire.'

She was startled. 'Claire?' she said.

'Yes. Your daughter.'

'I don't know where they're keeping her.' She looked around anxiously, then fixed her eyes on the door.

'I'm a friend of Claire's. She said to tell you she loves you. And that she's fine.'

She regarded me doubtfully.

'She's doing fine,' I said again.

She nodded slowly. 'Yes,' she said. But she seemed worried.

I reached into my pocket then, took out the photograph Claire had given me to bring, of her and her mother on Claire's wedding day.

I handed it to her. She stared at it.

'Margaret,' she said. 'On her wedding day.'

'That's Claire. She's a grown woman now. That's you and Claire, on Claire's wedding day.'

She examined the photograph again.

'They probably look alike,' I tried. 'That's Claire there.'

Her mouth pursed. She looked at me again. She started blinking.

'Claire is my daughter,' she said. 'She's at school at the moment.'

'She's not at school,' I said. It came out more harshly than I'd intended. I was feeling so tense, I suppose – desperate to get the job over. Then I reached across and tried gently to take the photograph from her. She didn't want to let go of it, though, and in the end I decided to let her keep it. What difference did it make?

'It might be nice to see a few trees,' I said, after we had been sitting in there in silence for a while. I gestured at her window again.

But she just made a sad little movement with her hands, as though to ask what she would know about the matter.

'Well, I'd better be going,' I said, and I stood. 'Claire just told me to say hello,' I said again. 'She will always love you. She said to say that.'

'No,' she said. 'That's not right.' Then she said it again, a little louder. 'That's not right.'

'It's okay. I'd say your friend will be back soon.' I couldn't think of the woman's name. The woman who had brought me down to her room. 'I'd better head back,' I said then. 'It's been lovely seeing you.'

'Are you leaving?' she said. 'I don't know you.'

'I'm a friend of Claire's. I have to drive back to Dublin now.'

'Wait.' She spoke the word urgently, as though something very important had occurred to her. There was lucidity in her expression, which hadn't been there before.

'What is it?' I said, trying to sound calm.

But she didn't say anything. She just kept staring at me as her hands slowly sank back into her lap. As though whatever thread of reality she had grasped had been lost again.

'Goodbye,' I said.

But then she stood, so that we were facing each other. The

curls above her forehead had somehow been pulled out so that they now slanted to the left. She looked around her room as though she didn't understand it. Then she turned to me, her mouth open.

'I really have to go,' I said. 'I want to beat the traffic.'

'Are you going into the town?' she said. 'I could take a lift off you.'

'No, no. Straight onto the motorway.'

There was just enough room for me to get past her. But as I tried to do so, she took hold of my cardigan. All the while she held onto it, she stared at me fiercely, her face sort of twisted. We were only inches away from each other. It was as though she wanted to say something, something urgent, but didn't know what it was. First I tried unpicking her fingers, but her grip was surprisingly strong. In the end, I had to call out.

'Hello,' I shouted. 'Can someone help me, please?'

Eventually the woman who had been at Reception appeared at the door.

'Now, Phyllis,' she said, and when Phyllis saw her, her expression slowly lost its intensity. She looked lost again. She let go of my cardigan.

'I'm not sure what happened,' I said weakly. 'I was about to leave and she seemed to get confused.'

The woman fixed a sharp gaze on me. 'You didn't mention her daughter?'

'No, of course not,' I lied. But I think she knew I was lying. I knew then that I wasn't going to raise the matter of the bedroom, as I had promised Claire I would. I said goodbye and left, as quickly as I could.

After sitting in my car awhile, anger took hold of me. More than anger – it was a kind of rage. Why was I putting myself in these situations, doing Claire's bidding, after everything she had put me through? Why wouldn't I just lie to her instead? After all, she had lied to me all those months without any compunction. Worse than that, she had tried to hurt me. She had hurt me. She owed me the truth, with or without any favours. And I owed her nothing. What was stopping me making up whatever it suited me to make up, the way she had lied to me? Surely that was nothing to feel guilty about. It was all she deserved.

And she wasn't the only person who owed me the truth, I thought.

Instead of going back to the motorway, I took a roundabout exit that brought me towards Dunlone.

I was going to confront Jason.

34

It didn't take too long to get to Jason's new workplace. I remembered where it was from the time we had driven out there on his first weekend down, when he had wanted to time how long his commute would be. I parked in the space assigned to his company, went inside the building and told the woman at the reception desk my name and that I was there to see Jason Maher. Then I took a seat, as she told me to do. Listened to her pick up her phone, tell Jason that a Beth Sheehan was there to see him.

He came through the door within seconds. He looked at me blankly. As though he couldn't speak. It was strange to see his face. He was changed somehow. Almost like a stranger. For a moment, I couldn't speak either.

He glanced at the receptionist, but very quickly, as if he couldn't afford to take his eyes off me for more than a second.

'I was in the area,' I said finally. 'Do you want to get a coffee?'

He glanced at the receptionist again. She was studiously staring at her screen. From somewhere behind her, a printer started up.

'Or could we catch up here?' I said. 'Is that handier?'

Without saying anything, he walked back in the direction he had come from, seconds later reappearing with his coat. Then he opened the door, waiting for me to walk ahead.

There was a huge Costa Coffee in the business park and we headed for it without either of us saying anything. He walked quickly, just as he had always done, and kept his eyes straight ahead. I quickened my pace to keep up with him, just like I used to do when we were together. It was important I didn't seem frightened, but it was as though my body had a different idea from my mind. I kept glancing back at my car, getting smaller and smaller in the distance. I couldn't bring myself to unfold my arms, even though that made it harder to walk fast.

Neither of us looked at the other once during that whole short walk. Or while waiting for our coffee, or even when we took a table by a huge wall-to-ceiling window in the almost empty café. As we sat, it started raining. Before long, it had gained a fierce momentum. I felt grateful to its sound, and to the speaker above our heads, blaring out an awful tinny pop song. They filled the silence.

I didn't let myself keep stirring my coffee long after I had added milk, even though I wanted to. It felt like a good idea not to be doing anything.

He didn't touch his espresso. He just sat there, his mouth tightly shut. He was so tense. I could see all this without properly looking at him. I could feel it.

Eventually, I spoke.

'Do you have the time?' I said.

He didn't look at me. But he took his phone out of his pocket and looked at the screen. 'Twelve twenty-two,' he said. He frowned a little, then seemed to check something, an email maybe. But I had a feeling he was pretending, that there was nothing there really. Then he put it back into his pocket.

'Twelve twenty-two,' I repeated.

Of course I didn't need to know the time, and if I had, I could have just checked my own phone.

He glanced my way then. Our eyes met. Suddenly, the table felt too small. It was too small. Our knees must have been almost touching, under its surface. His hand was too close to mine – he could reach out and grab it, if he wanted to. More than anything, I wanted to scrape my seat away from him. I wanted to run.

But I didn't do those things. Instead, I fixed my gaze on my espresso, the little biscuit in a plastic wrapper on my saucer, then his espresso, which he had not touched.

He was not going to apologise. That was already clear. He probably wasn't even going to acknowledge what had happened. All he was interested in was protecting himself. Getting to the other side of this encounter unscathed.

'Jason,' I said, and I forced myself to look at him. I immediately regretted saying his name. It felt too friendly. Almost intimate.

'What do you want?' he said. As he spoke, he made this sort of impatient gesture – glancing out the windows towards his office, then back at me. And even now, I'm not sure how to put it into words. It was as though I needed to see him again, to understand – not *how* what had happened had happened, but that it had happened at all. And I needed to hear him say sorry.

I had to get that, I decided. I couldn't just walk away with nothing.

'You owe me an apology,' I said.

'Oh, do I?' He looked angry. Like he was thinking, Here it is. The attack.

'Yes,' I said. 'Of course you do.'

He was all indignation then, as though he couldn't believe my nerve. Or not that he couldn't believe it, exactly; rather, that he wanted to give the impression of someone reacting that way.

'I'm not trying to catch you out,' I said. 'Is that what you think? That I'm recording this or something?' I took my phone out of my bag. 'Look.' I let everything else in my bag clatter down onto the table. There wasn't much. I handed my coat to him, so he could check the pockets. He didn't take it, though he seemed to hesitate for a second before returning his glare to me.

'I said nothing to the guards,' I said.

He was about to leave. I could tell.

'If I were you,' I said, 'I'd stay a bit longer.'

Outside, the rain was bashing against the window. I sipped my lukewarm coffee, looked directly at him.

'I don't know what you're talking about,' he said.

'There was this really nice one. Guard, I mean. A woman. She was very concerned about all my bruises. My two cracked ribs. Did I mention them?'

He had the biscuit in its plastic wrapper between his thumb and finger and was pressing the biscuit into a fine crumb. I don't think he even realised he was doing it.

'I told her I didn't want to talk about it and she said she'd leave it at that for now. But if I ever wanted to make another statement, I was to call her. She actually rang me the other day. Just to tell me there'd be no inquest. It was nice of her. She didn't need to do that.'

Now it was his turn, it seemed, to drink lukewarm coffee. Then he made this gesture with his hand, which I didn't understand at first. My coat. He wanted to check it after all. I handed it to him, watched as he put his hands, awkwardly, into the pockets, patted the front to make sure nothing was there.

After he had handed it back, he glanced around him. Then he stared out the window, at the rain.

'That wasn't me that night,' he said hoarsely.

'The specific problem I have is that it was you,' I said. My voice all steel.

He looked confused when I said that. Then he actually seemed to go paler. Took another sip of coffee. 'You can't understand the pressure I was under,' he said.

'What would you have done,' I said, 'if I hadn't got away from you that night? What else would you have done, I mean? If your flatmate and his girlfriend hadn't shown up?'

Again, he looked confused. It was as though he was having trouble understanding what I meant.

'Don't pretend you don't remember,' I said.

He frowned, shook his head. 'I wouldn't have done anything else. I would have calmed down. I had already calmed down.'

I could barely hear him.

'Calmed down. I was scared for my life,' I said.

'You come up out of the blue and tell me you've moved out of the house. That you've decided all by yourself that's okay. And that you've slept with our landlord, essentially. None of that's exactly irrelevant, is it?'

For some reason, it hadn't occurred to me that that might come up.

'Well, why *did* you sleep with him?' he said.

'I wasn't exactly in a good place,' I managed.

'No?'

'No. Thanks to you.'

'You can't blame everything on me. It was your idea to move down there in the first place.'

'It wasn't my idea. Not really. It was your plan all along. You *made* me offer to go down early.'

'That doesn't make any sense.'

'It does and you know it.'

'Well, what do you want me to say?' He tried to say it angrily, but he couldn't. It was almost disarming, the way his authority and control seemed to have dissolved.

'What I don't understand is how you could have done it – made me move down there on my own, all that, when you knew you didn't love me. I mean, would you have proposed to me, do you think? Would you have had children with me?'

He didn't say anything.

'Why me?'

He regarded me as though that was clearly a stupid question. 'It was a no-brainer.'

'What – the house? Not if we weren't in love it wasn't.'

'We were getting along.'

'We were *not* getting along.'

'We wanted the same thing.'

'I don't think so.'

'Yeah, well.' He did this sort of 'what-do-you-expect-me-to-say' shrug, then looked impatiently out at the rain.

And that was when I understood. Not only had Jason never loved me, for him this did not pose a problem. It was beside the point. The point always being Jason. Everything that had happened had been for his benefit. To enable Jason to be bigger and better than everyone else. A nicer house. More money. A more impressive career. All of which I had enabled – by moving down to hold the house on the estate for him, by having all my income paid into a joint account, which I still hadn't been given access to, by letting him control me.

By being so gullible. So stupidly blind.

For all I knew, he had been seeing someone else in Dublin while I had been living on the estate. That thing about his landlord not allowing overnight guests: it occurred to me then that it had never had the ring of truth.

But if he had been, I didn't care. It was an irrelevance. What I did care about was that I would have thrown my life away, at his bidding. I would have bought a house with him. I would have married him. I would have borne his children. And even after the estate, my life would have been more of the same. The lying. The controlling.

The violence.

Suddenly, I could see it so vividly – the way they say your life flashes in your mind just before you die. Except what I saw was my future. If I had stayed with him.

'I read somewhere once,' I said, 'that hatred comes from the heart, contempt from the head. Which was it, do you mind me asking?'

He didn't answer.

'That night, it seemed like you hated me. Now, I don't know. I suppose it doesn't matter.' I stood then. Put on my coat. 'I could still report you,' I said. 'In ten years' time, I could still report you.'

'It's not like I've nothing on you.'

'What does that mean?'

'What would Helen say, if she knew you slept with that guy?'

'Helen knows,' I said.

'Well, your friends don't.' He paused. You could tell he was trying to rummage up something – anything – else that would hurt me. That would give him some kind of leverage. 'Or your boss,' he said finally. 'What would he think?'

'I don't have a boss, Jason,' I said. 'I'm unemployed. Remember?'

I walked out of there, and back towards the car. But instead of getting in, I walked on, straight to his office. I wasn't sure exactly what I was going to do, even when I buzzed to be let in, even when I was back inside, the receptionist looking up at me expectantly.

'Jason asked me to ask you if you wouldn't mind checking his desk for his phone,' I said, the idea forming as I spoke. 'I don't know if he mentioned it, but his mother is unwell. He's expecting a phone call from the hospital. He would come and get it but he's actually a bit upset.'

At first I thought it wasn't going to work because she picked up her phone and I realised she was calling someone who sat near him. But they mustn't have answered because, after a few moments, she hung up.

'I'll just be a second,' she said, and she went through a door behind the desk, closing it after her.

I went around and sat at her desk. Quickly, I clicked on the mouse of her PC. Luckily, I had not been locked out. All those years of temping I had done after college were finally coming in useful. As I had hoped, they used Outlook, the email program that every company I had ever worked for used. And as with all those jobs, when I typed 'All' into the addressee line, it registered a list of the email addresses of everyone in the company. There must have been at least a hundred.

I had no time to think about what to write: at any moment, the receptionist would be back. In the subject line, I wrote, 'Jason Maher beat me'. And in the body of the email, I wrote, 'My name is Beth Sheehan. I am Jason Maher's ex-girlfriend. On 7 December 2008, Jason Maher punched my face, breaking my lip. When I fell to the floor, he repeatedly kicked me, leaving me with two cracked ribs. I didn't report this to the police because I was terrified of him. I knew he'd lie and I knew he'd probably get away with it. Jason Maher is very good at lying.' I pressed send and had just stood when the receptionist reappeared.

'It's all true,' I said to her. 'Every word of it.' And then I walked back to my car and drove away.

I had a final place to visit before returning back here, to my mother's house. Before long, I was back on that driveway, pulling over at that spot where that sad circle of houses comes into full view. I found I couldn't face going the whole way down to the house.

In that first glance, it all seemed just the same. Even the Portakabin was still there, without the yellow police tape around it any more. It was all the same, and yet it felt different. Smaller, sadder, robbed somehow of its power. I remembered how, coming down the driveway, the first thing I always used to do was check to see if Claire's car was outside her house. The relief I had always felt when it was. The vague sense of fear if it wasn't. Now, of course, there was no car outside Claire's house. But the Dorans' car was there, along with their makeshift fence. And Michael's house looked as it always had done. Skeletal. Unfinished. Cold. For a moment, I allowed myself to imagine that if I was to go down and bang on his door, he would open it. It felt so close to being true. But then I looked back at my old house and that awful night came back to me. Mr Doran pressing so hard and fast on Michael's lifeless body.

It occurred to me then that, for all I knew, Mr Doran might be watching me from his house, right now. He would recognise my car. He might come out and try to confront me. Or, worse, what if he walked down the driveway, while I sat there so furtively?

I turned the car around. It was time to return to this place. It was time to ask my mother for help.

35

12 February 2009

Dear Beth,

I don't know if you remember but I'm off to Lanzarote tomorrow morning. Well, by the time you read this it will be today. My flight is very early – five a.m.!

Ever since you came to live here, I've been trying to tell you something and I have realised I probably won't ever manage to tell you in person. We don't seem to be able to talk to each other very well, do we? You'd think after all these years we would have figured it out.

Do you remember that piece of writing I did that I gave you to read a couple of weeks ago? Well, I left out the last couple of pages. I'm putting them here for you to read now:

Someone might say it would be better if I told you all this in person. And I might have done, if you'd said something to me about the first bit I gave you. The bit about Helen. But maybe this is for the best. It will give you a chance to digest it all on your own, before I come back. And this gives you the whole story. Better than me just blurting it all out. If I did it that way, we'd probably end up arguing.

I've given up hoping Helen will tell you. If I've asked her to tell you once, I've asked her a thousand times. But that girl always suits herself in the end, no matter what she'll tell you.

Love

Mum

It didn't take long to read. There was a bit about how awful life had been for her in Brighton, those first few years. How it wasn't until Helen started school that things got any easier. And then about how she got a new, better, job in an office. How she started going out again, enjoying herself. How she thought Helen was doing fine.

I turned to the last page, expecting to read next about how she met my father. I even felt the old thrill of hope I used to feel when I was younger and thought she might be about to tell me something about him. Which, of course, she never did.

And then I got this.

Now, it seems to me that I always knew, even if I never recognised it. If that makes any sense.

And then the day came when Helen pulled up her sweater to show me her swollen stomach. She was sixteen years old. Three years younger than I was when I got pregnant.

When, a year later, one of my sisters wrote to tell me my father had died, I travelled back for the funeral with Helen and the baby. I wanted to go. I was hoping as well that maybe old wounds might be mended, with my mother and brothers and sisters.

But I also had had an idea.

I would tell them the baby is my own. And that the three of us have moved home for good.

Initially, Helen resisted. But when I explained, she went along with it happily enough.

Back in Ireland, you see, I could pretend the baby is mine. On the birth certificate, it is my name that is given as the mother. Eileen Sheehan. Not Helen Sheehan. Helen could be free again, if she wanted to be. I told her, once she was finished her last two years of school, she could do whatever she likes. A new scheme had been introduced in Ireland, making third-level education free for everyone, so I told her she could go to college, if she was able to pay her own way. Yes, she could even study drama; if she wanted to be so foolish I wouldn't stop her. Whatever she wanted. As long as she stuck out school for two more years.

And that is how I found myself home alone with a young child, for a second time. After Helen graduated, we saw very little of her for years, bar the occasional visit home when she would be full of plans and love for the little one, only to disappear again.

I made a decision in those early years back in Dublin. If I was going to be responsible for Helen's child, it would be on my own terms. So I found a crèche and went back to work. I started putting in long hours, to go out for a quick drink or coffee after work. I was even dating again. I was always being charged extra for being late picking up the baby. Beth her name is. Of course I dressed and washed and fed her. I did all that. And I loved her, of course I did. But this time it was different. This time, I was not going to let her take over. This time, I was going to leave some room for me.

36

I nearly didn't visit Claire today. After reading the letter last night, I drank some whiskey I found in a cabinet in the living room. It knocked me out but when I woke it was four in the morning and I didn't go back to sleep. So this morning, when it was time to get ready, I was not feeling good.

But I suppose I wanted to get it over with. Discharge all my duties.

I suppose part of me still wanted to understand all that had happened on the estate.

'You look even worse today,' she said, as I took the seat across from her.

'Cheers.'

'Seriously,' she said. 'I'm almost worried about you.'

'Fuck you, Claire,' I said, in a flat, quiet voice. I suppose I was so tired I didn't care what I said.

'Has something happened?' she said.

I started laughing when she said that. It just seemed funny – that, after everything, apparently Claire is still the closest thing I have to a friend. Because isn't that something a friend would do – notice something was up even when you don't say anything about it?

'What's so funny?' she said.

'Nothing.'

She shrugged, as though it meant nothing to her either way. Which, of course, it didn't. 'So,' she said, 'how did it go?'

'Fine,' I said. 'Your mother was delighted to hear about you. She definitely understood. And she's in a new room, with the nice view of the fields. She seemed quite happy.'

'Really?'

'Really.'

She frowned. 'You didn't take a photo by any chance?'

'Of your mother?'

'And the room.'

'The new room. No, I never even thought of it.'

'No.'

'Pity we didn't think of that,' I said.

You could tell she was kicking herself.

'How did she seem?' she said.

'Well. I just told you. Happy. I mean, she said she didn't know what to do, a couple of times.'

'Right.'

'She wanted me to stay for longer. But she said that after I left she was going to help lay the tables for lunch. She said she liked doing little jobs like that.'

'Good. She didn't confuse me with anyone else?'

'No, no. Not at all. Actually, she wanted to keep the photo.'

'Did she?'

'She did.'

'Right.' You could tell she wasn't reassured, not really. But what could she do?

'It went well with the girl too,' I said. 'A normal nine-year-old, if a little shy. Her mother said the doctors were happy. That she's made a complete recovery.'

As I'd been speaking, she'd been looking at me very carefully. She didn't say anything.

'So no need to worry,' I said. 'On either count. Actually, when I left, she and her mother were going for a walk.'

'Good.' I could barely hear her, she spoke the word so quietly. Then she seemed to recover herself a little. 'You have some questions for *me*,' she said.

'You'll really answer everything?'

'Probably,' she said. 'Why not? My solicitor wouldn't exactly advise it but I don't see that I've anything to lose. It's over for me, even if my sentence is lenient. That debt isn't going anywhere, is it? It'll be there, waiting for me.'

'One prison for another.'

'Something like that.'

'Okay, then. Was it you who hit me that night?' I had decided to barrel the questions at her so I could get out of there as soon as possible. With the last missing scraps of the picture.

She nodded.

'You could have killed me,' I said.

'I googled it first. How to knock someone out without doing real damage.'

'You googled it?'

She nodded. 'I was pretty sure I wouldn't do any real harm.'

'That was nice of you.'

She didn't say anything.

'Why did you do it?'

She focused her gaze on me for a second. Like she was surprised I'd had to ask that. And, of course, I did know the answer.

'I wanted to frighten you,' she said. 'I needed you to leave.'

'And the other times. The lights flashing. And the letterbox.'

'All me. It was easy to get back to my own house before you. Especially the first time, when you ran across the green towards Michael.'

'You were watching.'

She shrugged.

'Did Michael not do any of it?' I said.

'No. Michael was just there.'

Just there. And now, I thought, Michael was nowhere.

I was finding it hard to think clearly. But I had to keep asking the questions. I kept saying that over and over in my mind.

Just ask the questions. Just ask the questions.

'Did you kill Lurch?' I said.

'Rat poison,' she said flatly. 'In some minced meat. He devoured it. Poor thing was half starved.'

'Why?'

'Why did I kill him? I had to. You told me once if it wasn't for him you'd leave. Remember?'

'How did you get into my house?'

'Frank and Maura had given me a copy of their keys. No one ever asked for them back afterwards, so I held on to them.'

'Frank and Maura?'

'The couple who'd bought the place. Frank was the guy who hanged himself in your living room. Remember them?'

'I remember Jim Doran telling me about them. Why did *you* not tell me? If you wanted to get rid of me.'

'It worked better for the Dorans to tell you.'

'But—'

'I didn't want you guessing I needed you to leave. And I knew once I'd told you I didn't trust him that it would be only a matter of time before you paid them a visit.'

'Yes, but—'

'At first, you know, I told myself I was glad you'd moved in. I said to myself, "She's shaken me up. Knocked me out of this weird game." I even tried to make friends with you.'

I thought of all those questions she had asked me that night. The way she had won my trust, by first telling me her own story.

'That night you hit me,' I said finally. 'That was the night you took the girl, wasn't it?'

Another curt nod.

'You didn't bank on my sister showing up the evening after you took her.'

'No, I didn't.'

'Or Jason.'

'No.'

'She was there in the Portakabin, while all that was going on.'

She nodded.

'Why keep her there? Why not your house?'

'It seemed safer, you know, with people calling in on me all the time. And I kept thinking, What if she woke in my spare room and opened the curtains, got the attention of some golfer on the green? I couldn't paint that window black – it might have looked strange. But no one ever gave a second thought to the Portakabin. And if it all went wrong, well, anyone could have left her there. That was what I thought.' She shook her head. 'I'd actually got it ready in the summer, before you showed up.'

'Ready?'

'Painted the windows black. Put a new lock on. The builders had left it unlocked. They were in such a damn hurry to get out of there, once they realised the money had run out. And it's not like it contained anything valuable. I had an excuse too, if anyone had noticed the new padlock. I was going to say that the thing kept swinging open and shut.'

'The bed,' I said. 'The camp bed. It was in your hallway.'

'That's right. You saw it, didn't you? That wasn't until later. I saw it in a charity shop for nothing. I just picked it up.' She stared at me, as though trying to figure out if I would be able to understand. 'I hadn't decided yet, you know. To go ahead with it. The whole thing was like a game. For so long.'

'You were either planning it or you weren't.'

It was the first time she seemed unsure of herself. 'It started with this programme on TV, about a kidnapping in South America. Someone mentioned that many kidnappings are actually successful. Probably more than we know, because in the really successful ones, the police are never even called. That was when I started wondering. Might there be a way out of my situation? With the bank and the house, I mean. One I hadn't thought of. Like, what if nothing was holding me back? What if I didn't have a conscience? What might I do then? So even when I was doing all that, painting the windows and stuff, it was still only a game.'

'When did it stop being a game?' I asked.

'Hard to tell. Right up to when I did it, maybe.'

'Why her?'

'Oh, for God's sake, Beth. That must be obvious, even to you. There was no one else it *could* have been. They were my leverage – the Kennedys. My bit of expert knowledge. All that cash. The wood behind their garden. The girl young enough for it to work.'

'Grace,' I said. 'That's her name, isn't it?'

She just looked at me. Brazen.

'And you had insulin.'

'I knew how to use insulin safely as a sedative.'

'They said in the papers you couldn't have known. That you gambled with the child's life.'

'That's not true. I've been taking it since I was a child myself. And I researched it – how much would be safe to give someone else.'

'But she was unconscious when I found her,' I said. 'She had to go to ICU, in the hospital.'

'When I heard your car,' she said, 'I gave her a second dose. A smaller one. I panicked a little bit.'

'That's not true.'

She did this half-shrug and I knew then that it was true. That she had given her a second dose, just because I had shown up.

'Before then, it kept her sedated,' she continued. 'Most of the time she was asleep. If it had gone to plan, she would have woken with a headache in her mother's arms.'

For a while, I couldn't think what else I had wanted to ask her. I couldn't think of anything at all.

'They said on the television you had two passports,' I said finally.

'That's right. I couldn't believe it when the second one came through.'

'When did that happen?'

'The autumn. Not too long after you arrived. You know what that did? It reminded me that no one had a clue what I was planning. If you could even call it planning. No one suspected me of anything.'

'It motivated you,' I said.

She actually laughed, when I said that. 'I suppose that's right,' she said. 'It motivated me. By then the bank had started up their lovely correspondence again. I knew what I was facing for the rest of my life. Decades of paying back a huge debt that I could never actually pay back. All the while living in some depressing bedsit in Dunlone.'

'Going through with it, though. That's another thing, isn't it?'

'You think I'm a monster,' she said. 'But don't forget, Beth, if you had never shown up on the estate, Michael would still be alive. Wouldn't he? For all we know, he might have made it to his aunt's for Christmas. He might have been okay. And Grace would never have needed to go to ICU. She would have been perfectly safe, the whole time.'

'You can't blame me.'

'I'm not blaming you for anything. I'm just stating some facts.'

I should have left then. I should have walked right out of that awful room. I might have, if she hadn't said that Michael might have gone to his aunt's. That was too much. She shouldn't have said that.

'Here's a fact, then,' I said. 'Your mother had no idea who you were. Actually, she thought you were her sister in the photo. And they haven't changed her room. What would be the point? She doesn't give a shit about trees any more. She probably couldn't tell you what a tree is.'

Her face, when I said all that. Her face.

But I didn't stop. I kept going.

'I never visited the Kennedys,' I said. 'I saw them, though. The mother and the girl walking in their garden. I thought they walked very slowly. The girl didn't look right,' I said. 'I'd say she's a long way from being better.'

I left then. I left, without ever looking at her again.

So now I really have the whole story.

If it wasn't for me, Michael would still be alive. He might

even have managed to get clean and be living with his aunt by now.

If it wasn't for me, that little girl might not have a brain injury from which she might never recover.

And if it wasn't for me, Claire might be living her happy-ever-after in South America, instead of being in prison. Despite what she's done, it seems to me that even that would have been a better outcome for everyone.

All the new pain. Michael dying.

It's almost funny, when you think about it – that last piece of the jigsaw I didn't even know was missing, I mean. How I was never *supposed* to be. To exist, that is. There in the estate, or anywhere.

At least Claire taught me one thing. A parting gift, you might call it. No one does anything very terrible or shocking all of a sudden. What happens instead is little changes. You gradually edge yourself towards something until you find yourself right up against it, without really knowing how you got to such a place. So that the next thing you do, even if it seems terrible and unaccountable to other people, is really no big deal at all. It has almost become easy.

37

It is a couple of months since I've written anything in here. I'm not sure why I feel the need to come back to it. I suppose it's incomplete, if I don't. I always wanted to get down the whole story.

When I think of what happened after I'd finished the last entry, it's like when I think of what happened that last night on the estate, after I found the girl – more like remembering the actions of someone other than myself. The way I sat on that bed for I don't know how long.

Until I knew I could do it. That I was going to do it.

And then how quickly I did everything – pulled out a bottle of wine and unscrewed it, then the two jars of sleeping tablets and, without even thinking, put as many into my mouth as I could and washed them down with the wine. I did that a few times, until every single one was gone. Then I finished the bottle, as quickly as I could manage. All the time, I remember knowing that the important thing was not to think. Once the bottle was empty, I lay down on the bed and waited.

I tried closing my eyes but that made me feel sick, and I couldn't let that happen. So I kept my gaze on the view out the window – sunlight creeping up the laurel, the horse chestnut tree, still with no leaves anywhere. I remember it still had those hard, poisonous-looking things.

Until the drowsiness came and I let it take me.

The next thing I remember is waking up in a hospital room with a shocking headache, my mouth dry and my stomach feeling like it had been pummelled. In a chair beside my bed, Helen sat, slouched and sleeping. She was frowning in her sleep, as though she was in pain.

I tried to say her name but my throat was too dry to speak. For a few minutes, I lay there looking at her, until a nurse came in.

'She wakes,' she said.

At those words, Helen sat upright, her face all alarm.

'How,' I managed, after the nurse had brought a glass of water to my lips, 'did I get here?'

'Mum rang me from Lanzarote to tell me about the letter she'd left out for you,' said Helen. 'I got the first flight home, when she told me.'

I didn't know what to say.

'Am I okay?' I asked.

'You'll survive,' said the nurse. 'I'll leave you two for a few minutes, but then the patient needs her rest, okay?' She gave Helen a shrewd look.

'Of course,' said Helen.

Then it was just me and Helen. It was hard to meet her eyes. It was hard to know what to say.

'God, Beth,' said Helen, eventually. 'Will you ever forgive us?'

Spring has come, a lovely one, the days starting sharp and clear-skied, slowly bringing warmth, then cooling again in the evening. Yesterday Helen and I drove to Bull Island. The route took us down an avenue lined with horse chestnuts, like the one outside my mother's house, except these are full of new green leaves and pink and white blossoms. When we reached the coast road, we turned onto a narrow wooden bridge that links the mainland to the island. Slowly we drove down it, parking by that thin promontory with the statue of Mary at its end.

I still don't seem able to move very quickly. But we were in no particular rush. Neither was anyone else we passed – a couple holding hands, a man with his dog, a woman walking down steps and immersing herself in the water, as though stepping into a warm bath.

'It's not even a real island,' said Helen, as we walked. She was talking about Bull Island, which, long and thin, lies close to its mainland. 'It's artificial, if an island can be artificial. First they built that wooden bridge that connects it to the mainland.'

'Before there was an island?' I asked.

'Before there was an island. They built a wooden bridge that just went out into the sea.'

'Why?' I asked, despite myself.

'Because they wanted to build a wall, out there in the sea, to stop all the silt coming into the port.'

I nodded.

'The wall stopped the silt, but it just built up there instead.'

'And turned into an island.'

'And turned into an island. It's still happening, I think. It's still growing.'

At its end, the statue stands on high, frightening concrete poles. *Star of the Sea*, Helen told me it's called. Her back to the waves, she faces the city, her expression grimly resolute, or it seemed so to me. Her hands raised a little, in a sad, hopelessly inadequate but necessary embrace. Or in entreaty for something, maybe.

They had to pump my stomach in the hospital. That was why it hurt so much when I woke. If Helen hadn't arrived when she did, the doctor said there was a good chance I would never have woken.

'Have you emailed Sarah yet?' she asked.

I nodded. It had taken a long time, but the previous day I had sent Sarah a long email, telling her everything that had happened. Her reply had been so kind I didn't tell Helen about it in case I started crying.

'When is Claire's trial?' she asked.

'Next month,' I said. 'I'm going to write to her.'

'It weighs on you. What you said to her, when you visited her that time in prison.'

I nodded again.

Ever since I woke up in hospital, I've been frightened not to have Helen with me. I think she knows this, even though neither of us has mentioned it. She stayed by my side for the three days I was there. Now the only times she leaves me on my own, aside from when she's working, are when she drops me off at my therapist, and when I go to bed.

I go to bed very early, these days. I still get very tired. But I sleep pretty well now, most nights at least.

We haven't talked yet, Helen and I. Not really. I do have one blurred memory from the hospital, of Helen crying and saying things, but I can't remember what she said, or what I said, or if either of us said anything at all. It's been the same with my mother.

Grandmother.

I think they're scared to upset me. They're waiting for me to start the conversation.

'What will it be like from now on?' I asked.

'What?'

'Everything.' I glanced at her, then away. 'Us.'

'I don't know. We'll have to figure it out as we go along.'

For a while, neither of us said anything.

'Do you hate me?' she said. 'I wouldn't blame you if you do.'

'I don't think so,' I said. 'Maybe sometimes.'

'I wouldn't blame you,' she said again.

'You're my mother.' I tried to say it in a matter-of-fact way.

'That's right,' she said. There was a pause, and then she

added, 'I love you so much.' She said it flatly, almost as though that fact – because I believed her when she said it – was incidental. As though it didn't stand a chance against anything.

'You didn't show it.'

'I tried.'

'Was I the reason you came back from America?'

'Yes.'

'But why did you go there in the first place?'

She shrugs miserably. 'For acting. My career.' Sarcastic emphasis on 'career'. 'It didn't work.'

'Were you even around much when I was a baby?'

She nodded sadly. 'I was with you every day for the whole first year,' she said. 'Of course you can't remember that.' But she looked at me, as though hoping I might somehow remember.

'I should have told you sooner,' she said, when I said nothing. 'Or would it have been better if you'd never been told?'

'It's better to know,' I said.

We walked on in silence until we reached the end of the promontory and were standing right in front of the concrete poles, which stood heavy and strong on a base of rocks that trailed into the sea.

'Have you written that letter to the boy's aunt yet?'

'I'm working on it.'

'What about the meditation? Didn't the therapist say that might be a good idea now?'

'God, you're as bad as she is.'

'Sorry.'

For a while, we just stood there, gazing out at the waves churning sloppily around the statue's base and the rocks beyond, a huge ferry slowly moving towards the horizon.

After a while, Helen carefully stepped onto the rocky base until she was standing beneath the statue. She looked up at it, then out at the encroaching sea. Then she turned around to me. She was smiling apologetically. That was how I knew she was about to start reciting poetry.

'This fallen star my milk sustains,' she said. 'This love that makes my heart's blood stop.'

ACKNOWLEDGEMENTS

Heartfelt thanks are due to my agent Darley Anderson, and everyone in the Darley Anderson Agency, especially Rebeka Finch, for believing in *The Estate* and in me as a writer. I can't overstate how much this means.

A huge thank you is due to my editor in Hachette, Ciara Considine, for her support and encouragement, and for her brilliant insights and deft suggestions that really got to the heart of the story. Sincere thanks are also due to my copy-editor, Hazel Orme, and proofreader, Aonghus Meaney, for doing such a fantastic job.

I am especially grateful to Andrew Rosenheim, whose encouragement over the years has made all the difference.

Thank you to everyone in Audible, especially Robin Morgan-Bentley for producing the audio version to such a high standard. Thank you to Denise Gough for her amazing narration.

I would like to thank Westmeath County Council for the generous provision of an artist bursary grant, which was also a great vote of confidence.

Thanks are due to many others who have helped along the way, in major or minor ways. In particular, I would like to thank my sisters Anna and Emma, for their good grace and support that is always there, and my children Martha and Brendan for reminding me of the bigger picture. Last but not least, I would like to thank my husband John, unflappable rock and love of my life.